MARC A. BEAUSEJOUR

DIVINE
VENGEANCE

S.H.E. PUBLISHING, LLC

DIVINE VENGEANCE

For information contact : www.shepublishingllc.com | info@shepublishingllc.com | Tel: 219.515.8032

Edited by D.A. Goodwin | Front Cover photo by ID 48584570 © Ammentorp | Dreamstime.com | Book Photo by LaTisha Guster

Library of Congress Control Number: 2024936170

ISBN: 978-1-964061-04-7 (*paperback*)

Second Edition : May 2024

1 2 3 4 5 6 7 8 9 10

ACKNOWLEDGMENTS

First of all, I would like to thank my Lord and Savior, Jesus Christ, for blessing me with this extraordinary gift of storytelling, inspiring and entertaining readers from all walks of life. Without Him, I cannot do anything. I would also like to thank my parents, Jean and Lineda Beausejour, for supporting this journey through all the peaks and valleys. Although it was hard to see the light at the end of the tunnel, you have always taught me to walk by faith and not by sight. Your faith in me has given me a renewed sense of purpose to continue writing and offer insight for other potential authors in this industry. To all my supporters, friends, and extended family who have been in my corner every step of the way, thank you for continuing to inspire me. Thank you to my church friends and family, both in New York and Georgia, for the spiritual foundation that you have set within me. To all of my professors and educators at M.S. 217 in Queens, New York; North Cobb High School; Kennesaw State University, and Chattahoochee Technical College in Kennesaw, Georgia; thank you for the countless research papers and history papers that you've assigned me. They helped me in more ways than you know. It has been more than twenty years, but I want to thank my 3rd grade teacher, Ms. Bess, for helping to instill the love of reading that would evolve into poetry before expanding to authoring novels. Special thanks also to my editor, Dawn Goodwin, who had the pleasure of working with me for five years. Your editing expertise and feedback have helped bring a new dimension to the BlackCyrano Series. Shouts out to Mr. Clinton Holmes from Your Property Marketing LLC. Your cover designs helped bring the characters to life so my readers could visualize the story, and your contributions to the series cannot be overlooked. Finally, I want to thank my new publishing family, S.H.E. Publishing LLC, for relaunching my books as the BlackCyrano Series and for accepting me into your family of authors. Shenitha, I cannot thank you enough for re-introducing the world to my work and teaching me a great deal about the authorship industry. Your team has done an excellent job of formatting the font, look, and style of the BlackCyrano Series novels, and I look forward to working on future projects with you. Divine Vengeance is the last book in the BlackCyrano Series, and it has been a wonderful ride with all the characters involved from 2014 to 2023. As my characters grew and matured, they helped me grow and mature as a man and as an author. I am eagerly anticipating the next story and hope my readers are ready for it!

PROLOGUE

August 2002

THE COUPLE EXITED the lounge in downtown Flushing, New York. Walking towards his car with his date, Craig Hinton joked around endlessly, his arm wrapped around Jade's shoulder. He'd had more than a few drinks, and he was only a step away from complete inebriation.

Craig was twenty-two years of age, tall with an athletic build. A part-time student at St. John's University, he also worked as a trainer at the Planet Fitness gym in Springfield Gardens, New York. He met Jade while she was working out at the gym. He was taken by her astonishing figure, her womanly curves, and her cinnamon-brown skin that gleamed in the gym lights. As a trainer, Craig had worked with countless women of all different shapes, and he was always thorough during his sessions.

Women raved about the results that they saw from his workouts, and the more satisfied they were with their results, the more they became emotionally attached to their trainer. A single man, Craig had taken his work home on more than one occasion, leaving women more satisfied leaving his bedroom than they were leaving the gym.

Women were drawn to his chiseled physique, his boyish smile, and his charm.

Unfortunately for them, that was all it was. Craig was never interested in having long-term relationships with the women he held sessions with. He only used their bodies to get his rocks off. Craig's favorite movie was *Boomerang* with Eddie Murphy playing the suave, debonair marketing exec Marcus Graham, often patterning his liaisons with women after Graham.

Craig loved every part of the movie except the ending when Halle Berry's Angela character whipped Marcus long enough for him to fall in love with her. That part always bothered Craig because he felt that love was just another ploy to trap men into undesired relationships, and to him, the excitement of women was in the chase, the sweet talks, and finally the physical exploration and exploitation of his mates.

He realized that to women, he was viewed as a dog, yet he did not see a problem with how they viewed him. *God created men and women to have sex and procreate. I'm just using God's gift to get mines. I don't see nothing wrong with that. With the amount of women chasing other men day after day, using them for their own pleasure, why can't we have our fun? It's only wrong when men do it. Nah, baby, I'm flippin' the script. That's who I am, and if they don't like it, they never should have gotten with me in the first place. They knew what it was when they got with me.*

Little did Craig know that his advantageous pursuit of women was about to dramatically backfire and change the course of his life.

On the day he met Jade, she was struggling to adjust the weights on one of the functional weight machines. Seeing her struggling, along with her gorgeous body, Craig decided to play the role of hero helping a damsel in distress.

"What's up, girl? Need some help?"

Turning around to see her savior, Jade smiled. She had long brown braids that reached down to her lower back. "Thanks. I'm so clumsy sometimes with these things," she replied.

After helping Jade adjust her weights, Craig introduced himself. "Name's Craig Hinton, chief trainer here at Planet Fitness. I've never seen you 'round here before. First time?"

"Yeah, it's my first day here. I mean, I've trained at other gyms before, but due to crappy trainers and poor equipment maintenance, I had to leave them," she replied.

Craig nodded as if he understood, and in all retrospect, he could relate because nothing annoyed him more than people who did not take care of their equipment or place weights back in the racks after using them. But he was transfixed by this ebony goddess in front of him. Craig's shorts were baggy today, and he was thankful for that because, if he had worn his tight shorts, people would have noticed his pants tightening and the wood protruding.

"I feel you. So, do you have a trainer?"

Jade shook her head. "Not yet. But since you're here, maybe you can take the job," she replied, smiling.

Not wasting any time, Craig trained her, and during the training, they talked and laughed. He found this girl easy to talk to, and while they worked on different routines, he found out that they liked the same foods, had some similar hobbies outside the gym, and they both enjoyed going out on the weekends. It was the latter interest that gave Craig the opening he needed to make his move.

"So, since you like clubbing, there's this spot out in Flushing—the Moon Bar. It's a rooftop joint with a crazy view. You down?"

Looking at him as if he was a delectable treat, Jade decided to take him up on his invitation. "Yeah, I'd love to go, as long as you payin'!" she laughed.

"I got you. Don't even sweat that."

As they went to the front desk, they exchanged phone numbers, and Craig promised to call Jade before he picked her up.

As Jade left the gym, a man at the front checkout desk named Jake Hart witnessed his co-worker work his charm yet again. "Got another one, huh?"

Craig looked at Jake with a sly smile. "Aye, what I can I say, man? These girls can't resist me, dawg. You see the ass on her though? Oh yeah, I'm definitely tappin' that after the club."

"Whatever, man. Just please spare us the nasty details of your sexual exploits this time. I wanna keep my lunch in my stomach this time," Jake laughed, alluding to a previous exploit where Craig managed to seal the deal with another woman that he worked out with. Craig had spared no detail in bragging to Jake about his time with the woman, describing their evening together, even describing the explicit bits of their night.

"Bro, that was almost a month ago. Lately, I've been on a dry spell. The last two dates I've been on ain't been too good, especially the one I took out last week. Butch-ass chick too. She kept cuttin' me off while I was tryin' to talk, and she kept goin' on about some dude that she was feelin', but her best friend was dating him, or some shit like that. I lost the plot after the second sentence, dawg. I already knew I wasn't gon' get none that night, so I called a taxi to drop her ass off."

"What? You mean to tell me that you ain't even dropped her off yourself? That's a first."

"Nah, I didn't want problems. But I'mma make it up tonight with this chick."

Unfortunately, Craig would not fulfill that promise as the hopeful dream of sexual conquest would turn tragic that evening.

As they walked to the car upon leaving the club, Craig felt light-headed. "Yo, baby, give me a minute," he said, slowing his walk. His vision blurred, and the streets and sidewalk began spinning as he stumbled aimlessly.

"Craig, you okay?" Jade asked, a note of concern in her voice.

"Yeah, I'm good. I'm good. Just gotta shake this dizziness off. I think I need some Tylenol or something like that," he replied.

But the more they walked, it became increasingly difficult for Craig to keep his balance. Despite his remarkable physique, Craig was a heavy drinker, and he had passed out drunk more than once after constantly drinking himself into a stupor. But on this evening, Craig didn't feel drunk or groggy.

He felt dizzy, and he could feel his heart pounding rapidly in his chest as if it would explode. Suddenly and without warning, Craig fell onto the sidewalk, his eyes rolled back in his head.

Pedestrians shrieked in horror, and as Craig lie there collapsed on the sidewalk, Jade kneeled down beside him. "Oh my God! Someone, call 911! Quick!" she shrieked as a male witness pulled out his phone and called the emergency number.

Jade leaned forward, and from a distance, people believed that she was attempting to give mouth to mouth resuscitation and were waiting to see if Craig's eyes were open. But unbeknownst to the pedestrians, Jade was not providing CPR. Instead, she was checking to see if Craig's pulse had stopped yet.

The ambulance was not going to arrive on time, and if it did, there was no way the workers were going to be quick enough to save him. Sure enough, Jade saw the sirens blaring in the distance. Soon, she was watching as they loaded Craig onto a gurney in the back of the ambulance and rushing him to Flushing Medical Center's trauma center.

Later, as the doctor and nurses worked feverishly to revive him, Jade watched from a small window outside the ER. A small smile curved across her face. *There's no way this man is going to make it. He's gone.*

Earlier in the evening while at the club, Jade had sipped on her drink while watching Craig put away shot glass after shot glass. It had been a long day for him, and his primary goal was to get wasted so that he did not have to think about what he was going to do with his date later in the evening. But Craig had not anticipated that Jade was not the person she claimed to be.

With Craig making the fundamental mistake of leaving her at the bar to use the men's room, Jade looked around to make sure nobody was watching her. After making sure that all eyes were glued elsewhere, she took out a few Quaalude pills and a syringe filled with anti-freeze mixed with a clear poison solution, provided to her by her sister.

After quickly spiking his drink with what she knew was a lethal dose, Jade quickly placed the syringe back in her purse. A few minutes later, Craig returned and greedily drank his vodka before leaving the club with her.

Now, the doctors rushed frantically to save his life, but after fifteen minutes, Craig flatlined.

Before she could be questioned, Jade slipped out of the hospital undetected and walked into an empty alleyway. Removing the fake braided wig, she used a napkin to wipe away her makeup and then changed out of her outfit, replacing her heels with black and white Nike Air Force 1s. Taking out her mirror, she checked her reflection. She looked like a different woman, which would make it difficult for people to track her. Feeling no remorse for Craig, she took her prepaid track phone out and called her sister, LaToya.

That'll teach that flat-footed negro who hurt my sister. Next time, I ain't gonna use the name Jade. I'm a chameleon. I got to blend in, but I also want to be a sexy chameleon. Gotta give myself another name. I'll figure it out eventually.

After three rings, LaToya picked up. "What's up, girl?" she greeted.

"Chilling, Toya. Yo, remember the fool that played you last week by dropping you off in the taxi?"

"Yeah, what about it?"

"I took care of him."

"Word? Okay, I see you, Ms. Tina. Go on wit' yo' bad self, girl. Keep this up, and T gonna definitely add you to the family," LaToya replied.

"Appreciate that, sissy. Tell T that I said what's up." Ending the call, Tina threw the phone in the trash and walked down the subway steps.

Craig's unexpected death was reported in the news that evening, and his family called the police to open an investigation due to suspected foul play, but with no suspects or leads, the case went cold.

Tina Leigh Richardson had many hidden identities and aliases in the past, but she wanted a name that would divert suspicion from her. Looking in the mirror again, she adjusted the bang which partially covered one eye. *I look like Lola Bunny from Space Jam.*

Chuckling to herself, she finally found the name that would suit her for years to come. It was the first time Bunny killed, but it would not be her last. In a few days, LaToya would introduce her to Tadarius Hill, the leader of the notorious gang, M.O.B. Seventeen years later, Bunny would seduce another man by the name of Anthony Franks, which would lead to his abduction by her associates.

MARC A. BEAUSEJOUR

CHAPTER 1

DIVINE VENGEANCE

DRIVING DOWN QUEENS Boulevard, Tony Franks' girlfriend, Tina Leigh, caressed his thick beard and lower neck. He was wearing sunglasses to shield his sensitive eyes from the sun's glare, along with an Adidas hoodie, cargo pants, and classic Timberland boots. His girlfriend wore a thick North Face jacket with designer jeans and a long sleeve sweater. Even though they were dressed conservatively now, that had not been the case an hour earlier.

After a night of passionate lovemaking, Tony woke up to Tina staring lovingly at him. *How did I get so lucky to get this amazing woman?*

Despite criticism from members of his family and friends for moving abruptly in his relationship, Tony felt that he finally found the girl of his dreams. It was not only about their intimate moments in which there were more than frequent pleasurable experiences, but it was also the emotional support that Tina offered.

One day, Tony, who owned several supermarkets in New York City, found himself the unlikely victim of vandalism. One of his market branches had broken windows, multiple aisles of food and other products destroyed, and fire was set in the bakery, which set off the sprinklers and destroyed his perishable items.

When the branch manager called him at his office to report the incident, Tony rushed over to the store to assess the damage. *Who could have done something like this? What was the intent? Was it robbery?*

To Tony's surprise, after the New York Police Department's thorough investigation, the safe that held the store's funds was virtually untouched, which eliminated robbery as a motive.

One of the officers approached Tony with a different theory as to why his store was vandalized. "Somebody could have done this to send a message. Do you know anyone in this area that was dissatisfied with any of your products, or have you had any irate customers in this branch?"

Tony stared at the officer, looking baffled. "I don't know what you mean, Officer. My grocery stores had ranked near the top in sales and customer satisfaction each fiscal year. I can't imagine anyone who would want to do this."

His stores were not perfect, but which store could be categorized as perfect? Even though the investigation continued after that day, there were no suspects apprehended in connection to the vandalism. The unexplained crime also had a snowball effect, discouraging shoppers from returning to his stores, and as a result, the following quarter began to suffer a loss of sales. Tony was alarmed because he knew that if that trend continued, he would be forced to close one of his locations.

With the stress mounting, Tony could have resorted to drinking, which he'd had an alcohol addiction back in his early twenties. But it was not necessary because nobody was more supportive of him than Tina was. When she'd heard the news, she wasted no time in accompanying Anthony to the store, helping actively in the renovations, picking up garbage with the crews, and replenishing the shelves in the aisles. She had been nothing less than supportive at times where Tony desperately needed support.

With his four brothers otherwise occupied with their own lives, Tony was thankful for Tina, and although he did not want to admit it to any of his friends or family just yet, he found himself falling deeper in love with the woman that he had met only some weeks earlier. As Tony continued driving, Tina continued her caressing, navigating from his beard to the back of his neck, where her soft hands caused the hairs on the back of his neck to stand.

"Baby, come on now...I'm driving, and you're making me lose focus."

"I can't help it, baby. You are so sexy when you're focused. I keep thinking about last night. Oh, baby, nobody else know how to put it down like you do," she cooed as Tony stopped at a red light in a busy intersection.

"Well, you know I had to handle mine. You are insatiable, girl."

"You know, you didn't have to drive me back to my place. I could've taken an Uber or a bus to get back home. I know you gotta head back to work. I didn't want you to go through all the trouble."

But Tony shook his head. "Nah, Tina, I can't let you do that. You're my girl, baby. You ain't some ole' one-night stand. You deserve more than that. Besides, what I look like having my girl wait for a taxi or bus when I could get her back home?"

Despite the love he felt for her, the one trait of Tina that Tony never understood was the air of mystery surrounding her. Tina was extremely private. Ever since they had started dating, Tony had neither been to Tina's house, nor had he ever met her parents or anyone connected to her. If they weren't at Tony's house, they were either at the club or going out on dates in various places, but each time Tony insisted on driving Tina back home, she always declined, opting to take an Uber or a bus instead.

Tony never pressed the matter because he did not want to scare Tina away by being overly protective of her. If she felt herself being smothered, Tina was the type of woman that would not hesitate to walk away from a situation where she felt trapped.

But on this morning, Tony would hear none of it. He wanted to drive Tina home and show the same support that she showed him following the vandalism of his store. Tina did not refuse Tony, and he was eagerly anticipating the venture into Tina's world, where she lives, what she did with her spare time when she was not with him, and maybe even meet some people in her inner circle. As they finally arrived at the two-story house just outside of Forest Hills, New York, Tony parked his car and opened his door.

"Baby, please go on to work. You ain't gotta walk me in," Tina said, but Tony shook his head.

"Tina, listen. In my last relationship, I had the chance to spoil my lady and treat her better than I should have, but I missed that opportunity. I don't wanna make the same mistake. Please let me take care of you. I'll walk you to your door."

Tina lowered her head, and at first, Tony thought that she was going to refuse his offer once again. But then she replied, "Okay. Do you wanna come in? I can make you coffee, you know, that hazelnut flavor that you like."

Tony smiled. "See? That's what I'm talkin' about. Yeah, I would definitely love some coffee, baby."

Tina leaned in and gave Tony a long, lingering kiss and slowly guided him to her door.

I ain't gotta be in the store that early. Maybe if I'm lucky, I might get to go round two before I take off.

As Tina opened the door to the house, Tony followed her inside. The foyer and the kitchen area were connected. Tony looked around, unable to distract himself from the unusual layout of the home. Normally, a person would have picture frames hanging everywhere with plants, mirrors, and mixes of potpourri that made a domicile an actual home. But Tony saw that Tina's house was devoid of all those items. The walls were bare, the paint was peeling off in areas, and the floor creaked with every third step.

Man, this place needs a makeover bad. I need to hook her up with my home maintenance guru, Esteban Escovido. That dude worked wonders at my spot, so he can definitely work a miracle in this chick's crib.

As if she read his thoughts, Tina said, "Yeah, I know it looks kind of shitty right now, but I just moved here a couple weeks ago, so I'm still getting acclimated to this place."

"Nah, I ain't said nothing. I feel you. If you need me to come by and throw some elbow grease in here and spruce the place up, I got you."

"Thanks, but I got someone that's helping me in a couple days with the home décor. I just stored away the boxes in one of the bedrooms a couple days ago. I ain't in a rush, what with work and all and helping out at the store. Please, sit and I'll get you some coffee."

While Tony sat in the kitchen, Tina opened her cupboards and counter drawers, searching frantically for the coffee. After five minutes of searching, she said, "You know what? I might have not unpacked the coffee bag. It might be in one of my boxes upstairs. Give me a minute, baby, and I'll run up to get it."

As he watched Tina walk up the stairs, Tony looked around. Even with the sun's rays peeking through the window and a small light on in the kitchen, the dull gray paint color gave the kitchen an uncomfortable vibe.

Tina's got it going on in the body, but she knows next to nothing about home décor. I'mma help her with that though because the way it looks, it might as well be a dude with no taste livin' up in here.

After five minutes passed, then ten minutes, Tony began to feel uneasy. What was taking Tina so long? *It should not take that much time to look for coffee.*

If she did not have any, they could just run to Dunkin' Donuts and grab a coffee on the way to the store. Checking the time on his phone, Tony saw that it was almost ten. He had planned to meet the manager, Peter Kappolo, at 10:30 that morning, and if he stayed any longer, he was going to be late.

Then there was an eerie feeling that crawled down Tony's sides, a feeling that he was being watched. Tony was not one to be frightened, but he could not shake the uncomfortable feeling of being monitored. As he sat, a shadow loomed over him. Tony turned around, expecting to see Tina.

But it was not Tina who stood over him, but a gangly, tall male with various tattoos all over his arms and neck. Without warning, the man struck Tony in the face and knocked him out cold.

Forty minutes later, Tony opened his eyes. He was lying on a brown patterned couch in the living room. Rubbing his face, his eyes blurred as different images swam before him. As soon as they came into focus, Tina appeared, but she was not alone. A tall man stood with his arms around her, and he suddenly broke out into laughter.

"Damn, man! You got knocked the fuck out!"

Shaking his head after hearing the *Friday* reference, Tony began to sit up, rubbing his face. To his surprise, Tina laughed. *What the hell is so funny? What is going on?*

"Wake up, sunshine."

"Who the hell are you? Tina, what's goin' on?" Tony asked, dazed and confused.

"I'm sorry, baby. I failed to mention that this ain't really my house. I'm just bummin' it here for a few. You really should have let me take an Uber home."

There was a hint of snarky arrogance in Tina's voice that Tony had not heard from her before. Her appearance had changed as well. Previously she had been sporting a black weave when she walked up the stairs, but now she had short, cropped hair.

"Who the hell are you?" Tony asked the man again, but after his eyes refocused, there was no denying who he was. Tony had seen him before from news reports and from the descriptions mentioned by his half-brother, Antonio Franks, who had changed his name to Edward Reed just to escape from the one man who now stood before Tony.

"Funny, you don't know who I am. Figured your brother told you all about me."

"Yeah, he told me you were a deranged psychopath he used to run with before he wised up," Tony replied angrily. He was not going to let Tadarius or anyone with dangerous affiliations intimidate him.

"Then, I'm sure he told you that anyone who fucked with me was gonna suffer the consequences?"

Tony then turned to Tina. The woman who had once stolen his heart was now crushing it to bits right before his very eyes. "So, all this time you've been playin' me?" he asked.

"No, it was real to me, at least for the first couple months before I found out who you were related to. You Franks boys ain't too smart now, huh?"

"Look, whoever you are and whatever dealings you have with my brother ain't got nothin' to do with me, all right? I ain't even seen him in months."

"No, see that's where you wrong, B. You in it now, dawg. See, your brother took someone away from me, and he's gonna help me get her back. Then after that, he's gonna get dealt wit' and if you get in my way, then you'll get dealt wit' too." Tadarius's eyes gleamed in rage. "Do you think it was coincidence what happened to your store?"

Tony's eyes widened in rage as he looked at Tina. *There's no way he would've known me unless he had someone on the inside. Tina. She knew all about the stores, and she knew how to get in.*

Tony was convinced that Tina led Tadarius's gang syndicate, M.O.B., to the store locations where they looted and destroyed everything. The most infuriating aspect of the whole ordeal was that Tina pretended to care about the store being destroyed to the point of helping the workers in restoration efforts, even though she was the reason it was vandalized in the first place.

Tony looked at Tina as if he were seeing her for who she really was. "You're an evil, conniving bitch, you know that?"

"Tell me something I don't know," she laughed.

It was all a sick joke to them. They did not care whose lives they ruined, long as it fit their agenda.

"Oh, and in case you ain't aware, since you're our guest of honor, we would like for you to stay for a while, and before you ask, it ain't a request."

Tadarius lifted his gang-emblemed T-shirt to reveal the holster of a gun stuffed in his waist. "Give me his phone," he ordered Tina, who walked over to Tony and pulled out his cell phone.

She handed it to Tadarius, and he searched for Edward's number. When he found it, he pulled out his own phone and called the number.

"Now, it's time to tell yo' brother the happy news."

After the phone rang numerous times and went to voicemail, Tadarius left a sinister message that Edward would receive later in the day.

CHAPTER 2

DIVINE VENGEANCE

THE PHONE DROPPED on the floor as Edward Reed sat on his couch with his shoulders now slumped. Burying his face in his hands, he struggled to control his rhythmic breathing as he attempted to make sense of the cold message left by the notoriously liberated gang leader.

Feeling himself hyperventilating, Edward ran to his bathroom, turned on the faucet to his sink, and splashed his face with cold water. *This can't be happening. What's up with those sick assholes?*

Edward knew that Tadarius, known for his cruelty and natural disregard for others, was capable of murdering anyone without a second thought. Now, he had placed Edward's family in danger, and if Tony was killed, Edward knew his brother's blood would be on his hands.

Struggling to overcome the feeling of despair, Edward slammed his fist against the bathroom wall. As the sharp, searing pain shot up his arm, he stared at his knuckles, which had begun to draw blood. Taking a towel to wipe them, he was determined not to be Tadarius's pawn piece to be pushed around. He was not the Antonio

Franks that encountered Tadarius and his gang under the bridge where they had met.

I'm not going to play his game. He thinks because I'm a lawyer, I'm soft, and I'm just gonna let him do what he wants. He already killed Xavier and David, so he expects me to be shook. Nah, I ain't giving him the pleasure.

Walking to his room, Edward opened a dresser drawer and pulled out the Smith and Wesson handgun that he kept fully loaded. Gripping the chrome handle of the weapon, he reflected on his image in his room mirror. It was only a split second, but he saw his father, Phillip—again.

The memories of his father returning to their old home in Brooklyn when he was five years of age returned into his subconscious. Phillip had brought a loaded gun. Edward, not knowing any better at the time, had got a hold of the gun, and it was at that point that his mother, Isabelle, had made the decision to leave Phillip and move to Queens soon after the separation.

Am I cursed to live this life like my father did? Always looking behind me, wondering if I'm gonna be a victim...how foolish was I to think that this all was going to end with LaToya being arrested! Now they got my brother, and if they kill him, his blood's on my hands.

His heart racing in astronomical levels, Edward went to his drawer and searched through his clothes and other miscellaneous objects until he found a tiny gray pouch that had the green leafy substance that he was looking for. Grabbing a small piece of flammable paper, he poured the marijuana leaves into the center of the paper. After intricately rolling the paper into a joint, he found his lighter and sparked it.

Taking a few drags, he managed to slow his heart rate down as he paced his living room floor. Marijuana was able to keep him level-headed. He began to ponder his next move. Suddenly, he had a plan that would put him on the offensive, and if it worked to perfection, he might be able to save his brother and put a stop to M.O.B. in one fell stroke.

Grabbing his phone, Edward began to dial a familiar number, and while waiting for the recipient of the call to pick up, he began to concoct a plan. *Okay, Tadarius, you think you running things here? I'mma show you who's really runnin' things. I'mma destroy your whole empire, even it takes just me to do so.*

At Omega Studios, Andrea McAfee waited at her booth for producer and sound engineer Grover "Groove" Jenkins to play the track that she co-wrote and composed with prominent songwriter Deedee Underwood. The track was entitled "To the Ends of the Earth."

Andrea closed her eyes as she had done countless times and allowed the track to flow in her ears. Having been a recording artist for more than ten years, Andrea had grown wiser about the trappings of the music industry, and she was methodical and precise when it came to the selection of her team of producers and songwriters for her upcoming album.

But on this day when Andrea had closed her eyes, instead of the diving images of serenity and peace needed to sing the track, she saw and heard a different voice, and another figure appeared in her consciousness.

"Loree always had everything. Since we were kids, she always had it all—the best clothes. She had both her mama and her daddy. She was popular at school and in M.O.B. She was the little pampered hoe that everyone wanted."

The voice of her sister's killer played in her head over and over: LaToya—the one girl who had pretended to console her over the years after a lengthy absence turned out to be Loree's murderer, and she was completely unaware of it until the night Edward Reed visited her and exposed the truth about the fateful night. Andrea still saw the barrel of the gun pointed directly at her, and LaToya's insane expression had mired on her face as she prepared to fire the weapon.

"So, who finally told you that it was me?" LaToya asked as a cruel, cold smile curved her lips. She smiled gleefully as she pointed the weapon at the sister of her deceased former best friend. "Not that

it matters anyway because you're gonna be joining her and her man very soon..."

Unbeknownst to Andrea, the track started to play, but she had not shaken herself out of her trance.

"Yo, Adia, you good?" Groove asked as he stopped the track, snapping Andrea back to reality.

After taking a few days off, it was her first day back at the studio, and Andrea wanted to forget the events of that evening. But it was difficult to let go. She stared death right in the face, and the fact that her life could have ended at any moment still shook her to her core.

Against her better judgment, Andrea decided to return to the studio because if there was one activity that allowed her to transition through tragedy, it was singing for the Lord and singing for her soul. Music had to be soothing and loving to her, but she came to the realization that some wounds would never heal.

"I'm fine, Groove. Let's play it back."

Groove replayed the track from the top, and Andrea closed her eyes as she attempted once again to drown herself in the song.

"It's over, Mama. Let it go," Chris said, stepping out from behind the house with Edward.

"Chris, after everything Tadarius and I have done for us, you go and do this? You betray the Fam like this?"

"They're not my family. Not anymore. I ain't a pawn out here," Chris replied, defiantly.

"Like father, like son, huh? Well, I guess you overplayed yo' hand, and you lost too," she said, firing the gun.

Anticipating the gunfire, Edward dove at Chris, knocking him down. The bullet missed Chris and Edward by inches.

"Freeze!" Detective Shawn Wells yelled, accompanied by two police officers.

The scene played over in Andrea's head, and the more she played the scene, the more it nauseated her. Was LaToya really going to shoot her own son for the sake of the false family that M.O.B. portrayed itself as? If the detective had not arrived when he did, would she have survived the evening?

What alarmed her even more was that she questioned, if LaToya was fiercely loyal to the notorious gang, how did she know that Edward was not still loyal to them? How did she know that Chris, whom she discovered was later adopted by David Anderson's family, was not still loyal to the set? The amount of uncertainty caused a level of uneasiness within Andrea, and as the track started again, she had yet to sing one note.

"Adia, what's up? Are you okay?" Groove asked again.

When Andrea started to answer that she was okay, she realized it was far from the truth. She was not okay, and perhaps she may have returned to the studio too soon. "I'm sorry, Groove. I need to take a walk."

Placing her headset down, Andrea walked out of the booth and then outside the studio. The temperature had dipped from mildly cold to generally frigid, but she had to walk outside the studio to try to get her mind right. It had been tough to accept the fact that her sister was slain by gang members, but Andrea was always comforted by the fact that the supposed killer was behind bars.

When the revelation was made that LaToya shot Loree in a jealous rage and jumped town to avoid conviction, Andrea was monumentally upset to the point where if she would've had a pistol in her own hand, she would have committed a crime herself. She had been visited by thoughts of going out and eliminating all members of M.O.B. by herself, including the leader, Tadarius. *That piece of scum doesn't deserve to live after what he did.*

When Edward revealed to her that he may be part of a bounty where Tadarius was killing all former members that turned their backs on the leader once he was imprisoned, Andrea had half a mind to turn Edward from her door and tell him to deal with that situation himself.

After all, you made the decision to join that gang, knowing full well how dangerous those guys were. You were in the car the day my sister died. You could've gotten her out, and she would still be here today.

But Edward vowed to get justice for Loree on her behalf, and Andrea knew that it was out of guilt to atone for not saving her sister's life. With the emotional distress that it had caused her, Andrea was also forced to postpone the marriage to her longtime boyfriend, Quentin Stevens.

He was not thrilled that Andrea was postponing the marriage, and since then, their relationship cooled off to where both Andrea and Quentin appeared icy and indifferent towards one another. Although Andrea countlessly expressed her love for Quentin, she knew that he was crushed, and although he acted as if he was okay with the postponement of the wedding, she could visibly see that he was bothered by being placed in the background once again while the quest to put Loree's killer behind bars took precedence over their relationship.

Quentin had spent all high school pursuing Andrea before their lives took on different paths with him going to Morehouse College in Atlanta to study engineering while Andrea signed with Metro Records, becoming the R&B songstress, Adia. When Quentin returned to New York to find work, he reconnected with Andrea, who had just ended her high-profile relationship with rapper and fellow label mate De'Von Franklin. The relationship eventually blossomed, and although Andrea loved Quentin, she could not help but notice how meticulous and detailed he was about every facet of his life.

At first, it was a breath of fresh air for Andrea because she was in a relationship with a man who was all about his business, and his approach to daily situations was precise. But on the other side, it made Quentin appear paranoid. Andrea suspected that he had OCD or some type of compulsory issue because he wanted to know where she was at all times. He wanted her to be home at a certain time of night, and before all the events occurred with LaToya, Quentin had wanted Andrea to consider life outside of the music business.

"Andrea, I know that you are a great artist, and you're doing very well right now, but how long do you think that will last? Every artist has a shelf life."

"Okay, Quentin, I get that, but even if I don't sing anymore, I can still stay at Omega and help develop other artists. I can write songs, arrange, produce...there is so much that I can do. But don't ask me to just walk away from what I love to do."

"Andrea, there's nothing wrong with growing and developing a passion for something else. The music industry almost had you bankrupt, you've lost friends, and you've lost money. Besides, the landscape has changed now with everyone streaming music these days and not buying albums. How much do you think your brand will sustain? People are gonna eventually get tired of Adia."

The moment Quentin blurted that statement, Andrea furiously walked out of the house and was determined to go back to the studio. *If time off meant having to deal with Quentin's nonstop nagging and endless persuasion to leave the industry, I'd rather return back to work in the studio.*

As Andrea paced the outside of the studio, she looked through her phone contacts. As she passed Vanessa's name and number, she smiled. The only good that came out of all the drama with LaToya and her sister was that she was able to reconnect with her longtime friend Vanessa.

For years, the two friends were estranged, following a fallout from when Vanessa was raped by one of De'Von's friends. Vanessa then left to go to college, and the two had not spoken until they reconnected.

But Andrea looked for a different phone number. She needed professional advice, and only one person could provide her with such advice. *It's time to schedule an appointment with Dr. Ralwinski again.*

Lying down in his new bed in his new room on Saturday morning, Chris Anderson reflected upon the previous seventy-two hours. Within that span of time, his biological mother, LaToya Richardson, was arrested and charged with the murder of his biological father, David.

Raised under the tutelage of Tadarius, Pooh, and the other members of M.O.B., Chris had been tracking his father for years until their meeting at a club one night. It was a first meeting that he was all too eager to forget. David never acknowledged him and just brushed him off.

But after Chris met Edward Reed, a thought came to his mind. *Maybe I don't have to hustle out here to make my bones. Why am I begging for attention from a father who don't give a shit about me? My mom wants me to track him down, but what good is tracking him down if I can't even start a conversation with a man who was supposed to show me how to navigate this world?*

For the longest time, Chris never saw himself as anything more that the heir to M.O.B.'s empire, the empire that his father had walked away from and snitched on years earlier. Then, LaToya was doing some infiltration herself, hanging out and pretending to be friends with the sister of some old girl that she had killed years earlier.

Her plan was to destroy Andrea's reputation, and with that in shambles, the public would not miss her when the time came to send her six feet under. But Chris and Edward thwarted LaToya's plan and blew her cover and tipped off the police when LaToya unintentionally confessed to David Anderson's murder along with Loree's murder.

LaToya was arrested that evening, and after David was laid to rest a few days later, Edward gave Chris an ultimatum. "All right, Chris, your mom's in jail, and you have no other legal guardian, which means you're a ward of the state at this point. You've got two choices. Either you go back to the system and keep running with this gang that has no future, possibly facing life behind bars, or be raised the right way by the family you never had."

It was a no brainer for Chris. Word would have already gone out that he betrayed the gang affiliates that had taken care of him and his mother, and that would make him a likely target for the other members of M.O.B. With his future uncertain, Chris decided to give the stable family life a chance.

"I'm with door number two, Eddie. So what, you're gonna adopt me then?"

"No, not me, my friend. You have a chance to know who David really was by being raised by his family. What do you say?"

"All right, I'll do it."

"But you gotta promise me one thing, Chris. You gotta promise me that you ain't gonna drag this family into gang affairs, and you ain't gonna get the other kids in the family involved with your mess. You gotta let go all this 'hood G' mentality, keep a low profile, go to school, and be as much of a model citizen as you can. You got it? You've been given a second chance, so don't screw it up."

After Chris agreed to the initial terms, Edward drove him to the adoption agency that was adjacent to the courtroom in Jamaica, Queens. There, Chris met David's widow, Renee Anderson, who had agreed to take full custody of him.

Still reeling from the death of her beloved husband, Renee was not too excited about the prospect of taking in a former gangbanger, especially the son of the woman who stood accused of murdering her husband. When Edward had approached Renee with the idea, she had her mind set on refusing the adoption and making Chris a state ward. But Renee knew that it would not be safe for Chris to be in the system. He was also David's son, and if there was any cause that David sacrificed his life for, it was improving the condition of the youth and keeping them away from the streets.

Aside from coaching football during the school season, he ran off-season football camps and academic clinics with the purpose of cultivating young men's minds through education and football. Chris was the type of child that David would adopt for the mere purpose of keeping him off the streets and away from the influence of M.O.B. and other gangs.

Renee's kids—Dennis, age thirteen; Cree, age eleven; and Katrina, age eight—were already struggling to cope with their father's death. Dennis walked around the house aimlessly, randomly lashing out at his sisters, at times for no reason. He stopped hanging out with his friends, rather opting to stay home and spend hours on end playing his video games. Renee knew that Dennis was trying to internalize his grief, and each family member dealt with the loss differently.

Cree, once an aspiring gymnast, abruptly quit the gymnastics team and dove deeper into her studies. Renee would sometimes walk by her room and hear quiet, racked sobs from the room where Cree and her younger sister Katrina slept.

Out of all the children, Katrina was the most heartbroken over the death of her beloved father. He had been her teddy bear, someone that she ran and hugged whenever she felt sad, lonely, or fearful. He was her hero, and she was the one whom he lovingly gave the nickname "Tri-Tri".

Explaining death to an eight-year-old was not easy for Renee, and when she explained to her that "Daddy had gone to heaven to live with the angels," Katrina tugged at Renee's heartstrings when she asked the question, "When is he gonna come back, Mommy?"

It was the hardest conversation that Renee ever had to have with her kids, and it was all because some lowlife woman had decided to take the love of her life away from her.

After the adoption papers were signed and notarized and after the conversation between Edward and Chris's case worker, Renee was driving back home with the new addition to the family. At first, there was an awkward silence in the car.

But Chris was the first to break the ice. "Hey, Mrs. Anderson, I wanna thank you for accepting me into your family. I'm sorry for what my mother did to David—I mean, Dad."

After another two minutes of silence, Renee replied, "Don't worry about it, Chris. You were in a bad situation with your mom, and I don't blame David's death on you. You are a part of this family now, honey, and I don't ever want you to feel guilty over what happened."

"Yes ma'am."

As Renee rounded the final intersection to arrive home, she glanced at Chris, who was playing games on his cell phone. "Okay, so Chris, before we arrive home, I feel it's my duty as your legal guardian to let you know that we have a few rules for you to follow as a new member of our family."

"Sure, I'll do whatever I can."

"Good, so here's rule number one. In this family each of us does chores over the week, and these chores will vary each week. One week, you may have trash duty, the other week, dish-cleaning duties, and the other week, someone will vacuum and dust furniture. When David was around, everyone had their responsibilities, and I plan on keeping it that way now more than ever. Everyone shifts every week and does something different. David designed this for a reason: to show everyone a sense of hard work and consistency. Do you understand?"

"Yes, Mrs. Anderson, I got it."

Looking at her new son, Renee decided to pick his brain next as they pulled into the driveway of their home. "Another thing, how were your grades in your old school?"

Man, this woman is a drill sergeant. I'm starting to wonder if I should take my chances in the system. I had C's and D's in my old school, and for me and my mother it was good enough, long as I passed. "Well, I passed my classes, if that's what you mean."

Renee shook her head. *This young man is gonna learn today that we have a standard of excellence in this house, and we won't accept the bare minimum here.*

"Well, in this family, just passing isn't good enough. We want A's and B's around here, okay?"

A's and B's?? I barely saw a B last year, and I thought that was pretty damn good for what it was. "A's and B's?"

"You heard me, Chris. In a couple days, you're going to be enrolled in Townsend Harris High School. That's the school where your daddy was a football coach, and he didn't play with the grades, and neither do we, so I expect the same from you. No goofing off in class, no acting a fool in class, and most importantly, study for all your exams. Keep your mind on them books and not on them girls."

"Now, Mrs. Anderson, I definitely feel you about keeping my mind on them books, but you asking me not to think about the ladies?

Chris is all about the women. I make no promises on that one," he chuckled, not realizing that Renee did not share in the joke with him.

"I'm serious, Chris. I already told my kids about you, and you're the oldest, so they'll be looking up to you, and the last thing I need is for you to set a poor example for them. If I see that you are influencing my kids negatively, we're taking a trip back to the agency. You got it?"

"All right, all right...I'll just mess with the women outside of your home in my spare time. Is that cool?"

"And that leads me to the most important rule in this house, especially for you," Renee continued, disregarding his last statement. "Edward filled me in on your background, and I did my homework on you, so I'm gonna give you this final rule without mincing words. The moment you enter this home, you have renounced any association or affiliations with any gangs or organized crime groups as well as crime-related activities. That means no drinking, no smoking, and I already mentioned about the girls, but I can't stress it enough, being that you're fifteen and got raging hormones. I also see that you have a few tattoos on your arm, so those better be your last because as long as you're under my roof, you ain't puttin' any new ink on you. Understood?"

Damn, this lady runs a tight shift here. I don't even think the state pen got as many rules as she does. "Yeah, I hear you, Mrs.

Anderson. No drugs, no alky, no women. Next, you're gonna arrange to have me neutered, I suppose?"

Chuckling at the dry joke, Renee said, "You're a funny guy, Chris. You'll be fine. Just follow the rules that we've set, and you'll do well. So, get your stuff, and go upstairs, and it's the first room to your left. I've already prepared it for you."

Might as well get me a pair of handcuffs too cuz I feel like I'm locked up.

CHAPTER 3

DIVINE VENGEANCE

ON A FRIGID MONDAY morning, the Andersons were bustling and preparing to return to school. It was the first week of the new year and the beginning of a new decade, but for the Andersons, it would be a year of adjustment as they prepared to move on without the patriarch of the house. The tragic murder of David had occurred two days after Christmas, so the holiday season that had started with happiness and joy took a somber dive as the year 2019 ended.

The children still had not fully come to terms that their father was no longer around. Cree, who was a social butterfly in her school, withdrew and became very introverted following David's death. She had gone out for the cheerleading squad in I.S. 219 and succeeded in making the squad.

Now in sixth grade, Cree was starting to go through early stages of puberty, experiencing her first menstrual cycle. Renee began shopping for her daughter's first bra the week before school reopened, shedding a tear as she made her way to the juniors' female section of the store. *If only David was here to see how much his daughters have grown.*

Although they were young, Renee started to see characteristics of her late husband in her children. Dennis had started to bulk up, and while he grieved over his father, he was resolved not to let his emotions show. So, Dennis channeled his grief into his daily workouts, lifting weights in his room.

He was currently the leading scorer on his school's eighth-grade basketball team, and he was working on his dribbling and his jump shot. The court was the best outlet for Dennis, and he would often disappear during the day while the kids were on winter break, and he would go to the basketball courts at the park and play open pick-up games with local kids.

Katrina, who had experienced an unexpected growth spurt from ages six to eight and was at least two inches taller than everyone else in her class, had now stopped running track. Renee had flashbacks to her own growth spurt when she was younger. Because of that, combined with her young beauty, innocence, and gracefulness, her parents encouraged her to model in various beauty pageants, which kicked off her modeling career. Renee saw the same future for Katrina and had in mind to convince her to join in the yearly New York Young Debutante's Pageant, held each year in May. But with her father gone, Katrina focused more in school, excelling in science. Out of all the children, Katrina was the only student who still maintained straight A's on her report cards.

Then there was Chris, who in all respects was the prodigal son who had returned home in the wake of tragedy. After settling down in his room that previously served as a guest room, Chris tried his best to bond with his half siblings but with little results.

Dennis would merely nod at Chris whenever he passed him by, but otherwise, he would not carry a conversation with Chris. The children's worlds had been shattered just a week earlier, and it was just too soon to include anyone in their inner circle. Chris did not expect them to warm up to him immediately, but he figured after a week, they would finally accept him.

Unfortunately, that was not the case with Dennis or Katrina. The only one out of the group that showed him a warm reception was Cree but more so out of fascination of Chris than anything.

While alive, David had done his best not to expose his children to gang culture or any semblance of it. He did not want his kids going down the same path that he once walked, so he kept his kids as sheltered as possible. All they did was go to school, participate in school activities, and return home. They never enjoyed freedom beyond what was allowed in their home, and so they were not privy to gang members or anyone of the like.

So when Cree saw Chris, it was a novelty to her to see someone that had his hair unkempt, his upper arms tatted, and his strongly suggestive outfits, which consisted of tasteless T-shirts and skinny jeans, topped off with a North Face hoodie and Jordans.

Intrigued by her half-brother's look, Cree asked about the tattoos one day while they sat and ate lunch at home. "That looks so dope!" she exclaimed, taking a bite of her pizza.

"Yeah, just a little bit of ink I had done when I was thirteen. No big deal." Chris shrugged it off, taking a bite of his pizza and looking at the dragon tattoo on his arm.

"Didn't it hurt?" Katrina asked.

"Oh yeah, it hurt like a motha—" he started to reply before catching Renee's eyes, which glared at him as if to say, "Boy, I wish you would cuss in front of my kids. I will slap the taste out yo' mouth. You are going to censor your words in this house."

"Like a mother that slaps your arm a hundred times—that's how much!" Chris finished, editing himself, flashing a small thumbs up to Renee. *Nice save.*

Although they did not discuss it on the ride back from the courtroom, it was clear that Renee did not condone the use of foul language in her home. David, who often had loose lips himself, had worked overtime to make sure his children spoke intelligently and avoided using profanity.

"That looks so cool! Man, I wish I could get a tattoo," Cree said.

"Yeah, you can get one when you leave for college, but as long as you're under this roof, there will be no body art allowed. Do ya'll understand?" Renee asked sternly.

"But Dad had one, and Chris has one!" Cree protested.

"Those were special cases. Dad had his tattoo at one point late in his teens, but did he get anymore since then? No. Same goes for Chris...that tattoo you just saw will be his last as long as he's here. Right, Chris?"

"As you said, Mrs. Anderson, no more tattoos for me."

"No piercings in weird places either. Right, Mr. Chris? If it's not on your ears, I don't want to see earrings worn anywhere else."

"Roger that, Mrs. A.," Chris replied.

"Mrs. A.?"

"A for Anderson, of course. I gotta simplify these names."

"Chris, you 're a mess," Renee laughed before the other kids laughed also. The conversation broke the ice, and the family began to accept Chris into their family.

Even Dennis managed to crack a smile that morning. Now he was on his way to Townsend Harris High School for the first time, a school where his late father made his reputation. It was the first day of the new semester, and Renee dropped all her kids off, starting with Katrina, dropping her off at the local elementary school. Then she dropped Dennis and Cree off to I.S.219, the junior high school, which happened to be on the way to Townsend Harris.

As they pulled up to the high school, where Renee joined a series of other parents dropping their children off on the first day, Renee turned to face Chris in the passenger seat. "Okay, Chris. Here it is...Townsend Harris High."

Chris lowered the window so he could have a better look at the school. The main building ascended to at least four stories high, and it was adjoined to other buildings, including the cafeteria, the gymnasium, and the school library. Chris was also able to see large field lights that surrounded the vast football field.

"Okay, listen to me, Chris. David had a reputation here, okay? He was a beloved football coach here and a role model to the students, so I need you to be on point this semester."

Chris rolled his eyes. He could not bear to hear another speech from Renee again about walking the straight and narrow path. The goal was to keep his head low and not bring attention to himself.

He was sure that Tadarius, Pooh, and the other members of M.O.B. knew about his part in having his mother arrested in connection to David's murder as well as the previously closed case of Loree McAfee although there had been reluctance in the New York justice system to re-open the case, and the man originally charged with David's murder, Terrell Washington, still remained in prison.

"Okay, Mrs. A., I know where this is going. Look, I'm tryin' to lay low, so I ain't gonna mess up my pop's rep. You ain't gotta worry about a thing."

Although she was still unconvinced, Renee flashed her new stepson a warm smile, reached into her purse, and pulled out twenty-five dollars and a student bus pass. "Okay, here's your lunch money for the week and a bus pass to take the Q21 back home."

Handing the money and the pass to him, Chris shook his head, "C'mon, Mrs. A, twenty-five bucks? That ain't enough to last me a week."

"Boy, it looks like you gon' have to make it enough. I'm already on a tight budget, and with David no longer around, I gotta cover all the bills now. If it wasn't for David's life insurance, you wouldn't even have twenty-five dollars."

"Okay, I got you. So, what if I get a job? It wouldn't be full time or nothin' like that—just a lil' part-time gig—to help pay the bills?"

Renee smiled. Although she was still learning about Chris, she was pleased that he was trying to help out at home. "No, sweetie, I couldn't ask you to do that. I just want you to focus on school and get your grades up there. Then maybe we can talk increase on your weekly allowance. Show me that you can put the work in, and if you can maintain your grades, I will consider allowing you to apply for a part-time job after school."

"All right, bet. My grades gon' be so high, these ivy-league prep schools gonna be begging for me to come."

"Really? I didn't know Princeton, Yale, and Harvard accepted C- and D+ students. That's news to me," Renee laughed, winking at Chris, who shot her a fake exasperated look before laughing also.

"Oh okay, you got jokes, Mrs. A. Okay, just watch me work. Don't let the tats and the gang ties fool you. I'm smarter than Einstein. Just wait and see."

"Boy, if I wait that long, I'll be dead."

Damn, Mrs. A. is two for two on ragging on me about my grades.

When they arrived at the front of the school, Chris stepped out of the car, waved to Renee, and started making his way inside the school, joining the throng of kids entering the school. His first stop was the main office. Having already taken the photo during the registration process a week earlier, Chris soon had his schedule and his ID in hand. Looking at the schedule, he saw that his homeroom was located on the third floor. The office administrator had given him a map of the school, and now he had to find his way.

Studying the map before he left the office, Chris had already memorized the main corridors where all his classes were. He had made a mental note of where the cafeteria was and the library building. He placed the map in his pocket and made his way out into the hallway.

He did not want the kids to see him with the map in his hands, looking like a scrub that did not know where his classes were.

His homeroom teacher, Mr. Atkins, also happened to be his math teacher and taught Algebra II and Geometry. Looking back at his schedule, Chris saw that his next class was American History, taught by Sean B. Thompson. After History, five more classes followed, and his lunch time was wedged between the fourth and fifth periods. *This is gonna be a long-ass day.*

On the way to his class, Chris passed by a glass display that caught his eyes. The display was a memorandum of Coach David Anderson. His team pictures were strewn all over the display, which also had his conference trophy as well as his Coach of the Year trophy. As he looked at his father's endless array of photos, the deep-rooted envy for him began to grow like a bad fungus in his spirit.

These other students saw an accomplished family man that was a phenomenal football coach, a community advocate, and an individual that was admired in many circles in the school, but all Chris could see was a man who was too busy to show up for his first son. *Where was he when I was taking my first baby steps? Where was he when I learned how to ride a bike? Where was he when I was learning how to change a tire on a car?*

LaToya raised Chris to be an outspoken self-made man that did not ask for help from anyone. After all, nobody lifted a finger to help her when she was pregnant with her son.

Tadarius and various members of M.O.B. would stop by from time to time to help LaToya and Chris financially, and Tadarius always believed that Chris would soon run M.O.B. and be feared by other gangs and crime syndicates.

That day never came, and with LaToya now incarcerated, Chris had to move carefully because there was no doubt in his mind that he had become a high-value target under M.O.B.'s radar. Word would have gotten back to Tadarius, no doubt by LaToya, and to Chris's mentally-deranged matriarch, M.O.B. was a family, and any act of betrayal upon the family would be seen as treason.

Chris had not visited his mother behind bars, and presently, he had no interest in visiting her. *The way she used me to scout him so she could kill him was so low down, it's indescribable. I know my father did me wrong, but the man didn't deserve to die like that.*

Not wanting to focus too much on the glass-enshrined memorial, Chris kept on walking, looking around at the other students making their way to class, wondering if any of them had family as twisted as his own. When he located the History class, he made his way to the back row, threw his bookbag down on the floor next to his seat, and sat down.

More students began filing in, but Mr. Thompson was not in class yet. *Maybe if I'm lucky, he might not be here, and we might have a sub. No homework!*

While he was pondering the possibility of an easy first day, a beautiful Black girl walked into the class. She caught Chris's eye right away. Although it was January, and there was a chill factor outdoors, the girl was wearing black, nylon warm-up pants that accentuated her curves and backside. She sported a purple parka that was only zipped up to her chest, revealing a tight white low-cut T-shirt that showed ample cleavage. Her black hair was tied in a ponytail, and she had a caramel complexion.

There were other girls that entered the classroom, but none of them mattered to Chris except for the light-skinned ebony goddess that began to walk his direction. Chris had empty seats in front of him and an empty one to his left. The seat on his right was unoccupied until another kid sat down. He was also Black but with a darker complexion, and he wore a Nike hoodie with ripped skinny jeans and those hideous Keezy shoes that were hot on the market.

Everyone wanted a pair of those shoes and Chris had seen celebrities wear them, which boosted their popularity, but he was not a fan. The designs were hideous with the patchwork pattern and thick laces, and the shoe tongue stuck out like a sore thumb. *Well, he gets an "A" for effort but an "F" for show. He needs to burn them things.*

Focusing back on the girl with the ponytail, Chris prayed silently that she would sit close to him so that he could make his move before Mr. Thompson arrived. The girl initially did not know that she was being stared at. She was talking to another classmate about an episode of *Love and Hip Hop.* To his delight, she sat in the seat in front of him. *Thank you, God!*

The girl, still talking about the episode, had momentarily stopped talking to take her loose-leaf notebook out. Chris prepared to introduce himself.

But the boy who sat on his right spoke first. "Yo, what's good, ma? Damn, you lookin' right today. If I knew you was in this class, I would've sat by you."

The girl turned to look back at the boy. "Whateva, Marlon. I ain't about to deal wit' your shit this semester. By the way, you still messin' wit' that hoe Angela?"

"What? C'mon, girl, she's yesterday's news. It was never that serious between us. You need to give yo' boy another shot. So, what's up after school? You down to go to Harry's?" Harry's was the town deli and grille restaurant, a block away from the school.

"Nah, not today. I gotta get back home and babysit my little brother. You know my mama works long hours."

Watching the exchange between Marlon and the girl, Chris snickered lightly under his breath after watching Marlon's game fall flat, not realizing that the girl had shifted her attention toward him.

"And who might you be? I ain't eva' seen you here before."

"That's cuz it's my first day. Name's Chris."

"What's up, Chris? Shantay Monroe. So, where you from?"

"I'm from hea'. I just went to school on the west side of Queens last year—Bayside."

Upon hearing this, Marlon gave an arrogant presumptuous sneer. "Man, I heard about all them fools at Bayside. Fake, wannabe gangsta ass niggas roll at Bayside."

Chris looked at Marlon, who stared him down, piercing him with his eyes. *Yo, I know this fool don't want no smoke wit' me wit' his K-Mart store-brand Keezy's. Ain't nothin' fake about me. He better stay in his lane, or he gon' find out the hard way.*

"What, you got somethin' to say, Bayside? What's up?"

It took Chris everything he had to suppress his laughter. Marlon really did not know whom he was dealing with. Looking at Marlon, Chris discovered that he was not too big, he was not tall, and he did not have any muscles, at least not under the cheap hoodie he wore. *This skinny dude ain't worth my time and effort. I've seen and fought bigger dudes than him in the fam. This that type of nigga that M.O.B. would make quick work of in a minute. I'm tryin' to lay low, but I ain't no punk. If he think he 'bout to step to me, it's goin' down. Keep playin'.*

Just shaking his head, Chris turned to face the front.

"Yeah, that's what I thought, nigga. You don't want these problems."

Unable to hold it in, Chris started laughing, which infuriated his rival. "The hell's so funny?"

"Leave him alone, Marlon. He ain't said nothin' to you. He's probably laughing cuz you makin' yourself look like a fool out here, talkin' big game," Shantay replied.

"Thank you," Chris replied, feeling validated. *See, she knows what's up.*

"Thank you," Marlon mimicked Chris's baritone.

"What, you some kind of priest? Talkin' all low and shit. Speak up, son."

The room, which had been abuzz with various student conversations, went silent, as eyes began watching the exchange between Chris and Marlon.

Just when Chris was about to reply, Mr. Thompson walked into the room. "Good morning, class. My apologies for being late. For those who don't know me, I'm Mr. Sean B. Thompson, and I will be your History teacher this semester."

Inexplicably, his eyes fell upon Marlon. "Mr. Pierce, how many times are you gonna take this course? You gotta be the only junior in this class. Hopefully, third time's the charm?" he asked while the students burst into laughter.

Chris looked at Marlon, who thrust his head into his hoodie, trying to cover his eyes in embarrassment. *This clown's in eleventh grade, taking a tenth-grade class? Bet he got nothin' to say to me now.*

"C'mon, Mr. Thompson, why you gotta do me like that?" Marlon asked from beneath his hood.

"Do you like what? I mean, all you gotta do is apply yourself and pass all the exams and complete your assignments—a concept that you've yet to grasp."

Yeah, Mr. Thompson is one of them cool teachers. I can work with this.

"I mean, I saw you last year both semesters, and I see you this semester. At this rate, I might be the one standing between you and graduation."

"Whateva," Marlon grumbled.

"Anyway, let me go take attendance and see who else we got here." Mr. Thompson pulled the attendance sheet from his folder and looked over it. "Well, class, it seems we have a son of a community celebrity in here today," he announced.

Chris's heart dropped in horror. *Wait. Please don't do it, Mr. Thompson. It's my first day here, and what you're about to reveal is the last thing I want people to know.*

"It seems that in class today we have the son of our very own Mr. David Anderson, who passed away three weeks ago. Mr. Chris Anderson, are you here today?"

Although he didn't stand up, Chris furtively raised his hand. "Here," he muttered quietly.

There was a huge commotion in the classroom as students turned around to get a good look at the son of their beloved football coach and community beacon.

Shantay turned to face him with a look of fascination on her face. "How come you ain't tell me that Coach Anderson was your dad?" she asked.

Chris just shrugged.

"So, Chris, is this your first semester at Townsend Harris?" Mr. Thompson asked.

"Yeah."

"Well, your father was one of the greatest coaches we had here, and he was a good friend of mine. His untimely death was a tragedy and a huge blow to this community. We all miss him here. But welcome, and I hope that you're as much a hard worker as he was."

Chris only half-smiled, keeping his eyes low. It was Renee speaking to him all over again. *These people have these expectations of me and don't even know what I'm all about. I'm nothing like my father. I'm not a community leader. I'm not a well-loved coach. I'm a reformed former gang member that is trying to walk straight and avoid drawing attention to myself, and this isn't helping.*

As Mr. Thompson continued the roll call, Shantay, who had been whispering something to a classmate, smiled at Chris, which caused jealousy within Marlon. *This is gonna be a long day.*

At the end of the school day, Chris's bookbag was heavy, encumbered with textbooks that he needed to complete his assignments. Unfortunately, each teacher gave the class homework on the first day, which Chris could not fathom. Making his way over to the bus stop booth, he put his bookbag down and rubbed his sore shoulders. Sitting at the bus stop, Chris watched for his bus, unaware that someone had come to sit next to him.

"Hey, Chris Anderson, what's up?" Shantay greeted cheerfully.

"Yo, what's up? Just call me Chris, aight?" he replied smiling, not wanting to come across abrasive.

"Aight, cool."

"So, you normally wait for the bus here too?" he asked.

"Yeah, I live in New Rochelle, so it's a bit far from here. My mom lives in a townhouse a few minutes away from Greenbriar Mall."

"Oh okay, that's what's up. So, what's up wit' yo' boy Marlon?" he asked.

"Oh, Marlon and I just have a little history. That's all. We went out last year, and it was the worst two weeks of my life. He was controlling, rude...just not a good dude, and even after I broke it off wit' him, he stay stalking me."

"Damn, you know they got special mental wards for cats like him."

Shantay laughed, which relieved Chris. Most of the time he found it hard to break the ice with girls, but Shantay was different. She was easy to talk to and down to earth.

"You're funny. So, you neva' did answer my question, Chris. How come you never told me that David Anderson was your dad?"

Chris was hoping that she would let the subject go, but she was determined to know more about him. "Well, truth be told, I didn't really know my dad. See, he was wit' my mom years ago, and after she had me, he just took off. No letter, no note, nothin.' Just left me and my mom. My mom then enlisted in the Army, and we went everywhere: Texas, Georgia, even overseas...Iraq. Then she came back to New York, and it was just me and her and her family for the longest time."

Chris was extremely careful about not mentioning their involvement in M.O.B. because he did not know Shantay. What if she was a new informant for Tadarius? It was not unusual for him to recruit young women to put them on the streets to work for him. On the other hand, Shantay was different. Maybe all she wanted to do was to get to know Chris because she was feeling him. For Chris, the feeling was mutual.

"So, hold up. You mean his widow ain't your mom?" Shantay asked.

"Nah, she isn't my biological mom. But she adopted me after Mom left," he replied, being careful to leave out the detail that his mother was arrested for killing his father.

"Wow, I see. Well, I'm sorry about what happened to your dad. He doesn't seem like that type of guy that would leave his family high and dry. He was really cool when he coached here. He was always nice to me and my friends. Nobody deserved to die that way."

"Thanks. I appreciate that."

As the bus pulled up to the stop, he asked, "So, since you turned down that fool Marlon earlier, if you ain't busy this Saturday, you wanna roll to Harry's wit' me?"

Stepping onto the bus, Shantay examined Chris for a minute. "I don't know. I gotta think about it."

"Aight, it's all good."

"Boy, I'm just playin' wit' you. Yeah, I'm free to go wit' you this Saturday." Shantay laughed as they both sat inside the bus.

Edward Reed stepped out of his car in the building parking lot. He was fully suited and had his government ID with him. As he entered the Queens Women's Detention Center, he started to have doubts about what he was about to do. But if he wanted to keep Tony alive, he had no other alternative. The only silver lining to the entire ordeal was that his plan was in full motion.

After placing a critical phone call, he knew it was only a matter of time before his plan unfolded. If he was to save Tony and other people who were brainwashed by Tadarius, he had to play his game. Fortunately, from the weekly calls and reports that Edward was receiving from M.O.B., he knew that Tony was alive, but he was being forced to work the books for Tadarius and his cousin, Pooh, who were running the daily operations for the syndicate.

Tony counted the money, and because of his business and marketing background, he was able to obtain notarized documents needed for key transactions with other merchants and dealers. Tadarius began to view him as an asset and even rented out one of his apartments to Tony while still sending some members of M.O.B. to check on him routinely.

Walking into the facility, Edward checked his ID and walked into a small interrogation room. Then he heard a loud buzzer, and the door to the room opened as inmate LaToya Richardson, handcuffed and dressed in orange prison garb, entered the room.

CHAPTER 4

DIVINE VENGEANCE

FOR TWO MINUTES, the two individuals stared intensely at one another as if their eyes were shooting lasers to incinerate the other party. Edward gently laid his briefcase on the table and meticulously began to take out his notes without a word.

LaToya just stared at him, snickering. *Oh, he's putting on a good act right now. I know deep inside he's shook. This fool lucky I'm in here cuz if I had my piece wit' me, his brain matter would be all over this table right now.*

After she was arrested, LaToya had inwardly blamed herself for not realizing that she had been set up when she exposed herself to Andrea. LaToya's plan had been to stain the reputation of the gospel star to bring the party girl out of the person that many fans considered a saint. She could scarcely believe her eyes over the years when she had discovered that Loree's sister had become a music star and was sitting on thousands of dollars while she struggled every day as a single mother, newly discharged from the Army.

LaToya could not believe that she was dealt so cruel a hand in life after she had tried to fix everything around her. Loree's murder was supposed to reverse her fortunes and place her above everyone in the M.O.B. family. But it had elevated Loree's sister, and from that moment on, she had to go, but not before LaToya ruined her so that the public would abandon her, and she could get a dose of her personal hell.

Then when the time was right, LaToya would end Andrea's life and send her to join her sister. She had not counted on the traitor Antonio Franks and worst of all, her son, Chris, to join Andrea in exposing her, leading to her arrest in connection to David's murder.

While Loree's murder case was closed because the convicted murder suspect Terrell Washington was behind bars, new evidence had revealed that LaToya had been the one that pulled the trigger due in part to her mental lapse in judgement when she ranted proudly to Andrea about killing her sister. Then, when it all unraveled, the plan was to eliminate the only ones outside the family that knew the truth: David and Andrea.

LaToya was able to silence David, but she could not kill Andrea. *It's okay. I'm just biding my time, waiting for opportunity. This shit ain't over yet, Andrea. You gon' join your sister soon enough, and I won't have to think about that bitch Loree or anyone related to her.*

To LaToya, it did not matter that she was disrespecting the dead because Loree never respected her when she was alive, so why did she deserve her pity?

And as for Chris, I will deal with that boy as soon as I get out. He's definitely being punished for siding with that traitor, and he better fall back in line with Tadarius, Pooh, and the fam. If he doesn't, I'm just going to determine that he's got too much of his father in him, and he will have to go as well. I bought this boy into this world. I have no problem taking him out. Between deciding whether to kill Andrea or her own son, LaToya was now facing the man at the top of her hit list.

"Counselor, please keep in mind that you've got ten minutes. All the prisoners are on schedule, and we need to make sure Inmate Richardson is back in her cell," the guard told Edward.

"Yes sir, I won't be long at all," Edward replied as the guard walked back outside the room, closing the door behind him.

"Yes sir. Listen to yourself. You soundin' like a company man," LaToya mocked. "Is that who you is now?"

She knew that the room she was currently sitting in with Edward was closely being watched by cameras, and she wanted to remain discreet but at the same time show disdain to the very man that sat across from her.

"No, Ms. Richardson, I'm your defense lawyer, Attorney Edward Reed."

Just muttering the words was nauseating to Edward because he could not believe that he was being forced to defend a member of the gang that he loathed.

"So, you've been hired by a mutual friend to come to my defense then?" LaToya asked, her lips curling into a cruel smile.

Ain't nothing mutual about me and Tadarius. I think all of you should be locked up with the key thrown away or somewhere else six feet under, pushing up daisies. "Yes, I've been sent here to discuss your case and how we can appeal for a new trial."

"Okay, that's cool. So have the terms of our agreement been discussed with you by our mutual friend yet?"

Edward glared at LaToya more fiercely than he had when he first entered the room. He knew that she was referring to the abduction of Tony and the threat made by Tadarius that if he did not strategize a way to spring her out of prison, his brother would be murdered. *You're a cold-hearted bitch, and I wish nothing but the worst for you. I'm playing this little charade, but I like to play games too, and when I set my own plan in motion, I'm leavin' your ass right here.*

But he did not express his thoughts aloud, partly due to the level of surveillance in the room, and he wanted to somehow gain

LaToya's trust so that she could be convinced that he was trying to help her.

"Yes, those terms have been discussed, and we can definitely start creating a course of action to see if we can reduce your sentence."

"Wait, hold up. Reduce? Nah, playa', that ain't gon' cut it for me. You better be workin' on a plan to get me immunity."

Is this woman out of her mind? How does she think law and order work? "With all due respect, Ms. Richardson, on the night you were arrested, you verbally confessed to the murder of David Anderson, community award winner, Townsend Harris football coach, father of three children—"

"Did I ask for the man's biography?" LaToya asked, interrupting Edward abruptly.

Edward just stared at LaToya, shaking his head.

"I don't know what you mean, Mr. Reed. Sometimes I say a lot of things whenever I'm off my meds," she added, shrugging.

"Meds? So, what you're saying is that you have a chemical imbalance of the brain, and it causes you to spout incoherent statements?" *Even saying that is making me laugh. There's no way the court is gonna buy the claim that LaToya is legally insane.*

"Exactly. I went to my psychiatrist last year, and I was diagnosed with acute schizophrenia and bipolar disorder. I have the doctor's note at my place that will prove it too."

Edward pulled out a pen and paper while LaToya gave him her address, which he scrawled quickly. LaToya knew that if he had evidence of her bipolar diagnosis, it would increase the chances of her conviction being thrown away, and she would be removed as a suspect in the murder case of David Anderson.

"Okay, I have your address and the information regarding your medical diagnosis. So, if I can secure these documents, I may be able to use it whenever we get a new case."

"How long will 'whenever' be?"

"I'm not sure yet. I will petition right away for a new case, and when I have a date, I will keep you posted."

LaToya's eyes darkened once again as she started at Edward intently. "Then I suggest you get to it, counselor, and I want to hear something at the end of the week."

Edward, who was normally accustomed to calling the shots in a case, was taken aback by LaToya's propensity to take control of the case as if she were calling the shots.

Lowering his voice, he whispered, "After this is all said and done, ya better let Tony go or else I'mma make sure you, Tadarius, yo' sister, and all those punk asses that roll wit' M.O.B. get dealt wit', and I ain't talkin' about jail neither."

"Nigga, you think you callin' the shots around hea'?" LaToya whispered, grinning maniacally.

"Don't forget who you is, muthafucka, wit' a square-ass name like Edward, coonin' just to get butter biscuits from the man. I know who you really are, Tone, and yo' lil' dog and pony show ain't foolin' nobody. Underneath that corporate suit, you still the boy with them dusty-ass braids, beggin' for attention. You think I don't remember who you were? I still got yo' balls where you left them twenty years ago when you ran out the car like a lil' biyotch, so you betta' recognize. I did yo' dirty work for you, covering yo' ass. Then you punked out and snitched on the Fam in court."

"Covering my ass? Tadarius and his crew came back and beat my ass the next day. They don't give a fuck about me. They don't even give a fuck about you. They're only using you, and when they can't use you no more, they gon' throw yo' ass out to the streets where you belong anyway."

"Fuck you, you bootlegged Wesley Snipes wannabe."

While they were still throwing verbal jabs at one another, the guard walked back in. "Times up, Richardson. Let's go."

While standing up, LaToya said, "I want to see my son, counselor. I want to make sure he's okay. Where's he at?"

Packing his suitcase, Edward flashed LaToya a smile and a little wink. "Don't worry about your son, Ms. Richardson. He's fine, and he's being care for by folks that can properly raise him. Unfortunately, I advise that he doesn't visit you until after a court date is set. You have a good day now." *She don't have to know where her son is. It's better to keep her in suspense. She was talking way too much smack in here. Now I have the psychological edge. I don't know how my brother doing, so it's only fair that she don't know how her son is doing.*

Before the guard walked her out, LaToya mouthed silently, "Eat a dick."

Dr. Jan Ralwinski sat at the desk of her newly remodeled office in Forest Hills, New York. Sitting across from her was eleven-year-old Megan Plumgarten, a white Jewish girl who had visited the esteemed doctor for a session. Earning her bachelor's, master's, and her doctorate in Psychology, Dr. Ralwinski excelled in her role as a group therapist and grief counselor, who was able to connect to her patients and learned to treat them as more than just patients. She saw them as family members, and she connected with them on levels that other counselors could not reach.

Although Dr. Ralwinski served everyone, she felt a special connection with young girls. As a woman, she knew the uphill obstacles that young girls were confronted with—being marginalized or looked down upon because she was female, not being given the same opportunities as her male counterparts, and also being susceptible to the unfathomable consequences of naivety, such as teen prostitution, rape crimes, and early pregnancy.

As she was wrapping up her session with Megan, Dr. Ralwinski heard a commotion in the waiting area just outside her office. She had four more patients left for the day, but she had cleared a time slot for a fifth patient. She could scarcely believe it when she received the phone call from the surprise fifth patient because it had been years since she had spoken with her.

Hearing the commotion outside, Megan's curiosity got the better of her, and she turned around, stood up from her reclining chair, and followed the doctor to the door. When Dr. Ralwinski opened the door, she smiled when she saw Andrea McAfee again.

The other four female patients, along with their family members, were surrounding the one-time R&B artist and asking for autographs. Andrea was happy to oblige, signing autographs and taking pictures with several people before hugging Dr. Ralwinski.

"I should've known it was you, missy!"

"Well, I couldn't miss the chance to see you again, Jan. Wow, I like what you've done with the place. That mauve color's definitely you."

"Well, I was inspired by this former patient of mine who became some huge pop star," the doctor replied, winking at Andrea.

Andrea turned her attention towards Megan, who stood transfixed, unable to believe that she was standing inches away from Adia. "And what's your name, princess?"

"My name's M-Megan," the young girl stammered.

"Well, it's nice to meet you, Megan. I see that you've met one of my most favorite people in the world. I hope she's taking care of you well."

"Yeah, Dr. Ralwinski's great!"

Andrea's heart melted. She loved bringing joy to young girls wherever she went.

"She told me that she knew you personally, but I always thought she was just joking."

"Really?" Dr. Ralwinksi raised an eyebrow. "Now you know that I was telling the truth."

"Adia, I got all your songs on my Amazon playlist, and I love the first album that you released with De'Von. Are you still with him?"

Andrea smiled. It was not the first time she had been asked about her relationship with the bad boy rapper who was considered the king at Metro Records. Ever since their high-profile relationship ended, De'Von's record sales had plummeted, and although he released two more EPs with Metro, they did not perform well in the pop, R&B, or hip-hop charts.

Since then, De'Von remained behind the scenes, out of the public eye, producing other acts in the industry. Ever since he released a track where he thanked Adia for their time together and apologized for his reckless ways, Andrea had not spoken to him in person again.

"No, Megan, unfortunately we're not together anymore. But I'm sure he's doing well, and I wish him nothing but the best, and we'll always be friends."

After taking a picture with her and Megan's mother, Dr. Ralwinski invited Andrea inside her office. Andrea looked at the fish tank, which had since doubled in size and had more fish since her last visit.

"Do you let Megan feed the fish like you did for me?"

"Absolutely. Every time she comes in, I give her the fish flakes and let her feed them. You know, she reminds me a lot of you when you were around her age. Remember when we first met?"

Andrea remembered very well because their first meeting happened three weeks after Loree was killed. She was not Adia back then—only a shy, frightened little girl that wanted to hug her older sister, and although she could not get Loree back, Dr. Jan opened her office and her heart to Andrea, and they forged a relationship that lasted years.

"Yeah, I remember. What's Megan's story?"

"Now, Andrea, normally I would not reveal this information because in my practice I have patient confidentiality. But I'll break my own rule just this time because we're friends."

"Don't worry, Jan, your secret's safe with me. You know you can trust me, and I can trust you because you've never asked me to backstop you financially even after I became Adia."

It was the truth. Dr. Ralwinski never used Andrea for her celebrity status because she had grown to love Andrea too much to use her celebrity to boost her own popularity.

"Megan lost her older sister, Janice, last week. Drug overdose. She was eighteen years old. It was her freshman year in college, and she went go out with some friends, and they experimented with marijuana, opium, and coke. One day, her cocaine was laced with a lethal dose of fentanyl, and she took in too much and suffered a heart attack. She died in her dorm room, and it has broken Megan. Megan was really close to her sister."

Andrea stared out the window, brushing away a tear that had fallen from her eye.

I know how Megan feels. I still feel the weight of Loree's loss sometimes. We're all close to our sisters in one way or another.

Making a mental note to surprise Megan at her next birthday party, Andrea turned to face Dr. Ralwinski. "Drug abuse and murder. When is it all going to end?"

"If I had the answer to that question, I probably wouldn't be working here today. So, what brings Adia to my office today? As you can see, I still have the LP cover of your last album at Metro. Had it framed with my degrees."

"Really? I can't believe you still have that album cover. I ain't been at Metro for over seven years."

"Well, there are some things that I still cherish, and I kept that cover because you managed to rise above your pain and chose to live, and in living, you've given girls like Megan a reason to live. So, how's everything going at Omega Studios?"

Andrea sat on the reclining chair, which felt just as comfortable as she remembered it. She might as well have been twelve years old again, spilling her heart out to Dr. Ralwinski.

"It's good—no complaints. They've treated me really well, much better than Metro has treated me, but lately, Jan, I haven't been able to concentrate on my music."

Dr. Jan sat on her desk as she had done with countless patients throughout her career. "Well, you're in a safe space now, Andrea, so feel free to tell me anything. You have as much time as you want. I can reschedule my other appointments."

"No, Jan, you don't have to do that. I just needed to talk to someone about this because it just rocked me to my core."

After Dr. Ralwinski sat down, cup of tea in hand, Andrea revealed the events that occurred over the past two weeks, how Loree's old friend had come back to town and pretended to befriend her while taking her out to different nightclubs and also doing her best to enable her to act against her character and faith. Then Andrea explained how another figure from the past, a former gang member, who was polarized for testifying against his partners, had revisited her as a lawyer, revealing to her that Loree's friend was in fact, Loree's murderer, who had gotten away with the crime, leaving another gangbanger as the fall guy in the whole saga.

She also described to Dr. Ralwinski the night where her sister's friend, upon confessing her part in murdering Loree and her ex-boyfriend, David Anderson, pointed the same gun at her to end her life before law enforcement ended that confrontation.

As Dr. Ralwinski sat back and took in everything that Andrea described, she began to understand why Andrea could not concentrate on her music. *Poor girl. The endless violence that has confronted this young lady since age twelve is unspeakable. If I were her, I wouldn't be able to concentrate on music either.*

After hearing Andrea, Dr. Ralwinski sat and rubbed her chin in thought. "So, what you're telling me is that the man who was locked up for Loree's murder isn't the actual murderer? It's this LaToya person?"

"I know it's a lot to unpack, Jan, but yeah, Terrell Washington didn't kill my sister. We had the wrong man locked up for years. Thankfully, LaToya was arrested and taken into custody, but I don't trust it at all. What if she gets released? How am I supposed to deal with that? I've been convinced that they had Loree's killer locked up, and all this time, she had been running around scot-free without a care in the world. She's just too well connected, so I'm sure she's gonna be protected, either on the outside or on the inside." Andrea stood and then hit the top of the chair in frustration.

"Okay, Andrea, let's calm down now. Okay? Take a deep breath."

Andrea followed Dr. Ralwinski, breathing steadily and taking deep breaths, and sat down again to calm herself. All the visits that she was making to Terrell did not amount to a thing because he knew he was going down while keeping his allegiance to the gang.

"Listen, Andrea, you wanted my advice. Here it is. I think you need to take some time off work. I think you need to do some reflection and find some inner peace. I know that you're looking for closure in your sister's case, but don't be overwhelmed by vengeance. Please let the police see this thing through. As a matter of fact, I think I have just the thing. Next week, a group of friends and I are going on a hike through Mont Lawn Forest Trail. I would actually love it if you would join us on this hike, and maybe it will help clear your mind."

Andrea thought about Dr. Ralwinski's suggestion, and the more she thought it over, the more sense it made. Maybe she needed a few days to get away from the city, away from areas that would remind her of Loree, LaToya, Tadarius, Antonio, or anyone that reminded her of M.O.B. But after facing death, would Quentin allow her out of his sight?

"Yeah, I'll go with you. I just got to tell my fiancée about it. He's kind of keeping a short leash on my outside ventures for a while now."

CHAPTER 5

DIVINE VENGEANCE

August 2019

CHRIS WAS WAITING outside the two-bedroom flat where he lived with his mother, LaToya Richardson. Having bounced around from apartment to apartment all over New York City, LaToya and Chris were looking for a permanent place to settle down and put their plan into motion. For years, LaToya had been living off her benefits from the Army, but since she had been discharged, she was receiving funds from another source.

The inner-city crime gang syndicate, M.O.B. had overrun the city with its drug operation and infiltration of businesses and corporations. The gang experienced a period of great financial success through the early 2000s, spearheaded by the notorious, ruthless leader Tadarius Hill. With international contacts with other drug cartels and dealers based abroad, M.O.B. began to expand its territory beyond Liberty Avenue and 101 Avenue where the gang first laid its roots down.

But the early success met its untimely end, following a deadly shootout between the members of M.O.B. and members of the NYPD law enforcement officials. The fallout from the shooting resulted in four wounded officers and two dead gang members. Tadarius, who suffered a bullet wound to the leg, was apprehended that evening and was arrested for his part in the shootout as well as conspiracy to murder in the case of slain high school senior Loree McAfee.

With Tadarius behind bars, the general news reported that M.O.B.'s operations had finally crumbled. But unbeknownst to law enforcement and New York residents, M.O.B. continued its operations underground and out of the public eye. The infiltrating members of M.O.B. were unknown to the public, and while they continued to blend in with the population, the operations still ran daily.

People still brought drugs from individual dealers, who still had M.O.B.'s emblem tatted on their forearm, and as the year 2019 dawned, there were rumblings that Tadarius was going to be released from prison. In March 2019, speculation became reality as Tadarius was exonerated amidst general outcry of government corruption and insufficient evidence coupled with M.O.B.'s strong influence on the panel of jurors that reviewed the case.

While M.O.B. continued sending funds to LaToya and Chris, Tadarius checked daily to make sure she wanted for nothing. He had taken care of her ever since David Anderson left her pregnant and broke as a teenager. Chris had never seen Tadarius in person, but his mother would extol heaps of praise and gratitude to the man and the family that saved her life.

Her next goal was to eliminate the man that deserted her and the sister of her one-time best friend who was no longer breathing. LaToya decided that she would pretend to befriend Andrea McAfee before ruining her life and career while Chris scoped out the man whom he saw as little more than a sperm donor: his father, David Anderson.

LaToya would instruct Chris not to use his real last name nor disclose their address in public because she did not want to draw attention to her whereabouts. So, Chris used the tale of how he bounced around from foster home to foster home whenever people asked too many questions. M.O.B. became more than just acquaintances to Chris. They became a band of brothers and sisters to him, and it was only feasible that Chris would one day join their ranks.

Persistently tracking David for weeks, Chris knew his absentee father's routine by heart. Every day David went to Townsend Harris High School, a completely different high school from where Chris attended. He followed David home one night, and while they ate dinner, Chris happened to look through a partially-opened curtain in the side of the house, where he saw David and his family laughing and eating dinner together.

Every minute that passed, the feeling of resentment increased within because he would never experience a family dinner. He would never know what it was like to have a father that cared for him. On Fridays, David normally frequented a bar in town where he enjoyed playing billiards with other bar patrons. Chris knew both his mother and Tadarius wanted to kill David, but if he had a gun at that very moment, he would have shot David on his own and saved Tadarius some trouble. But he continued to wait for instruction from his mother while watching his adversary.

On this day, however, Chris was informed by his mother that he would not be spying on David because a member of M.O.B. was scheduled to pick him up. Chris had not been outside for more than ten minutes before his ride pulled up. The driver of the car—a strong, well-built, six-foot-five Black man with a bald head and goatee— rolled the passenger window of his car down.

Jermaine Jones looked up at Chris, who stared blankly. "Get in. Hurry up."

Not wasting another minute, Chris opened the passenger door and stepped into the car. Jermaine, a member of M.O.B., was tasked to pick Chris up that evening. His cousin, Malik Jones, had been murdered in the shootout back in 2003.

After dapping up Jermaine with the gang handshake, Chris asked, "Yo, where we goin'?"

"Don't worry 'bout it, B. You'll find out soon enough," Jermaine replied as he turned a corner. "So, how's yo' mama doin'?"

"Maintaining. You know how it is," Chris replied.

"I feel you. So, what about school? How's that goin'?" Chris just shrugged his shoulders. He could care less about how school was going. He just wanted to pull through to make it to tenth grade.

"School's whatever, man. I'm just tryin' to pass so I can get up outta thea', you feel me?"

"Oh, fasho. I'm takin' you for a ride-along, son."

My mother had to have planned this. Chris was thinking as the car weaved its way through traffic. A few minutes of silence passed between them.

"Aight, so you remember Anita—that Trini bitch that I was tryna holla at for weeks?"

After thinking it over, Chris did remember that the last time he met up with Jermaine, he kept talking about a woman he had met named Anita. At twenty-four years of age, Jermaine had an insatiable appetite for women, so much so that he was running through a different one every two weeks.

"Our time here's short, so if God put all these fine-ass shorties out hea' we gotta take advantage, one pussy at a time," he said.

"Yeah, I remember you mentioned her the other day. So what?"

"What you mean, 'So what?' Man, tonight's da' night. So, Tre' having a kickback at his crib to celebrate T getting' outta jail and shit, and Anita's gon' come through. I heard she bringing her lil' sister there too, and I thought it'd be dope if ya' met. Her name Serata or Sheronda, something like that. She go to Bayside High, and she seen you around, so she wanna get to know ya," Jermaine replied, smiling slyly.

"You mean Sharita?" Chris asked.

"Yeah, that's it. So, you know her?"

"Shit, I mean, I barely know her. I've seen her in the hallways, and I said hi or whatever, but I ain't neva' talked to her like that."

"Well, all that's gon' change tonight, B. We gon' roll into this kickback, and Anita's gonna be comin' through, so you know what that means. Open that glove compartment."

When Chris opened the glove compartment, he saw an assortment of condoms in varying sizes and colors.

"Pick yo' poison, man. Cuz one thing I know, if Sharita is anything like Anita, they both freaks, and it's goin' down tonight."

Chris chuckled and picked a blue condom from the pack. It was not his first time with a girl. He'd had fleeting relationships and hook-ups here and there, but he had never been sexually active with any of them. He knew he had to play it off because he did not want Sharita to get the impression that he did not know what he was doing.

"You know how to open it?" Jermaine asked.

When Chris started to use both hands to open the condom covering, Jermaine laughed and shook his head.

"Nah, nah. That ain't how it's done, bruh. Use yo' teeth to tear dat shit open. Tear from the corner like this." Jermaine grabbed a cream-colored condom with one hand while the other hand was on the steering wheel and used his teeth to tear the cover off.

"Aight, that was smooth."

"And after you open it, put it on yo' meat while it's still down. Don't wait till you get hard to apply the shit, or it might not fit. And if it don't fit, you can raw-dog her, but don't be surprised if you got another mouth to feed in nine months."

"Hell nah. I'mma make that shit fit. I ain't tryin' to be no baby daddy anytime soon."

After ten minutes, they finally arrived at a small, stucco house on the corner of 125th and Farmers Boulevard. Chris could see the lights inside and the party that was already in full tilt.

When Jermaine knocked on the door, he heard the commotion cease immediately, and only the music could be heard.

Tre' opened the door in high alert, gun in hand. Realizing that it was Jermaine and Chris, he let them in before closing the door behind them. "Damn, man, you gotta warn a brotha' before you come knockin' on this door, fool, breakin' down my door like you was Five-O."

"My bad, Tre', you know I be forgetting. But yo, this my lil' nigga Chris."

Tre and Chris dapped, doing the same gang handshake that tied their family together.

"What up, Chris? Yeah, you look just like him."

"Like who?" Chris asked.

"Who you think? Yo' daddy, nigga!" Tre' and Jermaine laughed as if they couldn't believe that Chris did not understand the comparison.

"Oh, yeah."

"You know, he joined the Fam at yo' age. That man didn't play. Anyone who stepped to Tadarius got dealt with by David. Except that one time with Theo—"

"Yeah, he ended that fool himself. Anyway, make yo'self at home. Mi casa es su casa."

Looking around the dimly lit living room, Chris saw various members of the family sitting around smoking weed and hookah and drinking Hennessey, wine coolers, gin and tequila with orange juice, and soda. They were watching a well-known movie on BET. The kitchen was filled with snacks, and Chris started to make his way toward the refreshments, dapping all the familiar members that he and his mother knew before hearing his name.

"Ayo, Chris, bring yo' skinny ass ova' hea'."

Walking over to Jermaine, Chris saw that he was standing next to a woman that he could only assume was Anita. Next to them was a younger female, mocha skinned, brown eyes, and long thin braids. When she saw Chris, she smiled. It was Sharita, and she was banging in her outfit.

"So, Anita, this is Chris."

"Oh, this is LaToya's son, right? What up, Chris?" Anita greeted, dapping Chris, which would have surprised him if he was not already accustomed to it. Girls and women were rolling in and out of M.O.B. frequently as some were initiated into the fold while others, like LaToya, remained dedicated informants for the family that held them together.

"Yeah, I know Chris. He goes to my school. He don't talk much though," Sharita said.

"Why you tryin' to play me? I be sayin' what up to you every time I pass you," Chris laughed.

"Hmmhmm. Well, we'll see."

A moment of awkward silence passed between them before Jermaine whispered to Chris, "Uh, Chris, wouldn't you like to go get the lady a drink?"

Taking his cue, Chris asked, "So can I get ya'll a drink?" he asked.

"Nah, I'm good. I've had like four shots already. Matter fact, I'm getting' tired. Lemme sit my ass down." Anita sat down on one of the small couches accompanied by Jermaine.

He shot a look at Chris as if to say, "Okay, beat it. I'm with my lady, and I'm about to make my move. Go make yours."

"Yeah, can you get me a shot of Crown with some cranberry juice?" Sharita asked.

"Cranberry juice, huh? Lemme find out you got some taste," Chris replied.

Sharita laughed.

After bringing her a drink and pouring one for himself, Chris and Sharita spent time talking about different topics, including their classes, favorite hobbies, and future goals. Three drinks later, they were still talking to each other.

"I actually tried out for cheerleader this year, but I missed the final cut," Sharita explained after sipping her drink. "They chose Kimmy Brown's narrow ass. She ain't got no rhythm whatsoever."

"Damn, that's cold. I've seen you dance at the homecoming dance, and you got skills. If I were the coach, you would've made my cut in a heartbeat."

Sharita then looked deep into Chris's eyes. She had heard guys just spitting pickup lines to get at her, but she sensed sincerity in Chris's response. "Do you really mean that?"

"You already know. What, you don't hear that very much?"

Sharita shook her head. "Other than Anita and the Fam, I don't got too many people in my corner these days. My daddy cheated on my mama, and she kicked him out, so it's just me, Anita, and her, and she ain't eva' around cuz she works long hours at the clinic."

"I know how you feel. I don't even know my dad. Man left my mama before I was even born. I just know about him through pictures."

"Sounds like yo' daddy and my daddy were both assholes."

"Yeah, I guess so."

As the night went on, some members left to return home, but a few people stayed behind. Jermaine and Anita were wasting no time, kissing intensely, not paying any mind to the handful of people remaining at the party. He had started to slip Anita's spaghetti strap halter top down while he was kissing her, so he knew that he was a few minutes away from carnal euphoria.

Sharita, by this time, was quite inebriated as well, and she began to coax Chris into an unoccupied bedroom in the house. The covers were wrinkled, so it was obvious that someone had been lying on the bed, but it did not matter to Chris and Sharita. No later did they sit on the bed, Sharita smiled at Chris as his heart began racing, scarcely believing what was about to take place.

"So, can I get you another drink?"

Sharita raised an eyebrow. "Why? You tryin' to get me drunk just to get some?"

Chris's heart dropped. Maybe it was not the right time for this to happen. He wanted his first time to be natural, not forced or contrived. Neither did he want Sharita to feel uncomfortable, nor did he want to give her any indication that he was literally petrified.

"Nah, it ain't like that. I just want to get to know you more and just chill wit' you. We ain't gotta do nothin'…" he started before Sharita abruptly lunged forward and kissed him on the lips.

Her lips felt soft, moist, and warm, and Chris would have enjoyed the moment more, had Sharita not bumped heads with him while moving in for the kiss.

"Oh, my bad! I'm sorry. I'm mad clumsy," she apologized.

"It's all good. You're so beautiful to me. It don't matter."

With that, it was all it took for Sharita to gently push Chris onto the bed and lift his shirt off him. She leaned forward, more slowly than the first time, to kiss him, and they both felt heat coming from each other.

Taking her shirt off, Chris began to relax and work his lips down her neck, breasts, and naval. While she enjoyed the smooth feeling of his lips, Chris took the condom out of his pocket and used his teeth to rip the covering off, just as Jermaine taught him. Making sure that he was not fully erected, he put the condom on and slid down Sharita's jeans before gently entering her.

That night, Chris lost his virginity and experienced a physical experience that elevated his status of being a step closer to joining the family.

JANUARY 2020

Waking up on a Saturday morning, Chris found himself reflecting on the emotional and sensual experience. He was not yet eighteen years of age, but he already knew what it was like to make love to someone. It was not until much later on that month he found out that the incident at Tre's house was all a clever ruse to bring both young teenagers together to perform the act of sex. Sharita was trying to join M.O.B.'s inner fold of female informants because of her sister's influence as well as Bunny and the other female members who had beguiled them into believing that Tadarius cared for them and would always provide for them.

As for Chris, it was later revealed that he was silently being initiated into M.O.B., and one of his first tests was to shed the blanket of virginity and become obsessed with constant sex escapades. It was no secret that Tadarius enjoyed being in the company of various women, and he had the habit of sleeping with two or three at the same time.

Tadarius had attempted to entice David into his way of life, but somewhere along the way, he became attached to Loree, and attachments were not part of the deal. Attachments led to betrayal, pain, and tragically, death. Each woman that Tadarius ran through was nothing more than exploiting his sexual appetite, and in order to be a confirmed member of the M.O.B. family, a potential member was required to share his lust and disdain for young women.

Sharita and Chris never interacted again after that evening, and when he saw her on the first day of school that September, she hardly even acknowledged him. He became a stranger to her, and the reality of the situation hurt Chris, but he never let his emotions show. The members of the family could not see how sad he was, and he had to hide his pain. So he moved forward and focused on doing what LaToya told him to do.

With all the drama behind him, Chris was looking for a fresh start and forward to the lunch date he had with Shantay at Harry's. He tried to focus on that date, rather than the similarities between Shantay and Sharita. They were both slender but curvy in all the right places. Both were athletic, and both had great fashion sense. But Chris was going to approach this new situation with Shantay carefully because he wanted to guard his heart.

After telling Renee he was going out to eat with a classmate, she almost ordered him not to go because she did not want Chris to be recognized by anyone who was in M.O.B. But after he convinced her, she allowed him to go.

"A date after one week of school...what are the odds?" she muttered under her breath as Chris headed for the door.

"What can I say, Mrs. A.? I guess I got it like that!" he exclaimed, shrugging as he took the house keys.

Since Chris did not eat any of the school lunch, he managed to save his money that Renee gave him, plus some money saved from his past dealings with M.O.B., which totaled $500. Nobody knew he had extra money saved, and Chris was determined not to reveal his extra ends to anyone.

After a quick bus ride, he met Shantay outside the school, and they walked to Harry's. It was already crowded because of the busy weekend, and after Chris paid for Shantay's lunch as well as his own, they walked over to a vacant table near the back of the restaurant.

"Yo, you ain't lyin' when you told me how good these were. I thought you was cappin' for a minute," Chris said after biting into his burger.

"I tried to tell you, boo-boo. Nothin' beats these burgers."

"So, Ms. Shantay, you neva' did answer my question," Chris mocked as Shantay laughed, remembering when she made the same statement to Chris.

"What question was that, Mr. Anderson?" she asked, playfully batting her eyelashes.

"What was up wit' you and Marlon, for real?"

"I told you. We went out once last year. It sucked, and I broke it off, and he kept tryin' to get wit' me."

"You sure that's it?"

Shantay stopped eating her fries and looked at Chris intently, and it only took a minute to realize that he was not joking. "Are you asking me if I fucked him?"

"Maybe. I just want to know if you had anything goin' on wit' homeboy. That's all."

Shantay rolled her eyes. *These boys and their silly competition over who tryin' to hit first.*

"Well, if you must know, we did get close to gettin' it in, but he was literally trying to have sex wit' me when I wasn't in the mood and when he got too handsy, I slapped the hell out of him and went home. You happy?"

"You already know." Chris winked and smiled.

CHAPTER 6

DIVINE VENGEANCE

TADARIUS HILL AND his cousin Pooh were waiting for their drug connect near the Verrazano Bridge. Taking a marijuana joint out of his pocket, Tadarius sparked up and took a long, deep drag.

Muthafucka's late. I hate waiting on people. Throughout his life, Tadarius was never huge on patience. Whenever he wanted something, he was accustomed to getting what he wanted expeditiously. He never waited around for his mother to reach out to him after abandoning him following his father's death. She was dead to him as far as he was concerned.

He never waited for David to come back around after he lost his senses and decided to take his relationship with Loree to the next level, pitting a dent in their operation, and he never waited to concoct strategies with his attorney to get out of prison.

Tadarius had been locked up at the Elmira Maximum Security Detention Center and the Queensboro County Jail for sixteen years, serving what was once a life sentence for his part in the murder of

Loree McAfee, aggravated assault with a deadly weapon, firing at law enforcement, and conspiracy to murder.

His lawyer, Perry Wilcox, was able to pull an exorbitant amount of strings to shorten his sentence from life to twenty years with the possibility of parole after convincing a jury panel that there was no substantial evidence to tie Tadarius to Loree's murder and that the testimony provided by Antonio Franks, a former gang member, was not credible because he was under extreme duress from the NYPD, who had coerced Antonio to tell a fabricated series of events. Wilcox also pointed out how Antonio's anxiety attacks had caused him to go into bouts of delirium and caused him to tell the court events that never took place.

When Tadarius's sentence was shortened, the attention shifted to Terrell Washington, a key member of M.O. B. who was last seen at a public restaurant with Loree the day she was shot.

The leniency that the court granted to Tadarius did not extend to Terrell, who remained in prison at the Queensboro County Jail, serving a life sentence. With Tadarius's sentence shortened and him exhibiting good behavior at the facility, Wilcox managed to petition for parole on Tadarius's behalf. In March 2019, the parole was granted, and Tadarius walked outside a free man after more than a decade.

Tadarius completely transformed in appearance during his stay in prison, having been used to wearing neat, thin cornrows on his head before his imprisonment. But during the period of incarceration, the officers cut his hair indefinitely, and since that moment, Tadarius opted to go for the bald look. He also spent many hours at the prison yard lifting weights, which transformed his once skinny frame to a lean, muscular individual. He had been in countless scrapes and fights in prison in which he won all of them.

Everybody knew to leave Tadarius alone, and unbeknownst to the officers, Tadarius began to establish connections behind bars. Various inmates that worked alongside him were promised membership into M.O.B. after its leader was released. He befriended imprisoned convicts, some who were ruthless convicts, which was not difficult because his reputation was well known. Loree's case was high profiled, and with Tadarius becoming a polarizing figure in the case, he was receiving countless letters from sycophants, women, and guys he referred to as "wankstas," or wannabe gangsters, that wanted to join M.O.B.

But the most important part of Tadarius's time in prison was the time he spent at the prison library. Ironically, Tadarius hated to read while growing up, feeling that it was a waste of time, and if he was not in school, what was the point of reading Ernest Hemingway, Mark Twain, or F. Scott Fitzgerald? But while he was imprisoned, he began to discover Black authors, and he was more interested in reading the works from Alice Walker, Toni Morrison, James Baldwin, William C. Rhoden, and other prominent Black authors.

Reading became a passion while Tadarius was imprisoned as it helped him deal with other physical urges that he had that were unattainable to him. His favorite book to read was *The Autobiography of Malcolm X* by Alex Haley. He was surprised when he discovered that Malcolm X was formerly Malcolm Little, a notorious hustler, drug dealer, and thief who went by the street name Detroit Red. He chuckled when he saw Malcolm's picture back when he had his hair processed and another picture of a mugshot. The man was a narcissistic mastermind and a cold man, which he related to in many aspects. The only mistake that Tadarius felt Malcolm made was getting involved in religion.

That Nation of Islam fucked with Malcolm's mind. If he'd left all that damn religion alone, he might still be here today. Tadarius saw no benefit in religion of any sort. It was all a scam to brainwash people to keep them docile and mentally and psychologically imprisoned. One of the other books he read was *The Art of War* by Sun Tzu, and what he learned was that the control of a large force was no different than the controlling of a few men.

Religion, whether it was God, Jesus, Buddha, or Mohammed was just individuals and agents of control, in Tadarius's opinion, and control can cause people to act against their best interests. He was determined not to allow himself to be controlled or manipulated by anyone. He was going to master his own destiny, and if he died, it was going to be on his terms. He made plans to strengthen M.O.B., and to do so, he needed more capital, and he needed to try to enterprise the syndicate.

As he waited on the dock of the Verrazano Bridge, Pooh asked, "Yo, you sho' 'bout this cat? I don't trust anyone that can't even get his ass here on time."

"I feel you, but we need to restock our supply ASAP," Tadarius replied.

"I got my young boys out there doin' work again, and we starting to get that money again, so quittin' ain't no option."

Pooh looked at his cousin taking a drag of his own joint. He knew that prison changed men, but what it had done to Tadarius was beginning to frighten him. Tadarius had been known to be extremely violent, reacting to anyone that angered him. He had a playful side, but at a flip of a coin, he was liable to lose control. Since his imprisonment, Tadarius still had his cool demeanor, but he was more calculating in his approach.

He learned from the past that overreacting drew unwanted attention to him, and to ensure that the operations of M.O.B. ran smoothly, he could not afford to bring attention to his operations. He still desired to work covertly with plans of getting involved in more real estate endeavors. His goal was to expand M.O.B. into a corporation that could operate within the system while the money circulated towards their organization.

He was no longer satisfied with just picking up little boys from the streets to become his drug dealers although business was now booming more than it had been in recent years. He also discovered that the opioid drug was increasingly becoming his bestselling substance lately. Out of all five boroughs in New York City, his largest sales generated in Manhattan and Staten Island, as opposed to Queens and Brooklyn, where sales had steadily declined since the beginning of the 2010s.

All Tadarius's operatives were still young boys, ranging from age fifteen to age thirty, and all of them had lofty expectations of growing within M.O.B. He was still breaking laws by selling drugs, but Tadarius felt that he was doing what he had been placed on the earth to do: take boys and girls out from the streets themselves and give them a family that cares for them—a family that was willing to work together to meet goals. Anyone that got in the way of achieving the ultimate family goal was ex-communicated from the family and silenced permanently. Tadarius silenced Theo. He silenced Loree. One of his girls silenced his one-time brother David.

I don't know what I'm doing that is so wrong that makes people want to bring me down. I'm employing folks to work and make their bones out here, giving them a job where The Man ain't gonna even look at 'em twice. My thing is, if these kids are gonna be in the streets, they might as well work for me.

Tadarius also saw that anyone who followed him must be able to handle a firearm with ease. He would have members of the crew teach the young hustlers how to load and unload a gun, how to aim it in the direction of the desired target, and how to hang on to the gun when it discharged.

"You sure about this goin' legit shit?" Pooh asked as he looked at his phone's clock, which displayed fifteen minutes after seven.

"Yeah. We gotta expand, B. We got a formula that's been workin' for years, and I know it got stalled while I was locked up, but I'm out now, and things are gonna pick up right where they left off. Only difference is I want to get M.O.B. a legit business license and taken seriously. I want to compete with other agencies, to do it legally."

"So that mean we out of the drug game then?"

"Hell nah. We still in the game. I'm just expanding it outside so we can compete with other agencies for representation. This is gon' increase our cashflow and give us competitive advantage."

"Who is you, and what have you done wit' my cousin? That's what I wanna know," Pooh laughed.

"Nigga, I'm still me. You know that ain't eva' gon' change. This is called evolving, son. You'll find out what it's like one day."

"Man, fuck you, T." Pooh laughed, and Tadarius laughed also.

Suddenly, Tadarius started coughing, and it took a minute for his coughing to subside.

"You good, man?"

"Yeah, I'm straight. Who you is—my mama?"

"I'm just sayin' B, you ova' here coughin' a lung out and shit. How many times I gotta tell you to puff, puff, give? You fuckin' up da rotation," Pooh laughed.

"Yo, this ain't *Friday,* B. Don't you think I know that? I've been smokin' since I was like ten years old."

Finally, a man of Italian-Hispanic descent walked over to them from the other side of the bridge. His hair was slicked back and greased, combed over neatly.

"Gentlemen, my apologies for being late. Tadarius, you lookin' thinner than usual, cabron."

"That's because I lost all that weight pumpin' yo' mama last night, Carlito."

Many other men would have taken Tadarius's insult seriously, but Carlito Savantes was accustomed to Tadarius's jabs, having been his supplier for more than seventeen years.

"Really? Because I just came back from yo' mama's house, and it was so good I had to stay and bang it out some more. Why do you think I came late?"

Pooh and Tadarius stared at each other with Pooh giving him a look as if to say, "You gon' let this fake ass bookie punk you like that?"

But after a minute, all three men laughed, and Carlito dapped both men.

"Aight, so I got another shipment coming in on Canal and 23rd tomorrow at six in the morning. One of my guys moonlights as a grocery truck driver, and he's gonna give you stuff. We got at least two months' worth of work in that truck, so you gon' need some hands to get that back to Queens."

"Aight bet. Yo' Pooh, pay the man," Tadarius ordered.

Pooh walked back to the back seat of the drivers' side of their car and opened it. In a few seconds, he re-emerged with a large briefcase that held the sum of over fifty thousand dollars. In classic transaction style, he opened the briefcase and displayed the money.

Carlito perused over the neatly lined up bills, and after a couple minutes he said, "Okay, everything looks good here. I see you've been maintaining out here. That's good because Perez was starting to wonder what to do with all the extra shit he had in his warehouses. I told him that his best seller was in lock-up, and once he got out, it was gon' be on and poppin'. For once, I was right."

"Damn right, you was right, dawg. I told you, this train's goin' too fast to stop. I still had people puttin' in work while I was inside, and everything's still moving."

"That's good. So, I heard that you got locked up for dealing with some bitch that was gonna blow the whistle on yo' operation."

"Yeah, but you can tell Perez we ain't gotta worry about her no more. We got it handled up hea'."

"You sure about that? There ain't nobody else in the way that could fuck up this relationship?"

Tadarius thought about it for a moment. *There is one person that could fuck it up. Antonio. But I got his brother on lockdown at the trap, so he gon' comply and do what I say in order to keep him alive. Then I'm gonna deal with him because blood gotta be shed for all the time I did in prison because of his snitchin' ass. But he's not in the picture right now, and everything's running smoothly.*

Tadarius did not reveal his doubts to Carlito. "Nah, everything's good. We got it. Tell Perez we'll double up next month, and we gon' need more. By the way, ask Perez if he could swing some girls this way. I'm sick of dealing with the same New York chickenheads out hea'. We need variety around these streets, know what I'm sayin'?"

But Carlito gave him an incredulous look and shook his head. "I'm already sticking my neck out importing drugs to you, and now you askin' me to import bitches in the black market to you? Why don't you try Los Angeles? They got girls to spare out there."

"Aye, aye, Carlito, man. I was just fuckin' wit' you, B. Damn, put yo' panties back on. We good ova' hea'."

Tadarius and Pooh laughed before Tadarius broke down into another coughing fit.

"Damn, bro. You don't sound too good. Might wanna get that checked."

"Don't worry about me. Just go back, and tell Perez we got shit handled over here."

They dapped Carlito one last time.

Before he walked away, he said, "Keep yo' phone on. I'll talk to Perez and see if he can scare up a few chicas for you too. Just don't break 'em in before you put 'em to work in da streets like you normally do."

After Carlito left, Pooh and Tadarius walked back toward their car, smoking the last of the weed they had with them.

"Yo, you sure you can still trust that Columbian fool? I don't know, somethin' about the way he moves, son."

"Pooh, yeah I still trust him. I mean, he more loyal than half these boys that rolled wit' me back in the day. If it's one thing David taught me, it's that nobody can be trusted out here. When people get a little taste of that money and that good life, they forget where they came from, and they start moving differently."

"Yeah, I feel you. Yo, check it. You know how you always sayin' that you wanna level up and go legit with this whole shit?"

"Yeah, what about it?"

"So, I was rollin' by Apple Kim's yesterday and spoke wit' somebody. He's a swole-ass nigga too. He heard about the plan to expand, and he wants in."

"What? Want in what? C'mon, son, you know I don't recruit no more, man. We don't need any more weight." Tadarius started the car, and they drove away from the edge of the Verrazano.

"Yo, hear me out for a second. I checked this cat out, and he runs these streets. He knows all the blocks that's hot right now. With the bank you'll be making from them extra sales, Perez gon' have to triple yo' supply. Yo, we ain't had anyone that knew the pulse of the streets since Xavier, and he's gone. We could use someone to replace him."

The last thing I need is another Xavier—a turncoat whose gonna go to the police and tell 'em about all the shit I did. I ain't goin' back to prison. They gonna have to kill me before that happens. Rubbing his sore temples, Tadarius reluctantly agreed to meet the man and test him.

"Aight, so I'm about to hit him up now and let 'em know that he can come through and meet us at the club tomorrow night at eight," said Pooh.

"Let him know not to come late. My time too valuable for muthafuckas to be comin' late all the goddamn time."

Looking for her athletic fitness pants and her sneakers, Andrea went through her closet and sighed as she came across some of Quentin's clothes. The couple had moved in together following their engagement, but since Andrea called off the engagement following a series of traumatic events, including one where her sister's old friend and confessed murderer held a gun to her, Quentin had been icy and indifferent. He was still open to staying with Andrea, but now he felt overlooked.

It was already difficult dating Andrea because of her huge following and her presence on social media, podcasts, talk shows, guest appearances, and concerts. Quentin endured the days where she went on tour for months and many nights he was relegated to sleeping alone. He knew it would be an adjustment being with a R&B and gospel artist, but he did not think it would be this challenging. In the last few months, Andrea had been going out with an old friend and had recently been in the news for partying, and he saw that it had taken a hit on her reputation. He wanted to protect her from the negative media attention, but Andrea only saw it as insecurity and overprotection. Their opposing views would lead to arguments, and Andrea would often cry herself to sleep, wondering what happened to the man that she fell in love with years earlier.

This morning proved no different as Andrea prepared for her hike along the Mont Lawn Trail with Dr. Ralwinski and her friends.

"Andrea, I don't think it's a good idea for you to be going on this hiking trip. Who is Dr. Ralwinski anyway—your shrink?"

"No, she's not my shrink, Q. She's my friend, and she helped me during the most traumatic moment in my life."

"Yeah, I know. Your sister being murdered was traumatic. I understand that. But given your status and especially what happened a few weeks earlier, should you think about being more careful? You told me that this woman you've been partying with had a gun pointed at your chest. I mean, if you have friends who can almost kill you at a drop of a hat, how do you know that this Dr. Ralwinski—" he started but Andrea cut him off.

She would not allow him to paint her beloved doctor and friend in a false light. "Save it, Quentin. Don't even finish that statement. How the hell was I supposed to know LaToya was trying to kill me? How was I supposed to know that she killed Loree? I admit, she played me, but I can't let her actions define my life."

"No, but your actions can define your career and your future. I'm just looking out for you, the same way I've always looked out for you. That's what a fiancé does."

Andrea walked over to Quentin, who was putting his work shirt on, and hugged him from behind. "And I appreciate you looking out for me. But I'll be okay. I promise. I just need to go clear my head, and once I do that then we can discuss our future."

"If we have a future," Quentin muttered quietly, but Andrea heard it and stepped back, staring at him.

"Hold up. What do you mean, if we have a future? What are you saying?"

Quentin walked into the bathroom, applied some wave gel, and brushed his hair. He could already see that it was going to be one of those days where Andrea was going to be at odds with him. "I'm saying, I'm always here to look out for you, but sometimes I feel like I'm not being appreciated for looking out for you. When was the last time we went out on a real date? When was the last time we stared outside at night and just stared at the stars, reminiscing on our future plans? It's like we never do anything together anymore. I see you less now than I did before we were engaged. If it's not your career obligations, it's this business with your sister and your obsession in getting justice for her."

"My sister deserves justice, Quentin! You know as well as I do how much she meant to me, and I will never stop fighting until I see LaToya, Tadarius, and whoever else that was involved with killing my sister get locked up for good."

"Are you willing to risk our relationship for this fight?" Quentin asked dryly.

Andrea stared at Quentin, her eyes boring right through him. *The nerve of him giving me an ultimatum to choose between justice for my sister and being with him. If this is how he's going to be, then maybe we shouldn't go through with it at all. I made it to this point without him, and whether we live out our futures together or not, I'm going to see this thing through, and I'm still going to be Andrea. I'm not changing for anyone. I can do bad all by myself.*

"Okay, well you know what, Quentin? I'm going to this hike with Jan, and nothing that you say is going to change my mind, okay? I'll be back tonight, and we can talk if you want to, but if you don't want to talk, then it's whatever. I've said my piece. I'm not about to be a prisoner in my own house."

Taking his coffee cup and his bag, Quentin walked by Andrea and opened the front door. "I'm not saying you should be a prisoner in your house. But I'd rather you be alive than dead. I wish you'd let the police handle this and not make any rash moves. I'll see you later."

With that, Quentin walked out, leaving Andrea to continue dressing up and then angrily brushing away a tear as she filled her water bottle.

After meeting up with Dr. Ralwinski and her hiking group, which were three other women, they looked at the map of the trail, which snaked around the Catskill Mountains, to locate resting points and sightseeing areas. Jan was accompanied by her sister Joan Giovanni, the associate CEO of Uptown Women's Fashion, a clothing retail chain with branches expanding vastly throughout New York state.

There was also Serena Ramos, the superintendent of schools in New York City, and there was Teresa Campbell, a pediatrician who had her own clinic in Bedford Stuyvesant, Brooklyn. All three women were excited that Andrea joined them and expressed how they enjoyed her gospel music, and their children enjoyed her gospel as well as her early R&B music.

Andrea also took the time to thank Joan for her creative designs in her clothing, as she had worn them on stage while touring on many occasions. The women forged a friendship and began the hike. The weather, which was susceptible to turning icy in January, was an unusual high temperature of sixty degrees, which made it ideal for outdoor activity.

For Andrea, it was refreshing to get away from the city for a few hours and walk the trail while taking pictures along the way. As the women hiked, even though Andrea was enjoying the quiet moment, her mind was occupied.

"I tell you, in my old age, I can't walk this hike as swiftly as I once did before. Promise me you won't get old," Jan laughed, panting rhythmically.

Andrea chuckled. She knew Dr. Ralwinski was trying to cheer her up.

"Is everything okay?"

"I don't know, Jan. Quentin and I got into an argument before I left. Because of what happened last year, he's trying to convince me to stay home and be more careful. I know he cares about me, but he's smothering me."

"Quentin—you mean the nice boy that took you out to prom in high school? I thought you two were a great couple."

"Once upon a time, he was. I don't know what happened to him."

"Maybe he's overreacting, not because of your situation, but because of his own insecurities."

What would Quentin be so insecure about? What does he have to hide?

CHAPTER 7

DIVINE VENGEANCE

RENEE ANDERSON SAT in the kitchen drinking her morning coffee, making sure to add an extra pack of sweetener into the simmering black liquid. She decided to omit the creamer because she needed to drink her coffee black on this morning after receiving an unsettling phone call the previous night. Tossing and turning in her bed, she barely slept an hour before her morning alarm blared from her phone.

Going through her normal routine of waking up Katrina, Cree, Dennis, and Chris, Renee hopped into the show, and after twenty-five minutes, she was dressed and in the kitchen. Checking the clock, she realized that it was fifteen minutes to eight. She yelled up the stairs, "Come on, guys! Let's move it! Ya'll are gonna miss your bus!"

Katrina was the first to make it downstairs. Then two minutes later, Cree shuffled downstairs, and not too long after, Dennis and Chris made their way into the kitchen. Chris grabbed a pack of Pop-Tarts from the cabinet while Dennis poured himself a bowl of Fruit Loops cereal. Chris had his headphones on, listening to music through an unlimited app on his phone, grinning from ear to ear. This was odd since Chris normally looked unenthused when it came to school.

"What you smilin' about over there?" Renee asked, suspiciously.

Chris saw Renee addressing him, but due to his speakers, he was unable to hear her question. "My bad, you said something?"

Rolling her eyes, Renee gestured him to remove his headphones. "I asked you why you over here smiling like Christmas just came early? You know this is a school day, right?"

"C'mon, Mrs. A., can't a brother be happy without being asked twenty-one questions? I'm just feelin' good, that's all."

But Renee knew what was up, and she was not a woman that was easily fooled. "Mmmhmm. So, I take it that your date with Shantay went well this past Saturday?"

Chris did not respond immediately, but his sheepish grin gave him away. "I mean, it was aight. You know we just kicked it at Harry's and talked about, uh school stuff."

"Boy, you think I was born yesterday? Ever since you got back from that date, you walking around this house like you on cloud nine. I see this girl got your nose wide open, Rover."

Cree and Katrina laughed. Even Dennis cracked a smile between bites.

"I have no idea what you talkin' about," Chris countered, taking a bite of one of his Pop-Tarts.

"Oooh, Chris and Shantay, sittin' in a tree…" Cree started singing.

"C'mon, bro, just admit that you feelin' her. So, when's the next date?" Dennis asked.

"It's gonna be the day after none of your business. Don't worry about how I get down, son. Besides, I can't help it if she's feelin' ya' boy. I'm just takin' it nice and slow."

"Right, and that's the way it better stay. Nice and slow. Don't be bringing no fast girls up in here. Okay, guys, let's hustle. Your bus is about to arrive in ten minutes."

As the kids finished breakfast, Cree took Katrina's hand and walked with her to the bus stop while Dennis grabbed his backpack and trailed after them. Since Katrina's elementary school and Cree and Dennis's junior high school were less than two blocks apart, they all took the same city bus. Chris took a different bus line at the opposite end of the street that usually dropped him just a few minutes away from Townsend Harris.

While preparing to leave, Chris noticed that Renee was not dressed in her usual work attire. "Hold up, you don't normally wear that to go to work, Mrs. A."

Renee hesitated for a moment. *Should I tell Chris why I'm dressed this way and where I'm going? I don't know how he'll take it.*

But she decided not to beat around the bush and be direct with him. "That's because I'm not going to work today."

"Well, where you goin'? Inquiring minds wanna know."

Turning away from Chris, Renee looked out the window. "Well, I'm going to the Queens County Courthouse today. I got a call from Edward Reed last night, and he said that your mother has a hearing today in court." Renee was waiting to see if Chris would react in surprise or anger, but instead he shrugged nonchalantly.

"Okay. Whateva." He grabbed his bag and started to place his headphones back on his ears.

While walking to the door, Renee grabbed his hand. "Look, Chris, I know that it's hard hearing that because she's your mother, but I don't want you to think any less of her—" she began, but Chris interjected.

"Check it, Mrs. A., I'm fine. You and Mr. Reed really looked out for me when ya' didn't have to, which is more than what I can say about her."

"Chris, your mother just got herself in some sticky situations, and she may be locked up, but despite all that, she's still your mother."

Upon hearing this, it was as if a switch flipped within Chris, and Renee saw a side of the young man that she never saw before, and it was frightening. For a moment, she did not recognize who was standing in front of her.

"No, she ain't my mother. Not anymore. She used me to scope people out so she could murder 'em. Let that bitch rot behind bars for all I care. I gotta roll. See you later."

With that, he walked out the house, and Renee watched from the living room window as he made his way to the bus stop with his headphones in his ears. *That went well, Renee.*

Finishing her coffee, she checked her blouse in the full-length mirror in her bedroom as she replayed her phone conversation with Edward the previous night.

Renee's phone rang at 1:45 in the morning, waking her out of a sound sleep. Ignoring the first round of rings, Renee continued sleeping, but before long, her phone rang again. Grumbling under her breath, she woke up and answered, believing it to be a spam call or even a debt collector.

But it turned out to be Edward Reed. Annoyed, she picked up on the third ring. "Edward, do you have any idea what time it is?"

"I know, Renee. I'm sorry. I know it's late, but I have important information to give you," Edward replied.

"What's so important that it couldn't wait until dawn?"

"Okay, I received word that LaToya Richardson's hearing has been moved to 9 a.m. today, and she is to be tried for the murder of David Anderson."

Renee could feel her anger welling up inside her. LaToya, the demonic woman that took her husband and her children's father, was finally going to be tried in court and hopefully convicted. "That's good. I was going to go to work today, but I can call out because I want to see this woman behind bars."

Edward did not reply for two minutes, and Renee wondered why he did not share her enthusiasm.

"Hello, Edward, are you still there?"

Finally, Edward replied. "I have to tell you something, and you have to promise not to tell anyone, and promise you won't be too mad at me."

"That depends on what you're about to tell me. Go on."

"I'm going to be representing LaToya in court as her defense lawyer."

Renee could not believe what she heard. It had to be a joke, a cruel joke that Edward was playing with her. Was Edward really defending the woman who killed David?

"What? You gotta be kidding me right now. You're defending that murderer? What game are you playing?"

"I ain't playin' no games, Renee. I ain't got a choice right now. Let's just say LaToya is very well connected, and they're not giving me a choice."

"Very well connected? Man, you work for one of the biggest firms in New York. You got NYPD on speed dial, and now you're telling me that you're defending her?"

"Look, he's got Tony, all right? He's my brother, and they kidnapped him, and now he's being held against his will. If I want to see my brother alive, I got to defend her and get her out of prison."

"Who is this woman connected to that got you so shook?"

"The same people David and I were connected to years earlier. I know how dangerous they are, and if I want to save my brother, I have to do this and get her out of jail, or else Tony's gonna die."

"And what if you lose?"

"If I lose, LaToya goes to prison, and my brother's gonna end up dying."

"God, just when I thought I knew David well, I'm finding out about his baby mama, his son, and all that jazz with M.O.B. What a nightmare."

"Look, I'm only gonna help her this once, and if I can get her no jail time and capitulate to their demands, they'll let Tony go. But look, it's okay. It's my problem to deal with. Anyway, please come to the courthouse around 8:45 a.m. because they want you to check in at the front door."

"What am I going to tell Chris?"

"I don't know. I wouldn't tell him because he's dealing with a lot right now concerning his mother, so I wouldn't tell him the news."

After she heard him hang up, Renee sat up in bed. What if LaToya got off? What if the verdict read that she was not guilty? Was she going to rejoin her gang once out to wreak havoc and destroy another family? Renee knew that she would not be able to sleep again that evening, but she decided to make plans to attend the hearing.

At the Queens County Courthouse, Edward adjusted his tie in the men's restroom. In less than an hour, he would have to do what he feared and loathed the most: defending a dangerous murderer. He had taken on cases in the past where he defended people accused of murder and other crimes, but this situation felt different. He *knew* LaToya Richardson killed David, and he knew she killed Loree McAfee years before, but there was nothing he could do about it on this day. For his brother to stay alive, Edward was tasked with convincing the panel of jurors and judge that LaToya was innocent.

The charges against Loree included assault with a deadly weapon, the unsolved murder of community stalwart David Anderson, and conspiracy to murder. Edward knew that she would not be charged with killing David because there was simply no evidence to tie her to the murder. M.O.B. did not leave any loose ends, and LaToya made sure not to leave any evidence behind. Another key to LaToya's freedom was the claim that she suffered PTSD and was diagnosed with schizophrenia while she still served in the Army.

Following LaToya's directions after his visit to the penitentiary, Edward went to LaToya's single room flat where she had lived with Chris before her arrest. The front of her door was littered with eviction notices and past due bill envelopes, and he was shocked to find out that the door was unlocked.

But then he suddenly remembered that LaToya had connections to the criminal underworld. *Yeah, M.O.B. left the door open, and they had one of their girls come in and routinely clean the place, so it looks like she's been here. Well played, Tadarius. I'm playing your game, but at the end of the day, you're still going down.*

There on the kitchen counter, was the note from the doctor's office, confirming her PTSD diagnosis, along with small bottles of Zoloft and Paxil. *I doubt that's even hers. She probably ripped that off some other person, and they slapped her name on this for the sake of the case. M.O.B. ain't slick at all.*

Taking documentation and the medication with him, Edward left the house but not before looking around to make sure that he was not being watched. He knew LaToya tipped off a member of the family to make sure he took the materials, and they were surveying his moves. Getting back into his car, he sped away from the house as if Tadarius were pursuing him.

As he stepped out of the bathroom, Edward saw a police car park outside the entrance of the building, which told him that LaToya had arrived. Sure enough, she was standing outside the court room. She had taken off the prison garb and was now dressed in black business pants with a white blouse and black pumps. Her hair was combed neatly into the back of her head and tied back into a ponytail.

Smiling at her lawyer, LaToya made her way over to Edward. "Showtime, Mr. Reed. Are you ready?" she asked, smiling deceptively, causing a brief wave of nausea to hit Edward.

She thinks this is a movie or a live TV production. She knows she's about to get off, and she's rubbing it into my face. I know what's about to happen, and when it does happen, I might need to run out of the courtroom because it is going to be sickening. The judicial system's gonna fail David and his family and let this witch walk, right in front of his widow.

As the courtroom doors opened, allowing the defendant, Edward, the prosecution team, and citizens to enter, Edward saw Renee Anderson among the throng. After telling Renee what he had to do, he could understand why she was upset and would not blame her if she decided never to speak to him again and send Chris to an adoption agency where she would not concern herself with him.

Judge Daniel Carson presided over the case, and Prosecutor Wendell Jones represented the State of New York as well as David Anderson's family. Renee sat behind the prosecution section of the courtroom. After the judge was introduced and the details of the case and charges against LaToya were announced, the prosecution wasted no time on their case against LaToya, calling witness Haley Potamkemps to the stand.

Haley was David's co-worker at Townsend Harris, working as a health teacher and one of the medical staff members of the football team.

"Mrs. Potamkemps, do you swear to tell the truth, the whole truth, and nothing but the truth, so help you God?" the bailiff asked with Haley's hand on the Bible.

"I do."

"Thank you. You may be seated."

Edward breathed nervously. *Now the chess match begins.*

"Mrs. Potamkemps, how would you describe Mr. David Anderson?" Prosecutor Jones asked.

"David was a family man, an individual who cared for his community and cared for kids in general. He was not just a football coach that won on the field, but he encouraged his kids to win in the classrooms as well. If he had any student-athlete that was behind in their grades, he would make sure they were tutored or assisted so they can graduate."

"So, it's safe to say that David was well beloved by everyone in Townsend Harris and the whole community?"

"Yes, he was well beloved by everyone in this community."

"Are you aware of any enemies that David may have had throughout his time there?"

"None that I'm aware of. If he did, I didn't know of it. He always treated me kindly, and his wife has always treated me kindly as well. In fact, I wouldn't have my current position as team trainer if it wasn't for Coach Anderson."

"Mrs. Potamkemps, do you know Ms. LaToya Richardson?"

Staring at LaToya, Haley nodded her head. "No, I've never seen her before today."

"You sure you haven't seen her anywhere—during the practices, maybe outside the school, or near the bar where Mr. Anderson frequents weekly?"

"No sir, I've never seen her."

Edward shook his head slightly and glanced at LaToya. He saw a small smirk at the corner of her lips. *She covered her tracks all too well. I'm not liking how this cross examination is going. She's not going to be charged for David Anderson's killing.*

After Mrs. Potamkemps, Renee Anderson was called to the witness stand. After taking oath, she sat down.

"Mrs. Anderson, how would you describe David as your husband?"

"David was a great husband and devoted father to his three kids. He never walked out on us. He always pushed them to excel in school. I never had any problems with David."

"So, David's never walked out on you or ever gotten involved in other relationships while he was married with you?"

"That's right. He loved his family."

Sighing, Edward knew what to ask next, and he hated throwing his deceased best friend under the bus and painting him as a deadbeat, but it was the only way to sway the jurors and keep the attention off LaToya.

"During your time with David, has he ever mentioned having a child from a previous relationship?"

There were murmurs in the courtroom. Many of the residents were in the Townsend Harris district, so they were mostly unaware of David's life before he coached at the school.

"No, he never divulged that information with me during our marriage." Renee was shooting Edward a look that he read right away.

You dirty bastard. Painting him as someone other than what he was, is low even for you. You have me looking over that child.

Unfortunately, Renee did not know how low Edward was able to stoop. She was about to find out.

"Did David ever tell you that he used to be in cahoots with Tadarius Hill and his gang syndicate, M.O.B.? I'm sure you remember Tadarius Hill, the gang leader who was locked up, then released a few months earlier?"

"I remember seeing that on the news, yes. But I didn't know who Tadarius was, nor was I aware of the connection between David and him."

"Okay, so is it possible the shooting of David Anderson, may have been either a robbery gone wrong or a member from his own set wanting revenge for him leaving?"

"I mean, yeah, it could be possible, but this woman confessed to doing it, and it was recorded too."

"Mrs. Anderson, you very well know that footage heard from recordings can be altered or doctored at any point."

"What? C'mon, no way! I heard what she said. There's no denying it. She killed my husband!" Renee was now at the point of tears and losing herself on the witness stand.

The murmurs in the courtroom grew louder, and the judge was compelled to pound his gavel to retain order.

"One more question...was there any physical evidence that suggested my client was responsible for David's murder?" *I am not doing this right now. I can't believe this is happening. She's not going to be charged for anything. LaToya Richardson is going to walk.*

"No, there isn't anything physical tying her to the crime, but why should there be if she said that she did it?"

"No further questions, your Honor."

After Renee tearfully left the stand, Sergeant Harry Werthers took the stand. He had been LaToya's sergeant while she was stationed in Iraq. Edward managed to call him to testify to seal up the case.

"Officer Werthers, how long has Ms. Richardson served in the Army?" Edward asked.

"LaToya Richardson has served for fourteen years."

"Can you please tell the courtroom why Ms. Richardson was discharged from the Army?"

"Yes sir. Ms. Richardson was discharged because, at the time, she was declared mentally incompetent, and after a standoff on base, she was sent to the VA for a psychiatric exam."

"Can you please describe the standoff in detail?"

Sergeant Werthers sighed. He was reluctant to relive the drama of that day. "Well, one morning, Soldier Lila Hernandez and Soldier Richardson got into a heated verbal dispute. It was unclear what the subject of the dispute centered around at the time, but knowing that Soldier Richardson has had a history of psychiatric episodes after being stationed in Iraq, people handle trauma differently. While over there in some battle zones, it's kill or be killed, and although Ms. Richardson was not directly in the battle zone, there's no doubt she's seen men screaming in pain as they were dying. You're always in a mode of self-defense, and Richardson was accosted physically by Hernandez, which caused Richardson to pull out her weapon, which was I believe, an MR-15, and pointed it directly at Ms. Hernandez. She was quickly subdued before any shots were fired and sent for evaluation. She was shortly discharged thereafter."

"Which is the same action as witnesses described took place the night on the property where the authorities were called. No further questions," said Edward.

Finally, LaToya took the stand, and Prosecutor Jones took the cross examination. He was on his last leg, and if he did not make a compelling case, he knew there was a chance that LaToya would walk or receive a reduced sentence.

"Ms. Richardson, were you present at the home of Andrea McAfee on December 22, 2019?"

"Yes. Andrea and I are old friends, and we've just been going out and catching up on old times. No big deal."

"Did you get into a dispute with Ms. McAfee?"

"We had a disagreement, yeah, but she's like a sister to me. I'm sure you've argued with your siblings more than once?"

"May I remind you, Ms. Richardson, that you're the one testifying on the stand."

LaToya rolled her eyes slightly at the smart remark.

"Is it true that you pulled a firearm on Ms. McAfee that evening?"

"Yes, but I had no intentions of shooting her. The firearm was not even loaded. We argued, and then I snapped. I didn't take my normal prescriptions for my schizophrenia and PTSD diagnosis that morning. I tend to forget."

LaToya bowed her head low as if she regretted her actions while, in his seat, Edward fought the feeling to vomit. *She's milking this, and she knows it.*

"What is your connection to Tadarius Hill, the recently exonerated former gang leader of M.O.B.?"

"He's my cousin, and he's been helping me financially since being discharged from the Army. My son and I had nowhere to go, and he provided us a home and some money so I can get back on my feet.”

Edward tried to hide his glare. *Liar.* “And he didn’t influence you in any way to murder David Anderson, who was once a member in his gang?”

“I don’t know what beef they had with each other, and honestly, it’s none of my business what Tadarius does. He helps me financially, but I don’t get involved in his dealings.”

“No further questions, your Honor.”

“The jury will now deliberate over the case, and verdict will be given soon,” Judge Carson said, but Edward already knew what the verdict was going to be.

After one hour of deliberation, the jurors came back out with their verdict. Everyone in the courtroom stood up.

“We, the jury, find the defendant, LaToya Jane Richardson, not guilty of the murder of David Anderson.”

LaToya closed her eyes, pretending to be overwhelmed with gratitude over the verdict as Edward’s head began to swim.

“We the jury, find LaToya Jane Richardson guilty on the count of assault with a deadly weapon. She is hereby sentenced to a year of house arrest along with sixty hours of anger management courses and monthly psychiatric evaluation.”

It was not the best-case scenario for LaToya, but she grudgingly took it as the alternative was four years imprisonment. Finally, the last verdict for conspiracy to murder was read in which LaToya, again, was not found guilty.

As court was adjourned, it took everything Edward had to feign being pleased that his client avoided serious jail time, but inside he felt sick because, once again, he failed Loree and Andrea.

He failed her family, and he failed himself. Tadarius beat him at his game, and the truth was too much to bear. Quickly making his way out of the courtroom, Edward entered the men's restroom, locked himself inside a stall, and retched heavily into the toilet.

CHAPTER 8

DIVINE VENGEANCE

AFTER THE TRANSACTION at the bridge, Tadarius and Pooh waited at Club Finesse, a new night spot that opened on Liberty and 32nd Avenue. Various members of M.O.B. frequented the club, and the location was discreet, not in the heart of the city, and although many people desired to visit the club, they knew that it was invitation only and that the owner had close ties to the dangerous gang.

Kevon Curtis, the owner was a member of M.O.B. in his younger years, but as he grew older, he went to business school, studied entrepreneurship, and with the cash advance from M.O.B. sales and the credit advance granted him by the bank, he was able to open the club. It was the perfect front for M.O.B. to scope out potential members, and it kept their illegal trades going, out of the sight of police surveillance.

Staring at the clock on his phone, Tadarius grew impatient. Pooh had asked the potential new member to meet them at the club at eleven o'clock, and it was already a quarter past midnight.

"Yo, where da' fuck he at, Pooh? If homeboy lookin' to make a good first impression, he ain't startin' off too good. My time is money."

"Chill, B. He on his way. Probably had to catch a bus at midtown, and you know how late they be runnin'."

As they talked, the security bouncer at the entrance of the club frisked a stranger outside. Although the club was a hangout spot for gangbangers, Kevon banned any type of firearms or weaponry at the club, having just secured the liquor license and gotten an A on the most recent health inspection. He did not want all the amenities that he fought so hard to acquire to be revoked. After he was frisked, the stranger entered the club.

It was not a busy night, and all the TVs at the club were showing various NBA games. Only Tadarius, Pooh, and a couple other members of M.O.B. occupied the club, and one of the members, Fariq, stepped up to the stranger.

"Can we help you?" he asked.

The stranger was slight in build with two gold chains around his neck, his cap worn backwards, and was wearing an Avirex jacket.

"Yeah, where Tadarius at?" he asked gruffly.

Fariq's eyes narrowed in suspicion. Anyone who was not a frequent guest at the club was either an uninvited guest or a member of law enforcement, which would put the other members on edge. "Who wants to know?"

"Nigga, I ain't got to say shit to you. Where Tadarius at?"

Fariq took the man's gruff tone as a challenge, and he stepped closer to the stranger. "Tell me what you want, and I'll tell T that you stopped by. If it ain't that important, you can roll yo' skinny ass out of here, or I'mma have to escort you out."

The stranger laughed at Fariq's threat and blank stare, unfazed by the dangerous element that surrounded him. "Bruh, if you think you got me shook wit' all that fake bouncer shit, you got me fucked up, B."

With that, he made his way to the bar, but Fariq blocked his way again. "I ain't gon' tell yo' square-ass again. I said get da' fuck out!"

"Who you squaring' up to?" The stranger stood up, staring at Fariq as boldly as possible. *If this man wanna fight, I'll throw hands wit' him cuz he don't know me.*

"Man, back da hell up!" Fariq exclaimed, punching the stranger hard in the chest.

Expecting the stranger to leave, Fariq did not expect him to retaliate. He pushed Fariq hard in the chest, and before long, both men were squaring up, and the stranger got his licks in, tagging Fariq in the shoulders and his midsection.

Fariq tried a few swings himself to put down the visitor but to no avail. The stranger ducked his punches and showed a level of dexterity that the bouncer had not seen yet. Finally, the bodyguard stepped out of the way, rubbing his bloody nose, finally allowing the stranger to go to the private suite, where Tadarius and Pooh were sitting.

"Yo, what up B?" Pooh greeted as he dapped the stranger, then offered his hand to dap Tadarius, but the gang leader was not interested in pleasantries.

"You got a lot of balls walkin' up in hea' like you own every gotdamn thing in this spot. Yo' ass couldn't even come on time."

"Yo, T, chill. Let's hear what he got to say," Pooh remarked as the stranger sat in the suite.

"Yo, my bad, man. I had to take two subway lines and a bus to get all the way out hea'. Ya' got this shit out in the boonies, son."

Tadarius glared at the stranger. For some reason, he did not like anyone that appeared more brash than he was. *I don't trust this Shaft-lookin' scrub. He don't look like much to me. I need soldiers in this family.*

"So, what they call you?"

"Wait till you hear his name, dawg," Pooh laughed.

"Cochise."

Tadarius raised his eyebrows suspiciously. "Timeout. Cochise? The same name as that nigga that got smoked in *Cooley High*?"

"Facts. My real name Randy Shaw, but they call me Cochise back at da crib."

"So, where you from, Cochise?"

"Born and raised in da Heights, big dawg."

Taking out a lighter, Cochise pulled out a Cuban cigar from his side pocket and lit it up, smoking in slow drags.

This nigga Cochise is confident as hell, just smirkin' right in front of me like nothin' phases him. Tadarius turned to Pooh. "You serious?" Turing back to Cochise, he asked, "Which Heights you from?"

"Where you think? Washington Heights, B, born and raised. I came up watchin' ya run these streets. I remember you and David applyin' heat to anyone that fucked wit' ya'll. Since then, I knew I wanted in."

"How old you is, Cochise?"

"Twenty-fo', finna turn twenty-five in two weeks."

Tadarius chuckled. "Damn, you young as fuck. You was probably just out da' crib when David and I ran things in Queens. But we ain't eva' stretched business out in Washington Heights. Tell me, why you wanna run wit' my crew, and why should I let you in?"

"Exactly what you said. I wanna expand M.O.B. to Washington Heights, Harlem, Manhattan, get all five boroughs investing in our product. I know all the streets, and I got connections to the Boricuas out there."

"Man, I ain't trying to fuck wit' them Chicanos out in the Heights. That's Serp territory. You a Serp?"

With his business picking back up, Tadarius did not want to draw attention with a gang war. The Latin Serps, another street gang that roamed areas of Queens, Brooklyn, and the Bronx, were just as ruthless, and Tadarius did not fear them, but a war would be crippling to his recovering economy.

"Hell nah, I ain't no Serp. But I'm cool wit' some of them cats, and if we could unite, we can have a stronger front and make more money. You got thousands, but I'm trying to help you get millions, dawg."

Tadarius thought it over. He was still not excited about joining an alliance with the Serps, but expanding his empire would double his yearly income. "Well, I'll tell you what. After I saw how you handled Fariq at the door, I'm intrigued. You got some dawg in you, and no doubt, you can help us. But I ain't all da' way impressed yet. So, Pooh gon' give you the spot where we gon' meet, and I'll give you yo' first assignment. Then we'll see if we can get you in the inner fold. Yo, waitress, bring a round of Moe' ova' hea' and bring the entertainment too."

Cochise, wondering what Tadarius meant by "entertainment," did not have to guess much longer as four scantily clad women in high heels walked into the suite. The gang leader had called an exotic dancer company for the evening. Tadarius took out a stack of bills. Popping the Moet, he poured a glass for his guest, but kept the bottle for himself.

"Aight gents, drinks up to Cochise being part of the Fam!"

The women went to work, stripping their lingerie off as their bare breasts gleamed in the glare of the club lights.

During the week that followed her Saturday afternoon hike with Dr. Ralwinski, Andrea felt refreshed. On Monday morning, she returned to Omega Studios with a sense of inspiration and renewed determination, recording four straight tracks in one session, a feat that she had never accomplished in her career.

With a clear mind, she was able to focus on her craft and allow the Holy Spirit to guide her and provide her the songs that she needed. And with her production and engineering team on top of their games, they were extremely confident that she was not too far from her next top single on the gospel charts. But the studio also served as a getaway of sorts for Andrea, for while her music career seemed to be back on track, her relationship with Quentin was beginning to come apart at the seams.

Aside from his neurotic overreactions whenever she went somewhere that did not involve work, he was strangely distant on other days. Whenever Andrea attempted to make conversation with him, he would appear disinterested and would offer generic responses to general questions.

Such was the case on Sunday night when Quentin and Andrea were lying in bed. Andrea was reading a book, and Quentin was working on his I-Mac Pro, creating a spreadsheet for his job. He had recently returned to wearing his glasses because he felt discomfort wearing his usual contacts.

Turning towards him, Andrea stroked the back of his head, envisioning the boy who was once nervous about asking her out in high school. "Hey baby, did I tell you how sexy you look in your glasses?"

For a moment, Quentin smiled, but the smile was immediately replaced by a straight face of concentration. "No, you don't tell me that very often. But thanks, anyway."

Andrea continued running her hands down his back onto his shoulders, where she proceeded to give him a massage. Usually, the massage would turn Quentin on, and he would respond immediately to the sensuous touch, which would lead into a night of lovemaking. But on this night, neither did Quentin budge, nor did his legs quake while his shoulders were being rubbed, which was unusual. So, Andrea tried a new tactic, rubbing her legs against his legs and raising her knee up to his groin area, but she saw that he was not aroused at all.

What is going on with him? Normally, the leg rub would get the party started with him, but he ain't budging. Time to turn the heat up. Moving closer, she kissed his cheek and worked her way down to his neck and shoulders. But instead of arousing her mate, she ended up annoying him.

"Look, Drea, I ain't in da' mood right now, all right? I got a lot of work to catch up on."

"I don't get you, Q. You always loved it when I caressed you that way. What's goin' on?"

"Nothing's goin' on right now. I'm just a little bit behind at work, so I'm making all of it up tonight cuz if I don't finish it, that's my ass."

"Ugh, whatever then. I'll leave you alone to work." Turning around in bed, away from Quentin, Andrea continued reading, but she never forgot what Dr. Ralwinski had warned her when she was hiking with her up at the Catskills.

"Maybe he's overreacting, not because of your situation, but because of his own insecurities."

"Hey Q, if something's bothering you, you know you could tell me about it, right?"

"Absolutely, baby. I'm good. You ain't gotta worry about me."

But Andrea was not convinced by his response. She knew that normally whenever he stated that she did not have to worry about anything, usually that was when she worried about him the most. "So, you're not still mad about calling the wedding off?"

"Drea, I told you I'm fine. I ain't gonna front, at first I was a little upset about it, but it is what it is. I know you've had some traumatic experiences, and I understand that you need some time."

"Yeah, I did. But trust me, there was never any hard feelings when I did it. I still love you so much, and you've always been in my corner and looked out for me." Kissing her boyfriend on the cheek, Andrea closed her book, turned off the lamp at the side of her bed, and fell asleep, leaving only the light from Quentin's laptop.

Feeling that she had reached an understanding with Quentin, she was able to put in work at the studio. But Tuesday morning would prove to be different.

When Andrea arrived at Omega Studios that morning, her producers and sound engineers were gathered around the television that was mounted at the lobby area. Patti, one of Andrea's producers, was watching the breaking news when Andrea walked over to her.

"Yo, Patti, what's going on?"

When she saw Andrea, Patti tried her best to guide her to the studio because she did not want Andrea to find out what was being reported. "Nothing important, Adia. Let's just go to the studio and work. It's no big deal."

"What you mean, 'It's no big deal?' Obviously, it's a big deal if all of you are gathered in front of the TV." Andrea turned back around to watch the news, and she soon realized why Patti attempted to guide her away. The breaking news reported on *New York City versus LaToya Richardson* and the controversial verdict that had New York abuzz. Andrea felt her blood boil as she watched the footage of her sister's murderer standing emotionless.

But the image that sent Andrea over the top was of the lawyer that represented LaToya. Andrea saw Edward Reed standing next to LaToya, and at that point, Andrea was enraged. *What the hell? Why is he defending that murdering Jezebel? That man had the nerve to come to my house and promised me that he would do anything to make sure LaToya rots in prison, and he turns around and helps her avoid jail time by sending her to anger management and for a mental evaluation?*

Patti, who was familiar with the story of Andrea's sister being killed by her best friend, tried to reason with her. "Andrea, listen to me. Don't do anything irrational. Maybe the prosecution will take it to the Supreme Court, and then they'll sentence her to jail then."

"Oh yeah? And what if they don't?" Andrea asked angrily. She could not believe Edward betrayed her. *I trusted that man, and he turns around and does this to me. He lets Loree's murderer get way scot free. Anger management doesn't transform evil. It enhances it, and Edward used the system to enable LaToya to continue killing people.*

"I gotta go, Patti. I'll be back tomorrow."

"Andrea, wait!"

But it was too late. Andrea was headed for the door and to her car. She was too enraged to continue working, and she was not going to let her sister's memory be erased and become a footnote. Andrea sped down the highway, weaving through other cars to arrive at her next destination.

Edward woke up hearing his doorbell ring several times. Taking a sick day off after the verdict, he made his way downstairs to the front door. His heart skipped, and he was suddenly alert when he saw who was ringing his doorbell and knocking frantically on his door. Rubbing his tired eyes, he opened the door. Before he knew what happened, the person behind the door slapped Edward, hard. Falling back in surprise, Edward held his cheek in shock.

"What the fuck?!"

Andrea stood outside his door, steaming in rage. "How could you? How could you call yourself an honest, changed man, and you go behind my back and pull that mess? How could you defend her when you knew what she did to David and Loree?"

"Andrea, hold up. Let me explain," Edward protested, but Andrea already stormed into his home and turned to face him, her eyes boring into his own.

"Explain what? Explain how you sided wit' that murdering she-devil to get her hours of anger management and mental evaluation? Are you freaking kidding me?"

"Andrea," Edward replied, rubbing his left temple, "it ain't what it looks like, all right. Tadarius one-upped me, and I had no choice."

"What the hell do you mean, you had no choice? You know what, this is all part of ya'll gang code, huh? All you M.O.B. gangstas rock together till the end, right?"

"Tadarius kidnapped my brother, Andrea!"

Suddenly, Andrea stopped her angry rants and looked at Edward. "Tadarius got yo' brother?"

"The day of David's funeral when I got back home he left a message on my phone, and he told me he got Tony, and if I didn't get LaToya out of jail, he was gonna kill him. I had no choice, Andrea. Tony's my family."

Tears started to stream down Andrea's face. "Loree was my family, Edward. You said you were going to help make sure the Loree's murder was avenged by making sure she saw justice, and you let her murderer get off."

"So, wait, you wanted me to sacrifice my brother just so you could see LaToya get locked up?"

"I don't care what needs to happen. Loree deserves justice, and if that woman gets anywhere close to me, she's gonna get dealt with."

Edward knew that Andrea was talking out of rage, and he did his best to calm her down. "Look, I know you're upset, and you have every right to be, but my brother means just as much to me as Loree meant to you, okay? I gotta play this game on his terms right now, and when my chance comes, I'll make sure he gets what's coming to him."

"You sure?" Andrea asked as she walked out of Edward's house. "I'm sorry about your brother. But the way you goin' about this, you might as well have stayed in the car that day when it all went down."

With that, she walked away, leaving Edward hanging his head behind her.

CHAPTER 9

DIVINE VENGEANCE

PUTTING ON HIS NIKE sneakers in the locker room, Chris tied the laces tightly and rolled his socks up underneath his P.E. sweats. There was always an advantage to having Phys Ed at the end of the school day, as Chris found out. First, he was able to work all his tension from the rigorous school day. It had now been three weeks into the new semester, and he had managed to keep up his end of the bargain with Mrs. Anderson.

His progress report showed that he was getting A's and B's in all his classes, a feat that he had never been able to accomplish at Bayside High School. He felt that the reason he never reached his full potential academically while at Bayside was because he spent so much time working for LaToya and the gang family.

Between running packages and spying on his father and other former members affiliated with M.O.B., it left little time for Chris to focus on his studies. But the new school and the new environment at home where Mrs. Anderson closely monitored her kids' progress had inspired Chris to perform better in class. He completed all his assignments by their due dates, and he even studied the night before exams and quizzes.

Occasionally, his phone would ring, and when he'd check it, it would be either Jermaine or Will G., two boys that ran with M.O.B., but he'd ignore the calls because he did not want to be involved in any more of their dealings. If he'd responded, they might have been able to track him, and it would have blown his cover because he was actively still avoiding the Fam at all costs.

The news that LaToya literally received a light slap on the wrist sentence for her part in David Anderson's murder and attempt to murder with a deadly weapon angered Chris intensely. So, he went out of his way to focus on school, and it was beneficial for Chris because now he was on a new mission. *I'm gonna prove to my mother that I don't need her to do good in my classes. I'm not going to be the loser that she turned out to be, whether bipolar or for a different reason.*

So far, the strategy worked, and Chris's hard work began to pay off. Due to him showing progress, Renee allowed him to start searching for a job. Chris filled out an application at Associated Food Source, a grocer retailer that had more than a hundred locations in the tri-state area. After a few days, he received a call from Bruce Pikes, the store manager, who informed him that he was strongly being considered for a part-time position, and he was scheduled to go in for an interview on Saturday.

For Chris, it came at an opportune time because his savings were beginning to dry up, and he was not going to make it through the week on Renee's weekly allowances. He also wanted to help Renee pay some of the bills in the house since she no longer had anyone to assist her, and it pained Chris daily to know that his mother was the reason for Renee's financial hardship. He could not bring David back, but he could do his best to contribute around the house.

Chris was also beginning to make headway with Shantay, who not only was in his History class but was also in his P.E. class as well. Between routine dates at Harry's and working together on some group projects, Chris decided to play it cool when it came to Shantay. He knew she liked him, and the feeling was mutual, but he knew getting caught up this early might distract him, and everything was going so well. He did not want to screw it up.

Still, Shantay did not make it easy with some of the outfits that she chose to wear to class daily: the blouses under the sweaters and the skinny jeans that showed her shapely legs, and the days that she wore the low-cut jeans were the best days because anytime she sat down, Chris saw her bright yellow thong peek out of her pants, and she would act as if she was unaware that she was providing him a peep show, but Chris knew she was teasing him. *Yeah, she knows exactly what she's doing. Well, I'mma let her rock. I ain't gonna say a damn thing.*

As tempting as Shantay was in History class, it was nothing compared to what she wore in gym class. She wore the same school gym T-shirt that everyone else wore during the period, but she would tie her shirt above her naval, revealing her belly ring. She would wear tight gym shorts along with some new designer sneakers or Jordans, depending on how she felt on a particular day. Those were the pros of Chris having access to a beautiful girl in two class periods of the day.

But with every pro came a con, and it came in the form of Marlon, who Chris had the unfortunate pleasure of sharing History and P.E. class with as well. It was not enough that Marlon was loud, brash, cocky, and just obnoxious, but he looked to instigate drama each day. Tadarius used to have a special term for people like Marlon, which was "habitual shit starters." People like Marlon would project their insecurity on others that were excelling above him and try to bring them down to his level, which was counterproductive to business and would become a liability. These types of people should be ignored, but if they came close to becoming a threat, it had to be dealt with.

The first day of school was only a microcosm of the misery that Marlon imposed upon Chris. Every day he roasted Chris on something new: his clothes, his tattoos, the way he sat and took notes, and the fact that he transferred from Bayside High School, a place Marlon felt was inferior to Townsend Harris. Chris had done his best to ignore Marlon whenever he went into his mindless diatribes, but the more Marlon talked, the more it irritated Chris, to the point where

Chris was tempted more often than not to hit Marlon in the face and shut his mouth, but he controlled his urges and just took everything that Marlon flung at him.

One day in gym class, it came to a head. Due to the cold temperatures outside, the students were inside in the auxiliary gym playing flag football in which they would pull a string of flags around a player's waist to replace tackling. Chris thought it was a corny way to play football, but he understood that the school wanted to take safety measures because they normally played football outside on the field.

The students that did not participate in the flag football game participated in open gym, which included jumping rope or climbing the small obstacle course wall that was located at the corner of the main gym. Shantay and her friend Pamela took time from their opening gym activities to watch the boys pick teams for flag football.

Chris, after being the third boy chosen on the Yellow Squad, tied a yellow flag around his waist. Although he would not consider himself extremely skilled, Chris knew how to play standard football and basketball. His eyes lit up when he saw Marlon tying an orange flag around his waist. *Oh, I'm gonna be facing this scrub? Okay, let's go. I'm 'bout to make this cat regret having to defend me out here.*

Marlon was slight in build, and he felt that would give him an advantage over his opponents in any sport. When he saw Chris on the opposing team, he gleefully walked up to face off against him. "Oh shit, I'm facing Bayside ova' here! This is about to be a blowout! I'm 'bout to work you, boy."

Chris rolled his eyes. *For all the things this man don't know how to do, does he at least know how to shut the fuck up?*

Soon the game got underway, and the quarterback of the Yellow Squad, Tom Peterson, threw the ball in Chris's direction as soon as it was hiked. Measuring where the pass would end up, Chris eluded Marlon who lunged for his flag before the ball was in his hands, which was illegal by the rules, but he was unable to fully pull down his flag, and Chris easily caught the pass and strolled into the end zone, which was identified by four cones on each corner of the gym.

"Hell yeah, Chris!"

"Show 'em how we do it on the west, Chris."

"Damn, Marlon, yo' ass got burnt, son!"

Halfway through the period, the Yellow Squad had a commanding 36-7 lead over the Orange Squad, and Chris was thoroughly outplaying Marlon, evading his flag pulls and ignoring the sneaky, dirty tactics where Marlon would stick his foot out before the ball was thrown, attempting to trip Chris up. But Chris was too fleet afoot and avoided being tripped.

As Chris breezed in for what would be his fourth touchdown of the game, Marlon, red with rage, began to increase his dirty level of play, holding Chris's T-shirt, forcing Chris to slap his hand off of him during the game. Chris employed a deft spin move that caused Marlon to scramble around until he fell on the ground on his backside. Hitting the gym floor in anger, he could only watch in jealousy as Chris waltzed into the end zone for another touchdown.

Throwing the ball back to the opposing quarterback, Chris walked back on defense with his squad. On the other side, Marlon could not shake Chris, who managed to pull his flag off each time he had the ball. Chris played defense on other players of the Orange Squad, partly because he wanted to get away from Marlon, who was getting increasingly angry at every failed opportunity he had to score. One such play was an unforced error, in which Marlon reached out to catch a pass, but it slipped right through his hands, prompting players from both teams to laugh at him. Even Chris did his best to suppress his laughter.

"I thought you said you was gon' blow us out. Check the scoreboard, son." Chris shook his head while lining up on offense.

Tom had the ball again, and after it was hiked, Chris made another beeline for the endzone, where he had been unstoppable. Marlon was in heavy pursuit of Chris, his eyes squinted deep in concentration, his mind mired with dirty intention. Once again, Tom threw the pass right in the pocket, and again Chris caught it, but Marlon was determined not to let Chris just walk into the endzone again.

While Chris ran into the endzone, Marlon put on an extra burst of speed and finally caught up to Chris, but he had no intention of just pulling his flag down. He ran headfirst into Chris, knocking the wind out of him, sending him sprawling past the cones into the wall. If Chris had not put his hands out, his head might have hit the gym wall and received serious injury.

Nonetheless, Chris fell hard on the ground, scraping his knee and his wrist. The other students watched Marlon's cheap shot and were waiting with bated breath to see what would happen next.

"I don't hear you talkin' now, Bayside!" Marlon yelled as he headed over to the other end of the gym.

Oh hell no. Now I'mma bust this nigga's ass. As soon as he gathered himself, Chris rose back up and ran towards Marlon, who had started walking the other direction, not expecting Chris to retaliate. But Chris was intent on breaking Marlon's jaw because he did not appreciate the cheap shot rendered to him. Marlon turned just for one second before Chris's fist smashed the side of his face.

Marlon fell from the force of the punch, but Chris was not done yet. He dove after Marlon and continued punching his gut, chest, and head. The other students formed a circle around the two boys as fists continued to whirl. Mr. Dartmouth, the P.E. teacher who was just outside the auxiliary gym, saw the commotion and waded into the circle and pulled Chris and Marlon away from each other.

Chris had a cut lip, scraped knee, and sore back from the cheap shot. Marlon's nose was bleeding, and he was holding his left side, which was sore from the assortment of body blows Chris rendered upon him. Both boys were immediately sent to the principal's office, where the principal decided on a proper punishment for them.

"Three days of ISS? Are you kidding me? What happened?" Renee asked after Chris arrived home following the incident with Marlon.

"Man, we were in P.E. playing flag football, and this fool Marlon ran straight into my chest on purpose to try to take me out. I've been dealin' wit' his bullshit long enough."

"You watch your mouth when you're talking to me, young man!"

Chris lowered his eyes in shame. "Yes, ma'am."

"Okay, so you just gonna let this kid Marlon get under your skin like that to make you lose control? Didn't you learn anything at all since you got here?"

Chris looked at Renee in disbelief. Leading up to the fight, he had been performing well in class, and he was on his way to get a job. He had been trying to walk the straight and narrow path for weeks, and it seemed as if Renee did not appreciate the work that he was putting in.

"I have learned some things, Mrs. A. But Marlon was getting on my nerves. For the past three weeks, he was jawing at me, and I ain't said nothin' to him. Then in P.E. he almost cracks my head open, and I'm still supposed to say nothin'? So, I can't defend myself?"

Renee held her temple in exasperation. She knew Chris had a point. He was a teenager still trying to navigate and understand life, especially a life that was as far removed from the streets where he was reared. *He was probably taught by his twisted mama to fight violence with violence, so I can't completely fault him for what he did.*

"Chris, there were a lot of things that you were taught early in life, and learning to stand up for yourself is one of the things that is taught to us at an early age. Because of who you are, people are going to try to test you to get you to react. But you've got to be the bigger man and walk away."

"Marlon don't know nothin' about me, Mrs. A., and I wasn't taught to run from people that put hands on me. I ain't on that 'turn the other cheek' stuff that you and David raised your other kids on. If someone steps to me, I'm gonna respond, whether you think it's right or not."

"Okay, I got you. So, what happened to Marlon? They assigned him to in-school suspension too?"

"Nah, they actually suspended him for four days. He got the good ole' out of school suspension because I told the people at the office that he started the fight by bum-rushing me like I was an NFL safety."

"Well, that's a relief, so you won't have to worry about seeing this boy for the rest of the week. Now can I trust that you'll do better to control yourself?"

"Yeah, Mrs. A., I got you. I'll chill."

Just then Dennis walked into the house.

"Hey, honey, how was school?"

"It was okay. I'm goin' up to my room. I'll talk to ya'll later."

As Dennis headed to his room, Renee looked at Chris, who just shrugged his shoulders.

I hope Dennis is okay. I know he lost his father, but he looks really out of it lately.

"So, this whole me scrappin' with Marlon deal, that's not gonna affect my interview on Saturday for a job, right?"

"No, it will not. You can still go to the interview. But remember what I said. Be mindful of where you are."

NetExplorer tech agent Kim Lee was taking her 15-minute break in her car after working a busy couple of hours into her work schedule. Normally at this time, she would be taking a coffee break or eating a snack from the vending machines on campus. But on this day, she happened to be someone else's meal. Her eyes closed in euphoric pleasure, and she sighed deeply as her legs quivered in ecstasy.

She was not alone in her car. A male co-worker was in the car with her, and he was extremely hungry, but he was busy sloshing her juices with his tongue. She covered her mouth and looked around nervously, hoping that nobody heard her moans.

With her right hand, she held his head between her legs as he continued to lick her crevices, and he was getting extremely close to her spot. Finally, his tongue lapped up her orgasmic fluids after her initial reaction.

"Oh my God, baby, your tongue feels so good!"

"Well, you taste extra sweet yourself, girl. What you been eating these days?"

Kim laughed as beads of sweat poured down her forehead from climaxing multiple times. "Boy, why you wanna know what I be eating?"

"Just curious. Damn, your break's almost over. I never got a chance to get mine off, so you owe me tomorrow."

Kim looked at the clock on her phone and gasped. He was right. It was almost time for her to return to work. Nudging his head away from her, she grabbed some paper towels and some wipes from her glove compartment and wiped herself before putting on her panties and pulling her blue skirt back up. Buttoning her white blouse, she put her blue blazer back on and checked her hair and makeup in the mirror.

Opening the door of her car, she stepped out first, and after looking around once again to make sure there were no other employees around, she beckoned her partner to proceed from her vehicle. Fixing his tie and tucking his shirt back into his pants, Quentin emerged from the car. Putting his glasses back on, he followed Kim back into the building as they went about their workday as if nothing happened between them.

CHAPTER 10

DIVINE VENGEANCE

June 2002

ELEVEN-YEAR-OLD Andrea McAfee was outside with her best friends Vanessa Roberts and Darlene Emmitt. All three girls were students at I.S. 139, where the school year ended, effectively beginning two long months of summer vacation. The temperature was in the mid-70s, and all the children in the neighborhood took advantage of the nice weather, playing in the public parks, going to the city pools, and playing basketball on the park courts.

The three girls took the time to play double-dutch jump rope outside the row of apartments where Andrea lived with her older sister, Loree, and their parents, Amos and Alisha McAfee. Although it was summer vacation for the kids, for the adults, it was still business as usual. Amos and Alisha worked at North Shore Jewish Hospital and were on call almost daily, which left them little time to spend with their two girls. But they were confident in Loree's ability to watch her sister while they were away, and Andrea had never shown signs of being neglected, and Loree was never short of adventure when it came to her sister.

On the weekends, Loree would take Andrea to the mall, the movies, or even shopping in some cases. Loree worked part-time at Grace's Department Store in addition to going to school and maintaining her grades. She always spent what she could on her sister and herself. However, Amos and Alisha were not privy to Loree's other job after dark. Loree, who was once a member of the infamous "Black Barbies" comprised of more than fifteen Black young women that exuded vibes of arrogance and pride, had joined another group: M.O.B.

Having been introduced into the gang's fold by LaToya Richardson, another former Black Barbie member, Loree, who was young and spontaneous, fit the ideal prototype of a female associate that Tadarius Hill and his other members searched for in their daily quest for members. But Loree and LaToya's roles within the gang were reduced to superficiality and some might say, demeaning and inappropriate behavior for young women.

They were tasked, along with other female members, to sell their bodies to the highest bidder. Prostitution, which was already at a high rate in the city, experienced a spike in the early 2000s, and with those numbers being driven up, and with his addiction to sex and promiscuous women, Tadarius took advantage of the young ladies as their night activities brought M.O.B. extra revenue in addition to what they earned in drug and weapons sales. Loree was also a nymphomaniac herself, feeding her lust with the endless interactions of different men, who all believed she was older than her actual age.

Had any of the men known how old she really was, they might have backed away from her to prevent being locked up for rape. Loree was only sixteen when she entered M.O.B., and throughout all the disguises, wigs, and enhanced appearances, nobody suspected her of being underaged. There were even days where she went to school extremely exhausted because she had been working the night before and only slept for two hours or less. When her parents asked about her unusual fatigue level, she would inform them that she picked up extra hours at Grace's, which was false, but her parents bought it and never second-guessed her.

As the month approached its final days, Loree and LaToya decided to spend the day together because Tadarius had not asked them to do him any more favors. Loree and LaToya were grateful for any of the little free time that they could get with school ending.

Sitting outside the little courtyard at the front of their apartment, Loree was busy braiding LaToya's hair, and they were engaged in rumor mill gossiping while Andrea jumped in sync to the double ropes that were spun by Vanessa and Darlene. Andrea, even as a young girl, was coordinated and athletic, and she jumped with ease. The girls were practicing for an inner-city double-dutch competition that was taking place in July in Brooklyn.

It was one of the biggest events in New York City, and the winner would retain bragging rights, not only for their neighborhood and school but also for the borough. Borough battles ran rampant through New York City, and kids competed to their limits to defeat their rival boroughs. It dated back to the Subway Series of baseball between the New York Mets, who played in Queens, and the New York Yankees, who played in Brooklyn. Local rap and hip-hop acts had rivalries dating back to the 1980s when Queens rap groups and Bronx rap groups were going bar for bar against each other.

Andrea and her friends trained daily for this competition, and she was at the top of her game, spinning around in conjunction to the ropes moving in circular motion. Her movements started to draw a couple of spectators and looks from people who were heading out to work to those returning from the store.

"Get it, Drea!" Vanessa shouted as she and Darlene spun the rope faster.

Meanwhile, Loree and LaToya were immersed in their own conversation.

"Girl, you crazy! Nick Hamby was not tryna' holla at me, okay? He was peepin' ole girl sittin' in front of him in Biology class. What was her name? Courtney?"

Loree stopped braiding for a moment, while trying to stifle her laughter. "Girl, stop trippin'! You know good and damn well Nick was lookin' at you. You tryin' to play it off like you don't know. It's okay. It's me. You can tell me what's up."

"Whateva. Just don't braid my shit too tight, Ree."

Watching Andrea freestyle with the double-dutch, LaToya said, "Yo' Andrea killin' it out there. She looks like she could be better than you," she laughed.

"Girl, stop. Who you think taught Andrea how to do that? You lookin' at the best double-dutch jumper in the family."

Watching Andrea perform her routine, Loree shouted, "Aye, Drea, you call that double-dutch? Yo' girls ain't turnin' that shit fast enough."

The girls stopped spinning while Andrea took a moment to breathe. Panting slowly, she turned to Loree, knowing that a challenge was on the horizon. "Oh yeah? I'd like to see you try. You ain't double-dutched in forever. You probably forgot how to do it."

Snickering, Loree turned to LaToya. "Girl, was that a challenge?"

"Oh, I think it was a challenge, Ree. You better go ova' there, and let her know what's up. Show her who runnin' thangs up in hea'."

Loree got up from the steps where she was sitting. LaToya, with a comb in her hair and one corner of her head still unbraided, watched with growing interest as Loree approached her sister and her friends.

"Move out the way. Lemme show ya'll how it's done. Turn the rope for me, Andrea. Vanessa, take the other side."

The girls did what they were told, and with Vanessa and Andrea turning the ropes, Loree timed her entrance down to the millisecond as she jumped in and skipped in rhythm to the rope.

"Let me know when you get tired," Andrea joked as she turned the rope.

"Tired? Girl, I'm just getting started. Watch me work. And please turn that rope faster."

Andrea and Vanessa increased their speed in turning the ropes, secretly hoping that it would not trip up or hurt Loree. But the faster the ropes spun, the better Loree seemed to perform, spinning counterclockwise and remaining in perfect harmony with the ropes. Andrea watched on in amazement. Loree had taught her to double-dutch, and she was good, but she never imagined Loree would up the ante on herself.

"Come on, spin the rope faster! Give me a challenge! I could do this all day!"

As she continued to jump, Loree was unaware of two young boys who were approaching her and the other girls. The boys wore identical gear, both black and white T-shirts, pants, and sneakers.

They also had identical gang tattoos on their forearms. One of the boys sported thick, short dreads.

When the jump-roping lesson concluded, Loree shouted, "What's my name?!"

After showing her sister up on the double-dutch front, she headed back to tend to LaToya but not before being approached by the two boys. When Loree and LaToya looked up, they saw the boys, and Loree's smile quickly dissipated.

One of the boys clapped his hands in mock celebration. "Impressive, Ms. Loree. I'mma need to pay for a show like that next time, only more privately."

"What the hell are ya' doin' hea'?" Loree asked. Clearly, she was not pleased to see the boys.

"Nothin'. Just came wit' a message from T. He wants ya at the spot ASAP. He got some work that need to be done."

"Aight. Tell T we comin' through in thirty minutes," LaToya replied.

"You plannin' on going by yourself? Cuz I ain't rollin' with you. Don't you see I'm babysitting right now?"

LaToya looked up at Loree disapprovingly. "C'mon, Ree, don't be like that. Andrea will be fine without you for a couple of hours."

"Exactly. And when lil' mama's old enough, she could join right in the fold wit' her older sister," the boy replied.

Loree, her face red with rage, stood up. "Listen, Malik, my sister ain't gonna have nothin' to do with this, you feel me? If T wants to talk, he knows where to find me, and that sure as hell ain't my house. So I'mma need you and yo' lil' brotha to roll up outta here, wit' his dusty-ass dreads."

Malik laughed as if he was told some long-lost joke. "Oh yeah, my bad. Where my manners at? This here's my man Tone. Just started rollin' wit' us a couple weeks. He just ridin' along wit' me a few days, learning the tricks of the trade and shit."

Loree stared at the younger gangbanger, eyeing him suspiciously, making him uncomfortable. "This boy look like he gon' pee in his pants. The least Tadarius could've done is get someone who could grow a pair."

LaToya laughed uncontrollably after the two girls dapped each other for Loree's undressing of the new M.O.B. member.

Tone, better known as Antonio Franks, looked around, trying to divert the attention off him. He had seen Andrea and her friends jumping double-dutch, and he watched Darlene at the center jumping in rhythm to the ropes. While she was turning the ropes, Andrea's eyes happened to look around before settling on Antonio.

The two eyed each other for a minute before Loree's sharp voice snapped him back to attention. "Yo, Bob Marley, you checkin' out my sista?"

"What? Nah, I was just checkin' out the jump rope routine."

"You better be cuz she ain't finna get involved wit' any of you nappy-headed boys."

"Fuck you, you low budget Tyra Banks wannabe." He was not going to allow Loree to diss him without responding for much longer, and he decided to go on the offensive.

"Yo, Malik, you betta' muzzle yo' dawg cuz he don't know me."

"I don't need to know you. I could ask half the block, and they know who you is, hoe."

Loree stepped to Antonio, and the two were about half a step away from throwing fists before Malik got between them. "Aight, aight, enough of that. Yo, Tone, Loree is still part of the Fam, so next time, just recognize who you talkin' to, B, cuz she don't play."

"I don't play either. Tell yo' girl to watch her mouth."

"You watch yo' mouth! Take the Similac out ya' breath before talkin' in grown folk business."

Antonio walked away, and unbeknownst to him, Andrea and the two other girls had stopped turning the rope and watched Antonio walk away from the complex to wait for Malik outside his car.

As soon as Antonio was out of earshot, LaToya said, "I ain't gon' lie, Ree'. Tone's got some flava. He definitely Fam material. He ain't scared of nobody."

Malik shrugged as if he knew Antonio had no fear.

"Yeah, okay. He ain't all bad. He just needs to learn how to respect his elders," Loree agreed.

"No doubt. So, T wanna holla at ya' about a couple of high rollas on the east end. They owe him money, and T thinks they'd wanna pay him if they got something back, you know what I'm sayin'?" Malik asked.

"When does T want us to get wit' 'em?" LaToya asked.

"T got ya'll ready to meet 'em on Sunday."

"Wait, hold up. Sunday? Nah, that ain't gonna work for me. I'mma have to pass the buck on that one," Loree replied.

"Bitch, are you for real? You ain't got a choice in this," Malik replied seriously.

"C'mon, Loree, this could be our biggest score yet. We do this, we could walk away with about three G's each," LaToya insisted.

"Sundays ain't good for me. You know I gotta be wit' my family on Sunday. I gotta go to church wit' my sista. Any other day would be cool for me, but Sundays are non-negotiable."

"Here we go with this whole church thing. You wanna know something about church that I found out? It ain't goin' nowhere. You got plenty other Sundays that you can go to church," LaToya argued.

"I said what I said. Sundays ain't good for me right now. My family's more important."

"So, what about this family? Ree, we got a good thing going right now. We makin' money, and we independent. We ain't waitin' for nobody to give us any handouts, and we call our own shots. Don't screw this up for us."

As Malik walked away, leaving the two girls arguing, he turned back and said, "I'll let Tadarius know ya still thinkin' about it, but ya better have ya asses in the spot tonight." Malik got back into his car with Antonio, and they took off.

As the car pulled away, Andrea was still staring at Antonio without paying attention to her two friends who were waiting for her to turn the ropes.

"Hello? Earth to Drea! Are you gonna turn the rope anytime soon?" Darlene asked.

"Nah, she too busy eye-bangin' Tone," Vanessa snickered, snapping Andrea out of her thoughts.

"Shut up, Nessa. It ain't that serious."

"Girl, don't come for me when you know I'm speaking facts. You like them roughneck types, don't you?"

"I never said I like him. He's kinda cute, but if my sister hates him, then I don't trust him."

"Mmhmm, okay, whatever you say. It's okay to like boys, Andrea. We ain't in grade school anymore."

"You know, I hear all this talkin' from you about who I like. How come you ain't made a move on Sean yet?" Andrea asked.

Vanessa raised her eyebrows. "Sean? You mean the little fat boy that sat behind us in art class? I thought he was your boyfriend, Drea!" she laughed.

"No, I think I heard him say that he likes Darlene. So, when is your first date?"

Darlene laughed uncomfortably, hoping her friends did not suspect anything. But she could not hide it for long. "Well, Sean kind of asked me out on the last day of school. I didn't want to hurt his feelings, so I said I would go to the movies with him."

Andrea and Vanessa both laughed. Andrea took her place back in the center starting point while Vanessa and Darlene turned the ropes again.

"So what movie are you guys going to see?" Andrea asked.

Darlene said, "Well, the new Spiderman movie just came out. I saw the trailer for it, and it looks nice."

"Well, enjoy the movie, and whatever you do, make sure you buy the extra-large popcorn for him. With butter."

Andrea could barely contain her laughter. Vanessa's humor knew no limits.

While the three girls chatted, Loree continued braiding the rest of LaToya's hair in silence. LaToya knew that her friend was contemplating going to the rendezvous spot where they were scheduled to meet Tadarius with instructions for meeting their next pleasure clients.

"What you thinking, Ree? You ain't said nothin' for about ten minutes since Malik left."

Wrapping up her friend's hair, Loree wiped her hands with a few paper towels from a roll that she took outside from her home. Eventually, she would have to accompany LaToya to meet with Tadarius, but for the first time, she was not enthusiastic about her job. Sneaking around behind her parents, concealing everything from Andrea, and sleeping with complete strangers, just was not appealing anymore. The thrill was gone, and it was replaced by concern.

"LaToya, what if we got out the game?"

LaToya, examining her hair in the mirror, gave Loree an incredulous look. "Girl, what you talkin' about?"

"I'm sayin', what if we got out? You know, just do our own thing without havin' to watch our backs or worry about fuckin' some unprotected fool out there. Ain't no security out here. There's a life outside of the street game."

LaToya could not believe what she was hearing. She knew the girls in the gang were not working under the best of circumstances, but she was not one to give up a lucrative payday, no matter how demeaning her profession was. The idea of leaving M.O.B. was unfathomable to LaToya.

"Why would you want out though? You out here making thousands of dollars and building wealth. You could get your whole family outta hea' if you wanted."

"At what cost?" Loree asked. "Getting sick? Running into a crazy cat that's gon' kill me when he doesn't get what he wants? Check it out. I've been talkin' to my guidance counselor at school and some of my friends. They like some sketches of my clothing designs that I've been working on lately. They feel like I can go to fashion school after graduation."

"Yeah, and then what?" LaToya asked. "You'll spend the rest of your life working some 9-to-5 for a boss who don't give two shits about you? Lemme remind you what time you on, Loree. This country ain't gon' give no po' Black girl from the hood any real shot at nothin' out hea'. There is a war on us, whether you wanna believe it or not.

Tadarius may not have all the answers, but he treats us a whole lot better than corporate America would. We control our destiny, girl."

"Really? Because if that's the case, then why is Tadarius the one callin' all the shots? Seems like he's controlling our destiny cuz whenever he wants us somewhere, we just go lock and step, no questions asked. I don't know if I can do that anymore."

As Andrea made her way back into the apartment to get a drink of water, the two girls lowered their voices so as to not draw attention to themselves. Although it was fleeting, Andrea saw a flash of anger on LaToya's face as she stared at her sister, but it was brief and replaced by the same look of consternation.

"Think about Andrea. Don't you want what's best for her?"

"Don't…just don't mention Andrea and M.O.B. in the same sentence. I don't want her doing what we do."

"Then for your sake, don't leave the Fam. We got you."

"Wait, what you mean 'for my sake'? You threatening me now?"

"No, I'm protecting you now. You don't know Tadarius like I do. It's best if we play along and do what he says right now because anyone that tries to dip out gets dealt with."

"You think that scares me? I ain't shook by Tadarius like everybody else is. The moment I feel like I've done what I can, I'm out."

LaToya shook her head. "Who's tellin' you all this? Your uppity friends? Ms. Flo-Jo Preacher's Daughter over there feeding yo' mind this garbage?"

Loree glared at LaToya. "Don't talk about Shania that way, you hear me? Whenever you're around me, I don't wanna hear you talkin' shit about Shania."

"Oh okay, I won't talk about Miss Goody Two-Shoes, who has both her parents. One of them is a poverty pimp preacher, and her mama's working in the community. She's got college All-American written all over her. You think that's yo' life?"

"Maybe not, but Shania's had my back ever since we met, and she's been real. You ain't gotta like her ,but you ain't gonna disrespect her in front of me."

Unbcknownst to the two girls, Andrea had stopped in her tracks and was eavesdropping through the other side of the door. *Why didn't LaToya like Shania Hillman? What was their beef? Most of all, what is my sister involved in that has LaToya all defensive?*

Almost eighteen years later, Andrea found herself thinking about the conversation that she'd heard between LaToya and her sister while she settled in for the evening. Had she heard what was to become the first sign of tension between Loree and the treacherous murderer whom she once called her friend? Had she known any better, could Andrea have confronted LaToya back then for threatening her sister? Could she have called the cops and gotten her sister out of the street gang cult she had found herself in? Andrea had to talk to someone. She tried calling Quentin again, but the call went to voicemail.

He must be working late again. He seems to be doing that an awful lot these days. But Andrea did not want to assume the worst about Quentin yet. After all, he was the only male in her life other than her father who had been there for her when she needed him, and although he was undoubtedly disappointed that their engagement was called off, Quentin never expressed that he wanted to leave her. Then again, he was a handsome man working at a high-tech firm in the city and would be considered a catch for any single woman looking to break up a happy union.

Ain't no proof that he's playing me. But I'm gonna keep my eyes open, and when he comes back in the house, I'm gonna press him for the truth.

CHAPTER 11

DIVINE VENGEANCE

DESPITE HIS THREE days of in-school-suspension for fighting Marlon in P.E. class, Chris's fortunes took a turn for the better. After serving his suspension, he went to his job interview at Associated Food Source on Saturday morning. Even if it was out of character for Chris to dress up, Renee made sure he did not leave the house without putting on a shirt and a tie. She was so pleased with Chris having a job interview that she took the time to buy him three dress shirts, an array of ties, two pairs of khaki pants, and one suit.

Chris knew how much Renee had to scrape and put aside to buy him clothes, and when she came home Friday evening with the new clothes and showed Chris, he instinctively hugged her while thanking her for her kindness and vowing that he would pay her back for everything she bought him.

But Renee would hear none of it. "Continue to perform well in school, keep your grades up, and no more school fights."

After he vowed to listen to Renee, Chris's phone vibrated. Realizing that it was Edward calling him, he excused himself to go to his room to pick up the call.

"Three days of ISS, Chris?" Edward asked, as a form of greeting when Chris picked up the phone.

Chris rolled his eyes as he undoubtedly realized that Renee must have told Edward about the school fight. "Look, man, he was the one that bum-rushed me in P.E. class when my back was turned. What you expect me to do? Fall back and let him do what he want, and I just gotta sit there and take it?"

"I expect you to control yourself, Chris. Remember, you're supposed to be laying low. Tadarius and M.O.B. are still out there, so you can't be drawing attention to yourself like that. If they even know where you are, they are gon' come after you. If you think the fact that you're LaToya's son makes you immune to them, better think again."

"Then what am I supposed to do if Marlon comes at me again? Or if anyone else tries me?"

"Don't do anything. Walk away. Avoid confrontation at all costs. Is that too much to ask for?"

Chris shook his head. Edward was clearly out of touch. *This is the guy that used to run M.O.B. with my father back in the day? I'm having a hard time believing this shit because no way a member of M.O.B. would take any of Marlon's dirty tricks lying down.*

"I ain't wired like that, Edward. You can't keep poking the bull and expect not to get the horns at some point."

"Okay, let me rephrase it. You better not blow your chance at this school. If you fuck this up, I'll take you back to court and make absolutely sure you get placed in foster care. Do you understand? I'll do that before I let you put David's family in peril."

"Peril? Yo, you buggin', Edward. It's dog eat dog out here, and it's all about surviving. If Marlon keeps playin' wit' me, his ass gon' get dealt wit'. It's that simple."

"See, that's M.O.B. talking right there. You got to break yourself out of that mindset. It's the only way you're going to make it out here. People are gonna try to test you every day. Hell, they try me every other hour at my firm, but I pick and choose my battles. There are bigger things at stake."

Edward knew that he was dealing with a reformed gang member, and one had to break out of certain habits to survive in among society, whether it be drug habits or violence. He had to remember that Chris was taught retaliation by his street family, and it could take months or years to break out of the mindset of vengeance.

"Anyways, let's get off that. What's done is done, and you've served your time. Please just keep your nose clean. In other news, I think congratulations is in order. First, I hear that you're making all

A's and B's this semester already. Good job staying focused in class. Not to mention, you also got a new job?"

Thankful that Edward changed the subject, Chris affirmed his accomplishments. "Yeah, well it ain't official yet. I got an interview tomorrow at Associated Food Source in Flushing."

"Yeah, but I'm making it official. You're gonna do well in that interview, and by this time next week, you're gonna have a job."

"Hope so."

But Edward's confidence in Chris was well-founded. After attending the interview in the morning, Chris received a call that afternoon from Human Resources, where he learned that he had been hired for a part-time position at Associated Food Source. Renee was so overjoyed at hearing the good news that she brought pizza for the whole family to celebrate the occasion. Chris could not have been more pleased with himself for getting his first job, especially a job that did not involve selling drugs, weapons, or spying on potential enemies. He had a real job, and he was going to get paid clean money even though all money was important.

Now it was Monday, and as the Anderson family prepared for school, Chris took the Associated Food Source shirt and tried it on to make sure that it fit. It was a royal blue color with white striped-trim on the sleeves and collar. He was allowed to wear any type of pants he wanted as long as the pant legs were not ripped. Jeans were accepted, but khakis were recommended.

While Chris was trying on his work shirt, Dennis walked out of the bathroom where he had been previously brushing his teeth. When he passed the room, he looked at Chris and laughed. "What the hell are you wearing?"

Chris turned around to see Dennis snickering under his breath. "It's called a work shirt, genius. I'm just tryin' it on. Today's my first day of work after school."

"Shit looks lame."

Unfortunately, Dennis did not see Renee walking out of her room, and she gasped. "Language, Dennis!"

"My bad, Mom. Sorry."

"Go get ready for school, young man."

After Dennis went to go dress himself, Renee looked at Chris in his issued uniform. "You look professional, sir. Are you ready for you first day of work?"

"Ready as I'll ever be, Mrs. A. Store's just a few blocks from the school, so I can walk there and change into my work shirt once I arrive."

"Okay, great. So, while you finish getting ready, I'm gonna go check on Cree and Katrina."

After confirming that his shirt fit to scale, Chris took it off and put his regular Nike T-shirt on with his hooded sweater. Later in school, he was making his way to class when someone tapped him on the shoulder.

"What's up, Chris?" Shantay greeted him, bubbly.

"What up, Shantay?"

"You all right? Feels like I ain't seen you in days. What happened? Were you sick or something?"

"Nah, yo' boy Marlon got me suspended for that shit that went down in P.E. last week. They had me in ISS for three days, but they suspended his ass for a week, so I guess it's all good."

Shantay covered her mouth with her hands as if she was in shock. "Damn, I'm sorry about that. Marlon was an asshole for pullin' that on you."

"Seems to me like he was trying to impress somebody a bit much."

"What, you think he came at you because he was tryin' to put on for me?" Shantay asked.

"I don't know. If he wasn't frontin' for you, then he's a hell of a good actor cuz he might still be feelin' you."

Shantay nodded her head in agreement. She knew Chris was right, but she did not want to give him the satisfaction of being right, just for him to gloat at her. "Maybe, but there are plenty other girls at this school. He needs to quit trippin' and find somebody else to act a fool for cuz we done."

"Seriously? Like you sure you ain't feelin' him no more?"

"Oh, I'm definitely sure. We through-through. So, are you busy this weekend? I was thinking we can go to Flushing Meadows Park and hang out—you know, play a lil' ball."

Chris looked at Shantay, not sure if he had heard correctly. "Wait a minute. Hold up. Hold up. You're telling me that you know how to ball? Like basketball?"

"Yeah, why is that so hard to believe? Because I'm a girl?"

"No, I've seen plenty of chicks that could ball easily. I just never took you to be the ballin' type."

Shantay was slender, yet curvy in her chest and rear areas, and she was not very tall. It was hard to tell that she played basketball from the untrained eye.

"Aight, follow me then. I'll show you." Shantay suddenly took a detour from walking to class and headed toward the gymnasium with Chris following closely behind.

He was careful not to press up behind her too much because he did not want to violate her private space, but she was naturally gifted in all the right areas, and he was very tempted to turn into a dog in that very moment just to grab her rear end. But he restrained himself, remembering the conversation he had with Renee and Edward.

"Where we going? You tryin' to bust out a game right now? We got class though."

"Boy, just hush and follow me." Rolling her eye and laughing, Shantay led Chris to a glass display that faced the main gym, reminiscent of the glass display at the front of the school.

Various individual trophies and team photos from the Junior Varsity and Varsity basketball teams from the previous year were plastered behind the display. Shantay pointed at a framed team photo of the JV basketball team that stood adjacent to the Varsity, and when Chris followed her finger and examined the photo, he saw Shantay posing as a member of the JV team. There were only nine girls on the team last year, and Shantay was its second-leading scorer. Plus, she led the team in rebounds and steals.

"Damn, I ain't know you had game like that. If you this nice, why you ain't on the team this year?" Chris asked.

Shantay lowered her gaze, and Chris wondered if he should have asked the question at all.

"Took a year off for personal reasons. That's all."

Chris could not help but to notice that Shantay answered his question uncomfortably as if she did not want to go into detail, and he decided that he was not going to press her any further. "Yo, we better get to class before the late bell."

Rushing back into the main building, Chris said, "I actually can't go to the park with you this Saturday. Not because I don't want to, but because I got a new job, and I work after school and on Saturdays."

"Word? Oh shit, that's what's up! Where do you work at?"

"Associated Food Source in Flushing Meadows. It ain't glamorous or nothing like that. I'm a courtesy stock boy right now, but I'm hoping to work my way up to cashier."

"That's dope! I actually got a lil' job myself. I didn't tell you, but I work parttime at Regine's Salon Boutique in Flushing Meadows mall. My mom owns the place, so I just stop by and work a few hours after school and on weekends upon demand. So, when do you start at Associated?"

"I start today, actually. I'm heading over there after school. Yo, maybe one day, I can stop by the boutique and watch you as you do your thing."

"Yeah, that's cool. And you know I'mma stop by Associated cuz I always need them groceries. Their prices are way cheaper than Key Mart anyways."

As the two made their way to class, Mr. Thompson was already at his desk getting the lesson plan ready. Chris and Shantay were making their way over to their desks when Chris felt himself being shoved from behind. He did not have to turn around to know who it was that shoved him. Marlon shuffled his way past the students to get to his desk.

Since his fight with Chris, Marlon's social life had been a living hell. His social media accounts were filled with comments from other students who were present at the gym during the fight, which he lost handily, and students were merciless, calling him all different names. Added to the fact that he was suspended for a full week following the fight, he was subjected to the taunts. One student had even recorded the fight on her cell phone and managed to create a meme out of the situation, which resulted in more ridicule. As a result, Marlon was determined not to let Chris get the better of him, and he wanted another chance to go at him.

Chris was not going to give him that satisfaction.

"Move out of my way, nigga," Marlon said gruffly.

Chris chuckled. "Someone a lil' tight cuz he got his ass whooped last week?"

Marlon slammed his hands on his desk, stood up, and made his way to Chris, who did not back down. "Listen, you got a lucky punch in, cheap shottin' me and shit."

"Oh, the busta who think he's Michael Strahan is talkin' to me about cheap shots?"

The two boys stared each other down as the class fell silent, waiting for a sequel to last week's altercation.

"Gentlemen. Are we gonna have problems again today?" Mr. Thompson asked.

"Nah, I'm good, Mr. Thompson," Chris replied, walking to the other side of the classroom, resisting the urge to smash Marlon's face in again.

After school, Chris took the bus to Associated Food Source, which was about ten minutes away. After Chris's arrival, Bruce showed him around the store. Even for a grocery store, Chris had to admit to himself that it was the best designed store that he had seen. Many stores that he went to in the past were rundown and were in serious need of renovations.

Bruce explained that Associated underwent an extensive renovation to stay afloat in the competitive retail chain in New York City and New York state. One of the renovations included a large employee area behind the store where the breakrooms were located, and there were lockers where employees stored personal items. Each employee was assigned a specific locker number and was given the combination for it. Each was responsible for his own locker combination and items that were stored in the lockers.

There were two breakrooms and each of them had two refrigerators. Every employee had to make sure all their items were out of the refrigerators by 8:00 a.m. every Monday because housecleaning would come clean out the refrigerators to prevent the spread of bacteria or insects.

But the one aspect of Associated Food Source that separated them from other retail chains was their unique employee clock system. Each employee was handed a specific ID card that had his or her employee number with a scan code at the bottom. There were two employee clocking docks that had a red scanner at the bottom.

Whenever employees clocked in for the day, they would simply scan their code from the card under the red scanner on the machine, and the machine would automatically place them on the clock. Whenever they clocked out, they would scan their code under the same machine either for lunch or at the end of their shift. Chris was only parttime, so he did not have a full one-hour lunch. His lunch was only thirty minutes a day, along with a 15-minute break before the end of his shift.

He worked Monday, Wednesday, and Friday from 4-9:30 p.m., and Saturday from 10 a.m.-5:30 p.m. Although Chris wanted to pick up a shift for Sunday, Bruce felt it was best not to overwork the young man so early. Because Chris was only fifteen years old, he only had a certain number of hours he could work a week due to labor laws, and realizing that Chris was a student at Townsend Harris High

School, Bruce felt the staggered schedule workday was best because it left time for Chris to stay focused in school and complete assignments on his off days.

Being a father of four, Bruce viewed Chris and the other high school employees as his own children and wanted the best for them academically. One of Associated Food Source's best incentives for those employees was the yearly scholarship program that the store held at the end of every school year. For all employees that were not in any negative disciplinary status, maintained a B-average in school, and participated in an extracurricular activity, including community service or joining school clubs, they were eligible to receive the $15,000 scholarship towards any college of their choice.

This program was especially attractive to Renee, who stressed education and informed Chris that Associated would be the best place for him to work because although Chris was only a sophomore in high school, if he kept his grades at a B-average or above, there was no doubt that he would be a shoo-in for the scholarship.

After arriving to the store, Chris headed to the employee area, scanned his ID card, and put his T-shirt and hoodie in the locker. After changing into his work shirt, he walked out and looked at the employee log where they had a list of tasks at a certain time for each employee. Chris was a courtesy stock clerk, which meant he was responsible for mostly stocking new items that were shipped from the warehouse onto the shelves of their respective aisles. But he could also be called upon to help with bagging groceries for customers if the front area of the store was overwhelmed with customers, which typically happened during a huge sale or holiday season or if the front area employees were severely understaffed.

Chris was also trained to help customers find certain items in the store, and he was obligated to ask, "Are you finding everything okay?" to each customer that he encountered.

Whenever he helped bag groceries, he also helped customers out to their vehicles in the parking lot if they had heavy carts full of groceries. Upon finishing, Chris would make sure to put the cart in one of many cart stations that scattered throughout the parking lot, which was vast. Associated Food Source had a dedicated team of cart employees that were tasked with pushing all the carts from the stations back inside the cart-holding unit for re-use.

Although Chris was relatively new at Associated, he recognized some of his co-workers. Michael Wilson, Kent Morton, and Charity Oscar were students at Townsend Harris. Michael and Kent were seniors, and Charity was a junior, who also happened to be in the same P.E. block with Chris. They were all receptive and welcoming to Chris, and they took the time out of their shifts to give him an impromptu tour of the store.

Chris took the time to walk each aisle after his hire to make sure he knew where all items were, but Michael and Kent, who were now cashiers, educated Chris on where the small potpourri items were and the locations of all over-the-counter medicines and pharmaceutical supplies. Out of all the employees that helped Chris settle in, Charity was the most helpful. She gave him advice on how to handle unruly customers and where the baby buggies were for customers with small kids.

After showing him the ropes, Charity asked, "So, now that you know where everything is at, you got any questions?"

"Nah, I'm good."

"Aight, cool. So now I got a question for you."

"What's up?"

"What's up wit' you and Shantay? Is that why you scrapped with Marlon at the gym last week?"

Chris laughed. It seemed as if the fight had made him an overnight celebrity at school, for better or worse. "I mean Shantay's cool or whatever, but we just chillin'. I don't know what was up wit' ole' boy last week. She probably ain't give him none last time, and he felt some type of way. I had to let him know that I ain't the one to run up on. I wasn't gonna dodge the smoke."

"I see," Charity laughed. "But if it was about Shantay, I feel like I should school you on her real quick. She ain't as innocent as she seems."

"What you mean by that?"

"Well, to put it quite bluntly, Shantay's a two-dollar hoe. She likes guys like you as long as she can get something from you—either money, rep, or she might just wanna fuck. But once she gets what she wants, she's on to the next one."

"Really? She ain't played me yet, so she must be serious about me cuz she sure wasn't serious about Marlon's dusty ass. How you know so much about her anyway?"

"Cuz she slept wit' my boyfriend. That's how." Charity turned away from Chris as she dropped the unexpected bombshell.

Chris looked at her in shock. *Charity can't be serious, right? I mean we all got raging hormones and shit, so we're gonna fuck each other at some point, but Shantay being a side chick and breaking up a relationship? I can't see it.*

"I know that sounds crazy, but believe me, that girl foul. My boyfriend Marcus and I had been dating for eight months last year. Everything was good. I was working, and I was on the cheerleading squad while Shantay played ball last year. Marcus used to do everything for me. He doted on me, held the door open for me, bought me gifts—the whole nine. Then he started acting suspect. The gifts stopped, and he wasn't showing as much affection as he was early on in our relationship. Then came the nasty rumors that Marcus had hooked up with some chick he met in his DMs at a house party after a basketball game. Turns out the girl was Shantay. She had sex with Marcus, bragged to everyone about it, and I was the last to know about it. Needless to say, I dropped his ass, and Shantay, who I was always cool wit' before then, became dead to me. Then without warning she dropped Marcus's ass and moved on to Marlon."

Chris was taken aback by the revelation. Something did not smell right about the story because Shantay had not displayed the characteristics that Charity just described.

"Look, you ain't gotta believe me, but watch yourself around her. I just hate for a nice guy like you to be another notch on her Gucci belt."

Heading back to the cash register at the sight of a customer, Chris headed to the back warehouse to await another shipment of items to stock shelves. As he stacked boxes of crackers in the cracker aisle, he did not see a customer behind him, asking him directions to the international food aisle.

"Hey, young man, what aisle is the spaghetti sauce on?"

"Spaghetti sauce? Yeah, that's on Aisle Three, sir," Chris replied before he turned around and finally realized who asked him the question. To his astonishment, it was his History teacher, Mr. Thompson. "What's up, Mr. Thompson? I ain't even see you behind me."

"It's all right, Mr. Anderson. You're hard at work. I'm happy to see that you're making money. Just don't let your schoolwork slip."

"Oh, I won't, sir. Are you finding everything else okay?"

"Yeah, I'm finding everything. Thank you. And don't worry about Marlon. He could be a bit of a hothead, but just pay him no mind. He'll see that he can't mess with anyone."

Easier said than done, Mr. T.

After returning to his work after ten minutes, Chris was called to the front area. "Hey, Chris, that man out there forgot his celery in this bag. He just walked out. Can you run out there and catch him?"

Charity pointed to a tall, Black gentleman that was just entering his car with his groceries. Realizing that it was Mr. Thompson who forgot his item, Chris ran out in time to see another man enter Mr. Thompson's car. But Chris could tell from afar that the man was not an ordinary citizen. He wore the alternating black pants, white shirt, and black and white durag on his head, but the dead giveaway was the tattoo on his lower arm.

The blood drops, gun emblem, and dollar bills were all too familiar. Mr. Thompson was being accosted by a member of M.O.B. While Chris feared blowing his cover, he realized that he did not know the man, which meant he must be a new member, so he would not recognize Chris from a can of paint.

Secondly, the man was talking with Mr. Thompson, not threatening him or stealing his car. The two men were conversing as if they *knew* each other. *What the hell is going on? What is Mr. Thompson involved in?*

CHAPTER 12

DIVINE VENGEANCE

KNOCKING ON THE driver window side, Chris held up the bag with the celery that Mr. Thompson left behind. Lowering his window, Mr. Thompson had a face that was mired in suspicion, and his passenger did not look too pleased either.

"Uh, you left this bag at the register, so I was just running it out to you."

Taking the bag, Mr. Thompson smiled, which put Chris at ease. It also became apparent that the man dressed in M.O.B. colors was his passenger or friend. Mr. Thompson did not appear to be in any eminent danger.

"Thank you, Chris. Wouldn't have been able to complete dinner without this. I'll see you in class tomorrow, yeah?"

"Yes, sir."

Rolling up his window, Mr. Thompson resumed talking with his friend. Chris made his way back into the store, secretly hoping that Mr. Thompson's friend did not notice the M.O.B. tattoo on his arm.

But he was sure the man had seen it and already made the connection. He did not know if M.O.B. would be coming after him after making the connection that he helped lock up his mother or if they would honor his mother by leaving him alone.

As Chris was walking back into the store, Charity could see that he was in deep thought. "You good?" she asked, after ringing up another customer.

"Yeah, I'm cool. I'm 'bout to head to the back. If you need help wit' anything, you know where to find me."

Walking to the back of the store, Chris prepared to stock groceries that were just shipped through the warehouse.

Pooh, Tadarius, and Cochise drove back to the spot where the rest of the gang members convened, a single-story house in Woodhaven, New York. Having moved out of the apartment that had served as their previous headquarters and domicile living area, the increase in the gang's profit from their drug and weapons distribution system afforded Tadarius and his family new digs in the city.

The house was currently occupied by other members of M.O.B. There were Alex "Armitage" Black, Dequan Lee, Wiles "Hitman" Paul, and Freddie "Pacman" Jones among other members. Armitage, Dequan, Wiles, and Freddie had been members of M.O.B.

for years, paying their loyalty to the family by performing whatever tasks needed to be done, whether they included intimidation, ransoms, or knocking people out who were agitators.

These men were part of the coveted inner circle of M.O.B. Former members like David Anderson, Malik, and Terrance previously held the positions, but with them now out of the picture, M.O.B. was revamped with new members, strong boys who were joined at the hip and would do anything to protect the Fam.

As Tadarius walked into the living room area, the other members were playing Xbox and rolling up weed in joints and smoking them, passing blunts everywhere. Cochise passed by two women, Raquia Harris and Jazmine King, both who worked for Tadarius and other members as informants and seductresses. They played their roles for M.O.B. Anita and Jermaine were still there as well although Tadarius instructed Pooh to keep an eye on them because he saw how close they were getting. But they were still loyal to the Fam and were already warned not to jeopardize M.O.B. chances at globalizing their brand.

Pooh and Cochise made their way to one of the rooms, where Tony was counting the money received from the dealers, and in return, Pooh and Tadarius named him an official financial operator, which kept him alive, albeit he was still being held ransom until the eventual showdown between Tadarius and Edward Reed.

Dapping each one of the members, Cochise held his hand out in front of Tony, waiting for him to respond, but Tony merely looked up from the stack of dollar bills that almost covered his face. Ignoring Cochise's hand, Tony went back to counting money.

"What up wit' him?" Cochise asked Pooh.

"Eh, don't sweat him. He good. He's here on a need-to-know basis. Nobody needs to know he here."

Tadarius excused himself to go the restroom, succumbing once again to his uncontrollable cough fits.

"He aight?" Cochise asked.

"Yeah, he good, man. Just probably got a lil' cold or some shit like that. Yo, since you in now, lemme show you something."

Pooh led Cochise towards the back of the house, an area that was rarely occupied. Cochise wondered what Pooh was about to show him. His questions were answered in two minutes when Pooh opened the door to the back foyer, and Cochise's eyes widened in surprise. There were about thirty boxes of C4 remote bombs and devices, makeshift pipe bombs, and grenades.

It suddenly became clear to Cochise that M.O.B. wanted to expand its inventory from firearms and drugs to selling war machines and weapons meant to devastate at a wide scale. "Damn, son. It looks like ya' bracing for war or something. Who pissed ya'll off to the point where you need all that firepower, B?"

"Yo, you know what T always says. 'When you stay ready, you ain't gotta get ready.' All this is like four hundred thousand G's, kid. World's changing now, bruh. Ain't nobody scared of pieces anymore. Guns don't send a clear enough message anymore. Gotta step our game up and start lettin' mufuckas know we don't play. Now if we gotta blow their shit up to make a point, so be it. Only Tadarius, you, me, and one other person knows about all this. We ain't told anybody else yet because we don't know who could be working for Five-O, you feel me?"

"I feel you. So, who the only other person that knows about this other than you, me, and T? Is he hea'?"

Pooh shook his head, chuckling softly. "Actually, she's out courting our supplier right now. See we just a couple G's away from a full purchase, and tonight's the deadline to make the final payment. So, once we clear that, we in business."

"Is she good at negotiating?"

"Man, trust me, she a pro. She'll be comin' through after she done. I'd watch myself wit' her though. She ain't yo' regular 9-to-5 bitch. She low-key crazy, you know what I'm sayin? Plus, she has a thing for gourmet chocolates. Fancy, but ratchet."

Cochise walked with Pooh through the house, taking the full tour, and while walking by one of the bathrooms, he could hear

Tadarius coughing and retching violently into the toilet. *Damn, what's up wit' him? He sound like he dyin' in there.*

On that same evening, more than two hours away from the safe house on Woodhaven, Igor Khaimov, a notorious arms dealer, was in his bed, poisoned by a woman he met through one of his buyers. Khaimov had been linked to the illegal importing of arms and other weapons from Russia to the U.S. His inventory included firearms, bombs, bazookas, and other high-end military grade weaponry.

A few days prior, he had met a potential buyer that was interested in purchasing from his inventory. Tadarius Hill, using the alias Todd Freeman, had called Khaimov and informed him that he would like to meet in Staten Island, where a clean transaction would be made. The meeting took place, and Khaimov was impressed by the appearance of Mr. Freeman. He appeared dressed in an Unlimited brand black suit and tie and shaven with his hair cut neat.

He was accompanied by fellow associates Paul Yarbrough, which was Pooh's alias, and a third associate, Tina Cabrera. Tina was dressed in a sheer, dark red long dress with the thighs slit, which showed all of her legs and left very little to the imagination. Khaimov himself was accompanied by two bodyguards, and as the two parties faced each other, Mr. Freeman gestured to Mr. Yarbrough to carry a Gucci bag filled with $300,000 to Khaimov.

One of the bodyguards took the bag and opened it to count the bands of money. Mr. Yarbrough rolled his eyes. The last thing he wanted to do was wait endlessly for them to count the money because they were going to find out what he already knew: they still owed $100,000.

"You're short," Khaimov commented in his thick Russian accent.

"Yes, we understand that, Mr. Khaimov, but I was hoping we can re-negotiate the cost," Mr. Freeman said.

"Mr. Freeman, we discussed that the cost of the high-grade military supplies was $400,000, and we agreed upon that sum yesterday. I was advised by your associate, Mr. Yarbrough that the amount would be ready today. Now if you do not have the total amount, I will be happy to take my business elsewhere."

But before the arms dealer walked away, he was approached by Tina. "Now, Mr. Khaimov, I'm sure we can come to a reasonable pricing agreement. Is there anything we can do to convince you to settle on the 300,000?"

Taking his hand, Tina ran it across her exposed cleavage across the top of her sheer dress. Running his fingers down her naval area into her legs, Tina closed her eyes, acting as if the entire experience was euphoric for her, but she had played the seductress role so many times in her life, it was second nature to her.

Mr. Khaimov, whose wife had been deceased for more than six years, was suddenly aroused by how strong Tina was coming on to him. "You are an exquisite woman, Mrs. Cabrera."

"Please, Mr. Khaimov, call me Tina."

Mr. Freeman and Mr. Yarbrough exchanged sly glances at each other. They brought Bunny to the exchange in hopes of seducing the arms dealer into reducing the price of his weaponry, and by the way she was buttering him up, it appeared that their calculated gamble paid off.

"Uh, gentlemen, I have decided to settle on $300,000."

Mr. Freeman and Mr. Yarbrough smiled and shook hands with Khaimov. "Thank you for your reconsideration."

"On one condition, however. Will Ms. Tina be my guest for dinner Monday night?"

"Mr. Khaimov, I would be honored to join you for dinner."

With that, the meeting concluded, and two nights later, Tina took an Uber and arrived at Mr. Khaimov's Victorian-style home in Staten Island. She wore a much shorter dress and applied more makeup than she had a couple nights earlier.

This man's got it made. He makes Tony's crib look like a street vendor at Queens Coliseum. You've hit the lottery, girl. Now put your game face on. Time to lay it on this simp thicker than peanut butter.

Answering the ringing doorbell, Mr. Khaimov, wearing his best two-piece suit answered and said, "Ms. Tina, you look extravagant! Welcome to my home. Please make yourself comfortable."

Bunny looked around. *This man lives in here by himself? With that much coin behind him, he's never found another woman? Shit, if I didn't have to do what I gotta do, I would keep him all to myself.*

But Bunny was fiercely loyal to the M.O.B. family and would not betray them. She was not going to go out like Loree did many years ago. Bunny sat at the table in the dining area while Mr. Khaimov checked with his personal chef to make sure that the dinner was ready. After ten minutes, the chef came out with filet mignon, lobster, Brussel sprouts, broccoli, carrots, and tartar sauce to dip the lobster, all topped off with red wine.

As they sat and talked, Mr. Khaimov revealed to Bunny that he had suffered bouts of sleeplessness and depression brought on by his wife's untimely death, and he worked very hard to hide his sorrow, but no amount of money could bring his wife back. To fight his depression, he took his recommended dosages of sleeping pills and depressants.

Unbeknownst to Mr. Khaimov, Bunny was compartmentalizing the information in her head, using it to start plotting the demise of the rich arms dealer. After dinner, Mr. Khaimov was throwing back glass after glass of wine, and he was becoming more comfortable around Tina, to the point where he was attempting to embrace her twice. Tina would laugh her pretend laughs at his jokes and coax him to drink more wine.

She began to realize that Mr. Khaimov was a lightweight, and the power of the wine was starting to overcome him. She could see him struggling to stay on his feet. "Are you okay, Mr. Khaimov?"

"Oh, I have not had this much fun in ages. Oh, I love you, Maria!" he exclaimed groggily.

Who the hell is Maria? Only a few moments later, Bunny realized Maria was Khaimov's wife, and for a moment, she felt sympathy for the man. He lived alone, he never really recovered from Maria's death, and all he wanted was to feel loved. *One of the largest arms dealers in known civilization, and all he wants is love. The irony of it all.*

A few more minutes passed, and Khaimov had drunk himself into a stupor. The red wine bottle was empty on the table, and Khaimov was slumped over in his chair. He was barely awake when Tina coaxed him from his chair and began to guide him toward his bedroom.

"Mr. Khaimov, I don't mean to pry, but as far as the weapon price, are you still reducing it to 300,000?"

Mr. Khaimov's eyes opened for a moment as if he were taken by surprise. "What? When did I say that?"

"You mentioned it two nights ago with my associates."

"Oh no, no. I don't lower the price on none of my weapons. Nobody can play Mr. Khaimov like that. Price is still 400,000 as it stands, and I expect the remaining amount to be paid this evening."

What the fuck? I know this fool did not just waste my gotdamn time for over three hours to have me dragging his drunk ass up to his bedroom, and he ain't even gonna bend on the price. I was gonna let him live, but nah, now he gotta go.

Looking around, Bunny did not see the bodyguards that accompanied Mr. Khaimov to the exchange two nights ago, and she had a feeling that he may have given them the night off because he did not expect Tina to be a threat to him during dinner, and he expected a happy ending afterwards.

Stupid man. You should've kept your guard up when it came to me, and all you had to do was stand on what you said, but now since you wanna make this harder than it needs to be, I'm gonna send you on a one-way trip to the sweet by and by. At least you'll be reunited with your wife.

After dragging Khaimov to his bedroom, Bunny began slowly unbuttoning his shirt and undoing his pants, kissing him seductively along the way.

"Ahh, that feels nice, Ms. Tina. It's been a long time since I've felt a woman's touch. If you can make me a happy man tonight, I still won't lower the price. But I'll make you a happy woman tonight, that I guarantee you."

Bunny rolled her eyes as she took off the rest of his clothes until he was lying there naked, and she shook her head, laughing to herself, staring at his privates. *Well, I must say I'm disappointed. There's no way he would've made me a happy woman with what he's got going on down there.*

Reaching into her bag, Bunny took out a syringe with a lethal dose of fentanyl poison. Mr. Khaimov had already passed out after mumbling incoherently for several minutes.

Old Mr. Khaimov thought that he could get some for free and not pay a price for his deception? You should've had your bodyguards with you. Now you're gonna die—another notch in the belt for Lethal Lola Bunny. Don't worry, it'll be quick and painless.

After injecting Khaimov with the lethal dose, Bunny waited for his heart to stop and his pulse to drop. She knew with the alcohol going through his system and the poison going through his bloodstream, his body would not stand a chance. After what seemed like thirty minutes, Khaimov's steady breathing ceased, and Bunny could feel his body temperature dropping. He was going though shock, and he was flatlining. It was only a matter of time before he would be dead.

Looking around frantically, Bunny searched the drawers in the room until she found the sleeping pills that he normally took. Opening the lid, she spilled the contents of the bottle out, spreading the pills all over the nightstand, and then she left the cap open.

Now it looks like a suicide scene. Mr. Khaimov retired to his bed after a long night of drinking, took a bunch of pills and accidentally overdosed. Oh well, it happens. Now we get to keep all our money and no one will suspect a thing.

After placing all the contents in her bag, Bunny took her bag and left the house. Instead of ringing her an Uber, she called Tadarius.

"You closed the deal?" he asked once he picked up.

"Yeah, it's closed," she replied bluntly.

Tadarius did not ask any further questions because he knew once she commented about a deal being closed, the client was most likely dead.

"Look, I can't get tracked anymore, so I need you to come get me." She heard him cough on the other end of the phone. "Damn, you all right?"

"Yeah, I'm good. Just feelin' a lil' under the weather. But check it, I'm 'bout to send someone over right now."

"Aight bet. I'mma send you a pin so you know where I'm at."

Bunny proceeded to pin her location and walked about three blocks away from Mr. Khaimov's house. Keeping her brunette wig on, she wanted to make sure nobody tracked her because she knew that if either Khaimov's chef or one of his bodyguards walked in and they discovered his body on the bed, then all clues would lead back to her, so she wanted to clear the area as quickly as possible.

But she was sure she made the scene appear as if he died from an accidental overdose, and she made sure she did not leave any of her things at the house or any traces of her DNA. She did not even sleep with Khaimov before killing him. Normally, she would at least get to second base with a potential victim before killing him.

She remembered when she got rid of Xavier, a former M.O.B. member, she had to engage in a portion of sexual activity with him before slitting his throat. To this day, his murder was still unsolved.

While waiting for her ride, her phone rang, and the caller ID read QUEENS MENTAL REHAB. "Hello?" she asked curiously.

"Bunny, is that the way to talk to you sister?" a familiar voice asked.

"LaToya? Damn, girl, where you been at? Where they got you at now?"

"Girl, they got me in some mental facility in addition to being under house arrest. Apparently, I have some unresolved family trauma that caused me to hurt people, so they're trying to get me right, I guess."

Bunny heard a loud crunching noise on the other end, followed by chewing and swallowing. "What's that noise?"

"Oh, my bad, I'm eatin' an apple right now. My bad if it's too loud, but I've been hungry all day. Ain't had a chance to eat."

"Well, can yo' hungry ass learn how to chew away from the earpiece?"

Her sister still ate loud and laughed loud. LaToya had acted the same way since they were kids, so she was not surprised.

"Listen though. I gotta ask you a favor. I need you to track someone down for me."

"Who you need tracked?"

"Your nephew—that's who."

Bunny did a double take. "You want me to track Chris? Girl, that boy went ghost since last month. He ain't returned back to the Fam or nothin'. I wouldn't even know where to look."

"I know someone who does. Edward Reed knows where he is."

Upon hearing the name, Bunny sighed. She knew her sister was not about to ask her to talk with anyone in conjunction to the law.

"All I want to do is talk to him. Explain things to him. Edward won't even let me see him, and I'm pissed about that, but if you find him, please tell him to come see me."

"Okay whatever, LaToya, but if you expect me to patch things up wit' him, I can't do that. It's yo' job."

"Trick, don't you think I know that? Look, when you see him, just let him know I need to talk to him, all right?"

After ending the call, a gray Honda Civic pulled up next to Bunny. "Yo, it's Bunny, right?"

After confirming that it was her, Bunny stepped to the car. Opening the passenger door, she glanced at the driver. It was neither Tadarius nor Pooh but someone else that she hadn't met yet. But he wore M.O.B. colors, and he knew her name, so it had to be someone that Tadarius knew.

"Um, who are you?"

Beaming widely at her, the man introduced himself. "Cochise. I was sent by T to come get you. He wasn't feelin' too well, so he asked me to come get you at this spot."

As she closed the door, and the car peeled away from the curb, Bunny still stared suspiciously at Cochise. Although she did not trust him, there was one factor that was undeniable about this new guy. *He is fine, girl!*

CHAPTER 13

DIVINE VENGEANCE

ARRIVING AT THE SCHORR Law Group building Tuesday morning, Edward yawned as he parked his car. After taking a lengthy amount of time off work following the fallout from the verdict of New York City vs. LaToya Richardson, he decided that he was finally going to return to work. It was vital that he resumed some form of normalcy because he was not a person to remain complacent, especially when one was in dire straits as he was.

Tony was still being held by Tadarius against his will under the threat of imminent death, but to the credit of the ruthless gang leader, he had kept his word. Tony was still alive. Edward also felt that his defense of LaToya and her reduced sentence might have bought him some time as well. He knew Tadarius wanted him out of the picture.

For some reason, the reality of Tadarius seeking to end him was not as threatening as it sounded weeks earlier. *Hell, he's been trying to kill me since I was fourteen years old anyway. The situation was unavoidable because I'm not a ruthless killer like the bitch that he had me defend.*

Looking at his predicament nonchalantly helped Edward with his anxiety attacks daily, and he was able to recover health-wise. But his reputation as a trusted attorney had taken a significant hit. After LaToya's case, Edward checked his approval rating on a trusted website where trusted professionals were given ratings by consumers who had used their services in the past or public word of mouth. Edward, who had always been held in high regard by the general public, began to see a decrease in public approval, and as if the low approval rating was not severe enough, people left comments under his name.

I always thought Attorney Edward Reed was one of the few honest, good lawyers out there, but after seeing him stand up for that vile woman, I've changed my mind. He ain't nothin' but a snake.

Another comment read:

Can't believe you decided to defend that evil witch. She held a gun to the head of my favorite musical artist, and you managed to get her anger management and house arrest? She deserved to be buried under the jail!

A third comment read:

What is she paying you, Reed? Or are you two screwing? Because whatever is going on there just got in the way of justice being truly served.

Edward finally closed the page because the comments of the public only got worse with every line. Taking the elevator up to his usual floor, he walked over to his desk, when he was greeted by Hank Kendall, a fellow attorney who worked at the group.

"Back already, eh?"

Taking out his folder of affidavits tied to previous cases, Edward shook his head, grinning furtively. "Yeah. Been a long week."

"Well, glad to see you back, man. I was afraid New York City was gonna run you out of town."

"Nah, it takes more than a few pissed off folks to run me out of here. New York can't get rid of me that easily."

"I gotcha. You know if you need more time off, I'll be happy to cover your cases during your time off."

But Edward firmly shook his head. "No, I'm good. I got way too much work to catch up on. I gotta get to it. Plus, it's better to be working here than to stay sulking at home doing nothing. Staying busy will keep my mind off things."

Later, as the other attorneys were making their way out for the day, Edward was still working on cases. At a quarter past midnight, with an empty bowl of what held Thai food that he had ordered for lunch on his desk, Edward finally decided to call it a night. After packing his suitcase, he left the building to go to the parking lot to get his car.

Usually, he would hit the Diamond Bar for a drink after a hard day at work, but he decided to avoid the bar this evening. He had already encountered pedestrians on his way to work that recognized him from the news coverage of the case, and they gave him disapproving, angry looks.

They were varied expressions that told him, "I trusted you, and you betrayed my trust. If I can't trust you in a high-profile case like this, how can I trust you when I need a lawyer?"

Going to the bar would only have the people express themselves while being inebriated, and Edward did not feel that it was worth it at this time, so he decided to head home for the evening. Upon pulling up to his apartment, he saw someone outside his door. He was an elderly Black man with short black dreads that had some gray strands sticking out. He wore regular blue jeans with brown Timberland boots and a green and yellow hoodie.

Over the years, the man had developed a small gut in his midsection, an area that he had religiously kept in shape for years in the past. But it did not stop him from embarking on his philandering ways, or did it excuse his absence from Edward's life during a time when he needed male guidance that did not involve drug dealing or killing people. Yet, Phillip Franks stood outside his son's home, and where most fathers would be met with enthusiasm and happiness after not seeing their son for more than twelve years, those feelings were not sensed by Edward in this case.

Phillip was a deadbeat father to Edward who left his mother, Isabelle, to raise him on her own. Edward would go years without hearing from his father, only to find out at the age of eight that his father had been arrested for illegally selling firearms and racketeering, and he was also up to his knees in debt, stemming from the child support payments that he made to Isabelle and his brothers' mothers.

After serving his time, Phillip was released and was now living with another woman, which infuriated Edward. Now Phillip stood at his son's door.

How the hell did he find me? He better not be asking for money because I ain't giving him a dime. I don't care if he's my father or not. Taking a step to the door, Edward tried to walk past Phillip.

Phillip was surprised that his son still had not acknowledged him yet. "What's going on, son?"

"How'd you find me?"

"Well, I asked your mother about you, and she gave me your address, so I decided to come by and check to see how you were doing."

"How'd you get out?" Edward asked. He was uninterested in anything that had to do with his father, and after a long day at work, this was bad timing on Phillip's part.

"Good behavior. What, is that so hard to believe?"

"It kind of is, Phillip. *Good behavior*," Edward replied sarcastically. "I need to find out who your parole officer is cuz this makes no sense."

"So, we on a first name basis, huh?"

"Yup, you're Phillip to me, and whenever you find my father, then let me know where he at."

Phillip hung his head as Edward turned the key to enter his home, and without waiting for an invite, he followed his son inside. "Look, Antonio, I know you're upset—" he began.

"First off, that ain't my name anymore. Secondly, I don't think I remember inviting you inside, so I think you better leave."

But Phillip stood defiantly in front of Edward, unwilling to budge. "Your name is what I named you. You'll always be Antonio to me. I don't give a fuck what the government says."

"Well, seeing that you've been on the wrong side of the law for a long time, I think that's pretty clear. Listen, I'm very tired, and I've had a long day at work, so what do you want? Money?"

"No, I want to know why you gave up on who you are. The name change that they had you do years ago...did you do that to spite me?"

"To spite you?" Edward asked. "Everything is always about you. Maybe I had my own reasons for changing my name. Has that ever occurred to you? Maybe I did it because Antonio Franks was a marked man."

"I don't care if you had the National Guard after you. I didn't create you to show fear. You don't run away from your problems. You face them, and you protect yourself. You don't take no shortcuts."

"Right, because you're the paradigm of facing your problems? You couldn't even bring yourself to see me after you got out of prison. Well, let me catch you up on how life has been for me since you left. At the age of thirteen, I got caught up in M.O.B. and became a gang member, much like my father. Guess it runs in the family, huh?" Edward replied sarcastically again.

"Then after I leave them, they come back and threaten to kill me," he continued. "Because I didn't have my pops there to do anything, I had to change my identity so they don't find me because, believe it or not, they're hunting my ass, and they will stop at nothing until they get me, even if it means kidnapping a family member."

Upon hearing this, Phillip sat on a kitchen chair, listening to his estranged son share his account of traumatic events. "Who they got right now?"

"They got Tony right now. M.O.B. is literally dangling him in my face, daring me to do something, and if I don't listen to 'em right now, they could kill him."

"So, let me help you, then. Tony is my son. If anything happens to him, it falls on me too."

"Phillip, this gang is different from the crack-addled boys you hung out with in the eighties. These guys are next-level killers with high grade weaponry and access to explosives. I can't draw police into this situation right now, and I can't draw attention to myself, so I've had to attack from a different angle."

"What angle is that?"

"Look, I know Tadarius. I know how guys like him get down. You can't treat this guy with kid gloves. To destroy his empire, you got to play his game his way or else he'll be a step ahead. This is chess not checkers."

Hearing that statement made Phillip smile. During the few visits he paid to Antonio during his younger years, he introduced him to the game of chess. He taught him the significance of the rooks, knights, pawns, kings, and queens. For starters, there were no court jesters anywhere on the board.

"A battlefield is no place for a clown," Phillip once said as he made his first move on the chessboard.

Antonio, then age six, looked at the chessboard before moving his knight. After making his move, Phillip moved his rook a couple paces across the board.

While his son contemplated his next move, Phillip said, "Make your move, Antonio. Remember this is all for fun now, but in real games, they got a timer, and you gotta move within a minute."

Antonio made his next move, relocating his rim pawn, which left one of his knights open for Phillip to knock the piece off the board. "There are some moves made in life where you have to sacrifice some of your knights to keep your queen safe."

As the game continued, Phillip was impressed by how fast Antonio was catching on to the game, and he even made a few smart moves on his own, and had Phillip underestimated him, he would have lost the first match to his son. But Phillip proved that he was a better chess player, and finally he was able to checkmate.

"Great game, Antonio. Not bad for your first game. Always keep in mind that there are some situations in life where you have to outsmart your opponent, rather than to fight him. Not everything is about using strength and force. Sometimes it's about using what's up here," he said, pointing to Antonio's head.

"You're very smart, you know that? What is your mama feeding you?" he laughed and said as he then treated his son for ice cream.

Now years later, father and son faced each other once again, only there was no chessboard for Phillip to use to break the ice. "So, we're in a new game, huh?" he asked.

Turning to face the window and the dark street, Edward nodded his head, confirming what his father already knew.

"So, you've moved a pawn in there among the knights to expose the queen. Great strategy, son. Now, you gotta know what you're risking, and are you prepared to make the ultimate sacrifice to bring down your opponent?"

With a look that defined determination, Edward stared at his father intently. "You damn right I am."

On Thursday afternoon after school, the I.S. 219 eighth-grade basketball team held a brief walk-through and light practice in preparation for that night's game against I.S. 112.

The Bears and the Barracudas had been rivals for years, and each school's students would take to social media to bash one another. Dennis Anderson, who was the starting guard for the Bears, had been waiting for this match for days. This would be the second time the Bears faced off against the Barracudas.

In their first match, which was played in the main gym at I.S. 112, the Barracudas defended their home floor, winning 59-49 with their best player Frankie "Smokes" Scott dropping twenty points, corralling eleven rebounds and dishing out four assists. They executed their game plan to perfection, trapping Dennis at every turn and forcing him to mishandle the ball at certain points of the game.

It was one of Dennis's worst games, as he went 2-15 from the field and finished the night with only nine points. It was uncharacteristic for a player of his caliber because he averaged better than fourteen points per game and was one of the go-to players for the Bears.

Demetrius Herring, the center for the Bears, was about six-foot-three, long and lanky, and what he lacked in pure athleticism, he made up for in length, shooting touch and ball anticipation. The Bears also had a lightning quick point guard, Ramel Devereaux, a shifty ballhandler who was able to stop at the drop of a dime and shoot little mid-range jumpers, which was extremely helpful to stop opposing teams' runs.

The rest of the starting lineup for Bears included Michael Scott and Forest Williams. The Bears and the Barracudas were jockeying for position in the standings where each team was neck and neck for the top two seeds in the conference. While their early season victory over the Bears gave the Barracudas an advantage in the standings, the Bears knew that if they could beat the Barracudas at home, they could tie the series and still had a chance to lead their conference.

It meant a great deal to Dennis that he got some payback for the loss because while it was a painful defeat for the team, it was especially painful for Dennis because it was the last game his father watched before he was murdered.

The last memory Dennis had of his father was the look of sympathy combined with disappointment after the tough loss. And on the drive back home, David was reminding Dennis of all the things he did not do well during the game and areas of improvement.

"Look, I know you're a guard and everything, but you've got to get in there and box out," he said, during the ride.

"What you think Demetrius is in there for? He's the tallest player on our team."

"Son, size and height isn't everything in sports. You gotta have the heart and the hustle to go in there among the trees and grab the board. The Barracudas had thirty-eight rebounds. You guys had had only eighteen rebounds. That's the ball game right there, Dennis."

Dennis remembered thinking to himself: *What do you know about it? You played football your whole life. Basketball's a different game. Sometimes a team just doesn't have it.*

Dennis was a great football player as well, playing tight end and wide receiver during football season, but he loved playing basketball even more than football. Soon he concentrated on basketball, working on his ball handling, his three-point shooting, and his drives to the basket.

He would stay after practice and work on his fundamentals. Coach Wes McNair saw Dennis's perseverance, and he was confident that the Bears would have a phenomenal season due to Dennis's improvements.

But when David Anderson was murdered a few days before Christmas, the town was stunned and saddened, and Dennis contemplated whether he wanted to continue playing after the tragedy. Renee even attempted to talk Dennis out of playing because she did not think that he would be able to concentrate in school, much less on the basketball court.

But to his credit, Dennis did not fold or buckle in the face of unspeakable tragedy. Instead, he bottled up his anger and fury that he felt towards David's murderer and channeled it into the game. Coach McNair had also given Dennis the option to step down from the team to mourn for his father, and he would have understood if Dennis were to call it season. After all, it was only a game, and losing a loved one was never easy for the victim's family.

Dennis decided to keep going for his father's memory. Before his passing, David told him the story of an individual back at his old high school who dealt with a tragedy that caused him to quit basketball and turn to drugs. He was also a Division I prospect that had all the gifts and talent in the world, but amid the crack epidemic of the 1980s, he almost succumbed to his addictions. Then his friend was killed while he held her in his arms.

Years later, the man found a job at David's old high school as a janitor, which many people saw as a fall from grace, but one day, a cocky high school basketball player unwisely challenged the janitor to a one-on-one game, completely oblivious to the janitor's history and background. The janitor proceeded to beat the player handily to the astonishment of the other students that watched this match, and he was one day elevated to become the school's next head basketball coach.

It was a great story, but Dennis would always question the validity of the tale because it had all the makings of a bad sports movie that his father watched and just made up. However, David always contested that the story of the janitor was true.

While Dennis continued putting up shots, Coach McNair, who had been at the office reviewing plays, came out to see him on the court. He was working his way around the top of the key, draining jump shot after jump shot.

Coach stood watching his protégé for five minutes. *That boy is a star athlete just like his father. He's definitely D1 material. There's no doubt about that.*

"What's up, Dennis? Save some for the 'Cudas tonight."

Dennis looked back and saw that it was Coach McNair who addressed him. "Gotcha, Coach. Just gettin' ready for Frankie Smokes tonight."

Coach walked up to Dennis. "Listen, Dennis, I know you have extra motivation tonight to go out there and get him back for last game, but remember, this is a team game, all right. Don't get sucked into making this a one-on-one game between you and Frankie. That's what happened last game. You were forcing the issue and not letting the game come to you. If you do all the little things—play defense, rebound, and take care of the basketball—we'll be fine."

Dennis nodded to indicate to the coach that he understood.

"By the way, how's the situation with your brother?"

Dennis rolled his eyes. No matter how much he tried, he could not bring himself to trust his half-brother. What did he really know about Chris? All he knew was that he was his father's son from a previous relationship, and the woman was connected to his father's death. But that was all Dennis needed to know.

Cree and Katrina welcomed Chris, but Dennis was skeptical. Chris could not be trusted, and he did not care where Chris slept in their home, he was no brother of his, at least not at this time. Chris had tried to break the ice between them, sometimes giving Dennis extra money, which he gladly took, but the two boys never saw eye to eye. But Chris vowed to be at the game that night to support his brother.

"It's aight, I guess. He should be at the game tonight."

Just then, Renee walked into the gym, waving to Dennis. She was picking him up from school on the way back from work.

"Okay, son, go home. Get some rest, and I'll see you at 6:30. We gon' have some fish fry tonight!" Coached McNair exclaimed, while Dennis laughed.

"No doubt, Coach. I'mma be ready!"

In the second quarter of the showdown between the home team Bears and the visiting Barracudas, the Bears trailed 28-20 with two minutes to go before halftime. From the onset of the game, the Barracudas jumped out to a 17-4 lead, surprising the Bears with an early full-court press that stymied the Bears' attack.

Ramel was flustered as he found himself swarmed on each possession by Barracuda defenders. Each time he turned the ball over, it was an easy lay-up for the Barracudas, forcing Coach McNair to burn through three timeouts in the first half alone.

But in the second quarter, Dennis found his shooting stroke and had converted on three consecutive 3-point shots that narrowed the lead down to 23-20.

But Frankie Smokes also caught fire and went on a personal 5-0 run to stretch the lead back to eight. It was apparent that Frankie saw Dennis heat up and was taking the challenge to match him point for point.

The Bears huddled up at their next timeout. While Coach McNair was drawing up backdoor plays, he also warned Dennis, "Okay, Dennis, they know you got the hot hand right now. They're gonna send Frankie at you over and over again to try to up under you. I need you to remain poised, and use your team. Do not get drawn into a *mano y mano* game with him."

As the whistle blew to resume play, the teams stepped back out on the court as the Barracudas prepared to trigger the ball in. Anticipating the pass, Dennis stole the ball, and the fans roared their approval. I.S. 219's gym was filled at capacity as this was the biggest game of the year for the Bears. After Dennis stole the ball, the Barracudas got back on defense.

Frankie then ran to defend Dennis after he passed the ball to Ramel. "What up, boy?" Frankie taunted. "Where your daddy at?"

Dennis looked towards the ref, expecting a taunting foul, but the ref had not heard Frankie. Dennis knew that Frankie was talking trash to throw him off his game, but he ignored Frankie and continued to execute the play drawn up by the coach. Eluding Frankie, Dennis cut backdoor as Michael Scott found him for the easy layup. 28-22.

Frankie inwardly cursed at himself as the Barracuda's head coach James Lionel yelled at him for not watching his man. Coming down the court, Frankie called for the ball as Dennis defended him. "You think you the shit cuz you scored that lil' wack-ass layup. Watch me score on you now, bitch."

Frankie rose up to shoot with Dennis draped all over him defensively. Nothing but net. 30-22. As he ran back on defense, Frankie intensified his verbal attack on Dennis.

Watching from the stands, Chris, who attended the game with Renee, Cree, and Katrina, saw Dennis getting agitated on the court. *Come on, man. Keep yo' cool. They fuckin' wit' you. Just keep ya' head in the game.*

As much as Dennis tried to tune Frankie out, he kept pushing, and the Barracudas were starting to play dirty, fouling players hard.

"Where yo' daddy at, nigga?" Frankie kept asking during the game.

It was less than a minute to go before halftime, and Barracudas held a slim lead over the Bears. Dennis had eleven points, easily surpassing his point total from their previous game. But Dennis was close to the breaking point with Frankie's taunting. Then Frankie pushed the wrong button.

"Oh, that's right...yo' daddy dead, ain't he? Guess I'm yo' new daddy now, son."

That was all Dennis needed to hear, and he snapped, pushing Frankie hard from the chest, causing his opponent to sprawl across the court. A whistle blew.

"Technical foul, Number 12!"

Who's ya daddy now? Told you, don't fuck with me.

CHAPTER 14

DIVINE VENGEANCE

IT TOOK TWO PLAYERS to pry Dennis away from Frankie, who used the opportunity to milk the moment by lying prone on the ground as if he had been bulldozed by an NBA center. With the fans at the gym already loud, the technical foul sent them into a frenzy. The Barracuda fans were yelling for Dennis to be ejected or disqualified from the game while the Bear fans wanted Frankie to receive a taunting violation.

However, neither action occurred, and Coach McNair tried to get Dennis's attention amidst the noise. "Dennis! Dennis!"

Jogging over to the bench, Harry Turner, the Bears' backup shooting guard, checked into the game while Dennis sat on the bench. It was only a few seconds before halftime, and after Frankie knocked down the technical free throw, it was 31-22, Barracudas, with both teams heading into their respective locker rooms.

Coach McNair wiped the perspiration from his head. Normally, he did not get rattled during regular season games, but this game was one of the biggest of the year, and he knew he was in peril of losing for a second time to the Bears' biggest rival. He had to get his star player re-engaged.

"Guys, listen. We've played one half of basketball, and do you know what I've seen so far? You're playing right into their hands again like you did last game. You are not hustling to get the rebound. I don't see anybody calling out picks, diving for loose balls—there are no effort plays. The Barracudas want it more than you guys right now. What is it going to take to turn this thing around in the second half?"

The players, some with their heads hung as if they were already defeated, looked at one another.

"Make all the hustle plays. Rebound, play tough defense, and score on each fast break opportunity," Michael Scott replied.

"Exactly! We should do all of those things, and we will come back and win this game. More importantly, we must remember to keep our composure and close our ears to outside noise. Barracudas will stop at nothing to throw you off your game. It's part of their game plan, and if we let their words stick to us, it's gonna be a long night." He stared at Dennis while giving the statement.

The buzzer, suddenly went off, signaling the players to return to the court. As the players filed out of the locker room, Coach McNair pulled Dennis from the group. "Are you okay, son?"

Dennis, who took the message of the coach to heart, also had time to reflect on his sudden outburst. "I'm good, Coach. I'm ready to go."

"Good, because we need your contribution tonight, or we won't win this game. Even Frankie knows this. That's why he ain't gonna quit. He's gonna keep bringing up your father every chance he gets because he knows it's gonna get under your skin. I know you're defending your father's memory, but your father would want you to keep your head in the game and win. Okay?"

Nodding his head to confirm that he understood, Dennis ran out onto the court. Looking at the stands, he saw Chris and his family in the stands.

Chris pounded his chest and pointed at Dennis. He was telling him, "You got this! I got yo' back, homie. Just come back out there and let 'em know who you are."

When the second half got underway, the Bears came out focused on the defensive end. Coach McNair implemented a full-court press that threw the Barracudas off. Nate Brandis, the Barracudas' point guard, who was normally quick enough to dribble out of double teams and traps, found himself surrounded by Bear players early and often.

The Bears would capitalize from their press, converting three Barracuda turnovers into six points. Then Frankie missed a shot, and

Demetrius caught the rebound. Dennis leaked out towards the basket, and Demetrius threw the ball as far as he could before the Barracudas' defense got set. Catching the ball, Dennis laid it in easily.

Now the Bears trailed 31-30, and over the course of the third quarter, the game was evenly matched. The Barracudas would score, but the Bears always had an answer. Ramel knocked down a 3-point shot from the corner where Dennis previously found him all alone in the corner.

On the ensuing play, Dennis dove for a loose ball, managed to corral it, and passed it to Michael Scott, who scored from the steal. Frankie watched the lead dwindle and knew that the Bears would be making their run. He had to rattle Dennis again.

With under a minute left, Frankie stepped forward to Dennis. "You know what they told me? They said yo' daddy was a horrible player as a kid. You think you can shoot better than him?"

But this time Dennis followed Coach McNair's advice. He tuned his ears out to Frankie's taunts and began playing within the offense. By the end of the third quarter, Dennis had fifteen points, but the Bears held a slim lead over the Barricudas with 45-43 heading into the fourth quarter.

In the fourth quarter, the teams battled to gain an advantage with the best players of both rising to the occasion. Frankie started to flex his All-League muscle, scoring off the dribble and blowing by his defender for layups.

The Barracudas regained the lead, and after a quick timeout by Coach McNair, Ramel and Dennis ran the similar backdoor plays with each player finding the other player cutting across the baseline, exposing the Barracudas' weak interior defense. As the 2-minute mark approached, the Barracudas led by four, and then Dennis decided to take over the game for the Bears. Michael found him out on the perimeter, and Dennis shot the 3-point shot. *Swish!*

That cut the Barracudas' lead to one with less than two minutes remaining on the clock. Frankie eluded two Bears' defenders, but Dennis recovered and swiped at the ball but caught Frankie's arm instead. The whistle blew, and Dennis clapped his hands in frustration. It was his third foul, and it could not have come at a worse time. Frankie was eighty percent from the free-throw line during the season, and here he was stepping up to shoot his free-throw shots.

Dennis crossed his fingers behind his back, and the Bears' fans yelled themselves hoarse in hopes of causing a miss, but to their dismay, Frankie knocked down the first free throw. The Barracudas led by two—62-60, with Frankie stepping up to shoot one more free throw. But the ball rolled around the rim then fell out.

Demetrius caught the rebound, and Coach McNair called another timeout. He was advised by his assistant coaches that he had only one more timeout left, so he had to make the most of this stoppage of play.

"Okay, men, here's what we're going to do. We're going to run a 5-out offense, where I'll have Michael and Demetrius outside the paint to clear up the middle, and Ramel will isolate his defender. Dennis, once they approach the key area, set a little flair screen for Ramel, and then dive toward the basket."

Once both players were parallel, Ramel passed to Dennis. The play was executed to perfection, and Dennis converted the layup with Frankie trailing him defensively. Frankie was unable to deflect or block the layup.

The game was tied once again with under a minute to go. After the Barracudas called timeout, the ball was swung around the key until it found Frankie. Dennis had the assignment of guarding Frankie as the clock dwindled down. Because there were no shot-clocks in middle school, teams held the ball to spend precious clock time, but Dennis was not going to allow it to happen.

When Frankie began to make his move, Dennis watched his waist and the ball together, and the next thing he knew, he had managed to swipe the ball out of Frankie's hands. Frankie was planning to cross Dennis over with his dribble, but Dennis anticipated the direction, and the ball was in his hands with under ten seconds to go. Dennis streaked towards the rim and laid it off the glass with Frankie, once again, trailing him.

The Bears led 64-62. The Barracudas called their final timeout, and the play was once again to get the ball to Frankie and let him create. Dennis watched Frankie like a hawk. There were only four seconds for the Barracudas to work with, which did not leave enough time for most players, but Frankie was different.

As first team All-League, Frankie was already primed to become a Division I basketball player. There were various high schools in New York that were lining up in hopes of him attending their school in the fall. Frankie chose to attend Roosevelt High School, which also happened to be the same high school where the legendary former professional basketball player Julius "Dr. J" Erving had attended school.

Frankie had hit his fair share of buzzer beaters during the year, and he smirked when he saw Dennis guarding him again. Dennis had a phenomenal game himself, scoring twenty-one points and handing out five assists.

Now Frankie had twenty-seven points, and he measured the distance between Dennis and himself. His goal was to rise up to shoot the 3-point shot over Dennis to win the game. Sure enough, the shot was up, and Dennis contested the jumper, closing out on the shooter without fouling. It was as if everything had stopped, and the ball was rotating in perfect form in slow motion as all the fans at the gym held their collective breaths.

The Barracudas were bracing themselves to celebrate another game winner from their best player, but instead of witnessing a triumphant victory, they would experience the sting of defeat as the ball clanged the side of the rim, and the Bears' players stormed the court in celebration. They had beaten the top ranked Barracudas and now held sole possession of first place in the division.

Frankie untucked his jersey and hung his head in defeat. Although Frankie had been relentless in his trash talk and berating of Dennis throughout the game, Dennis still shook Frankie's hand in an act of good sportsmanship.

"Good game, bro."

Frankie looked at him in shock, almost as if he could not believe he would shake hands with him. But David had taught his children manners and fair play, and after each game, whether it was football or basketball, it was common courtesy to shake the opponents' hands after a game.

"Yeah, good game, B. My bad about the shit I said about yo' pops. You got game, Anderson. I'll see you in D1 soon."

With that, Frankie walked off with his team, and Dennis was mobbed by Renee, Cree, Katrina, and surprisingly, Chris.

"Yo, I don't even know if I'm worthy to touch this man right now. I should be askin' for his autograph!" Chris exclaimed.

Dennis smiled and dapped his half-brother. It was the turning point in their relationship.

Chris, who normally rested on Thursdays after school because he worked on Fridays, had taken the time to support and attend the game.

"Yo, Dennis!"

Turning around to see who had addressed him, Dennis saw an old friend, Gerard Blaine, who had attended I.S. 219 a year earlier but transferred out prior to the current school year. He was a year older than Dennis, having been held back a year in elementary school.

"Yo, what up, G?" After telling Renee that he would catch up with them in a few minutes, Dennis walked over and dapped his friend.

"Look at you out here, bustin' niggas' asses in ball! But you lucky you ain't had to face me. Don't forget who ya' master is, boy!" said Gerard.

"Man, shut yo' clown ass up! Nah, but where you been though? It's like you went ghost since you got up outta here."

Gerard shrugged. "Shit, I ain't doin' nothin' much. You know I been on my grind makin' money all year. Yo, I heard the news about yo' pops. I wanted to come through to show love, but I had to work."

"Appreciate it, B. It's all good, man. Just tryin' to deal. So, what up wit' you though? Where you at these days? What school you goin' to now?"

"I go to I.S. 193. I mean that ain't no big deal though. I've been stackin' all year, kid. Check this out." Gerard reached into his pocket and pulled out a wad of dollar bills.

"Damn, man, where you work at?"

"I guess you can say I'm a salesman. Speaking of that, I got a business proposition for you. You wanna know how to make some extra money on the side?"

"Oh, fasho'. Hold up, lemme get to the locker room and change."

While the two boys were talking, Chris, who had been following Renee and her daughters back into the car, suddenly felt uneasy. When the boy dapped up Dennis after the game, Chris had a feeling he recognized him from somewhere, but he could not remember where he had seen him.

But when he saw the boy pull out the wad of cash to show Dennis, Chris recognized him immediately. It did not take more than two minutes for Chris to finally identify the boy.

He had only met him in passing, but he recognized him as "G-Block," and he was one of the newer recruits into the gang. Although Chris had only been part of M.O.B. less than a year prior, G-Block was the type of young hustler that Pooh and Tadarius were looking for: young, ambitious, ruthless, and money-minded.

I'm not gonna let G-Block talk Dennis into joining M.O.B. He ain't got no clue how the story ends.

AUGUST 2019

Chris was napping in the trap house after selling his stock for the day. The temperature was just below ninety degrees, and being out in the hot sun for most of the day had sapped his energy. His mother was still out working, but he did not know what she was selling—drugs or herself. Still reeling from the harsh reality that Sharita merely used him as a sex object, Chris was determined not to let another female butter him up again. *If I want to fuck someone, it's gonna be on my terms. I ain't lettin' any of these females use me.*

The relationship between Jermaine and Anita had somewhat cooled off because Jermaine was out looking for the next conquest.

While Chris was lying in rest, he felt liquid dropping on his forehead. Wiping off the liquid with his left hand, he looked up and saw Yvens "Whynot" Jean, another gang member, jokingly emptying the bottle of water that he had been previously drinking from onto his forehead.

"Yo, what the hell?" Chris reacted, angry, as he wiped the drops from his forehead.

"I damn near poured the entire bottle over yo' head, and you still ain't felt a goddamn thing," Yvens laughed.

"I bet you'd feel my fist breakin' yo' teeth. Shit ain't funny."

"Damn, man, I was just playin'! Chill, B. Yo, Boss called a meeting. Must be important cuz he ain't called one of those unless someone 'bout to get smoked or we get some new soldiers, you know what I'm sayin?"

Although Chris still never fully grasped how Tadarius ran his operation, he knew one important rule: Not to get on Tadarius's bad list. It was the last place anyone wanted to be, and if there were any doubts about what happened if anyone crossed him, all people had to do was reflect upon what happened to Theo Brunsen.

Theo was one of M.O.B.'s chief informants, and he carried his duties out successfully, but there was a problem. Theo discovered that Tadarius was mishandling money and never paid anyone what they were fully owed. Theo grew increasingly unhappy and confronted Tadarius about the money he was not receiving.

Tadarius on the other hand, felt that Theo was stealing money from him, so an impromptu meeting was set. Theo was accompanied by a young lady, and when he met with Tadarius, he mentioned the financial disparity and became more demonstrative when Tadarius finally snapped and with a small switchblade, sliced Theo's neck without warning. Gasping for air, his eyes watering in pain, Theo was doing all he could to staunch the blood flowing from the open wound in his neck. Four more slashes of the switchblade followed. Then Tadarius stabbed his adversary repeatedly until Theo finally collapsed.

Believing him to be dead, Tadarius arranged to have his body dumped in the lake where nobody would suspect him. At the time, Chris was not yet born, but his mother was there when Theo was stabbed.

The door opened. Tadarius, Pooh, D.J. Warren, and Stacey Davis, accompanied by Anita, walked in. Also with them was a boy who looked like he was no more than thirteen years of age. He was short and stocky, but he was already scarred on his arms and legs. It appeared that he had already been initiated into M.O.B., and it was confirmed when Pooh introduced him to the other members.

"Yo, give it up fo' the new member of the Fam: G-Block!" Pooh shouted as the other members cheered.

Each member performed the gang dap with G-Block, and when he finally got to Chris, he accommodated him, and they performed the gang handshake.

"This hea's my boy, Chris," said Pooh. "Definitely one of the best hustlers in the game. Man sold out all my stocks one day. You wanna learn from da' best? There's the man to talk to."

After Pooh and Tadarius walked away, Chris decided to give G-Block a tour of their house, showing him where they secretly had a stash of weed hidden from Tadarius's eyes because Tadarius wanted profit for all his sales, and if anyone was short on any day, they would be dealt with. Chris was the mentor to G-Block for one day. As they walked outside, they decided to visit the spots where G-block would be selling.

"Yo, Chris, they said that you came from M.O.B. royalty. Is that true, or was it all play-play?"

"What you think?" Chris asked.

"Well, yo' mama is in M.O.B. right? Who was yo' pops?"

"My pops was one of M.O.B.'s founding fathers. Ever heard of David Anderson?"

"I only know one David Anderson, and he's my boy's father. He live out in the sticks now. Same dawg?"

"I don't know. I guess. I've been tryin' to tail him for a while."

"What for?"

Suddenly, Chris regretted saying anything to the new recruit. *Why does this scrub want to know so much about me?*

"Never mind, bruh."

"I mean, I know where Mr. Anderson goes every day. I'm cool wit' his son, Dennis. I used to go to his school last year before I moved."

As they walked the streets, G-Block asked, "So how long you been crew wit' M.O.B.?"

"My whole life if you want to be technical about it. I was born into this."

"Damn, so you couldn't get out even if you wanted to."

"I mean if I wanted out, I would've been got out. Don't get it twisted, son. I'm my own man. I could leave if I wanted."

G-Block laughed obnoxiously. "Yo, if you dipped out now, forget T, ya' mamma would whoop yo' ass. Don't even front."

The more Chris got to know G-Block, the more he was naturally disgusted by the kid. *This arrogant flow he on right now's gonna get him capped. He better recognize where he at.*

"So, word on the street is that you and Sharita got it in the other night."

Chris stared at G-Block, bewildered. How would he have known about his sexual tryst with Sharita? "How you know about that?"

"Cuz Sharita's my cousin. That's how. And no, you ain't the only one she played for a chump. She's played other niggas too. Yeah, she told me how you came back tryin' to hit it again, and she had to turn yo' thirsty ass down." G-Block walked ahead, laughing hysterically.

Okay yeah, I definitely don't like this cat, real talk. I hope we posted up on different blocks because if they have me next to him, he gon' come up missing.

CHAPTER 15

DIVINE VENGEANCE

EVENTUALLY, DENNIS CAME out of the locker room fifteen minutes later and joined his family in their car. During the ride back home, Chris had to sit through twenty minutes of the family reminiscing about Gerard. The entire trip was nauseating for Chris because he knew the type of person Gerard really was: a gangbanging con artist. Whether it was Dennis talking about the classes they had together the last two years, or it was about attending his birthday parties, the family had nothing but fond memories about the boy Chris knew as G-Block.

According to what he heard, apparently David Anderson was accommodating to Gerard as well while he was still alive, often assisting him with his homework or giving him car rides to school. Cree and Katrina were so used to seeing Gerard at the house, as he visited every other week, to the point where they saw him as an older brother. Chris contemplated bursting everybody's bubble to expose the wily poser so that he could arrive home without puking over these so called "happy memories" of G-Block.

Finally, they arrived home, and as Cree and Katrina prepared for bed, Chris walked by their room and knocked on Dennis's door. At first there was no response, so Chris tried knocking on the door again. After about ten more knocks, Dennis finally opened the door, shirtless and wearing shorts while listening to music on his Bluetooth pods. Chris walked into the room. Dennis had different posters on his wall, mostly of NBA players LeBron James, Steph Curry, and Chris Paul.

After a few more minutes, Dennis finally removed his wireless headset. "Yo, you saw how I put in work tonight, right?" Dapping Chris, Dennis walked over to his closet and pulled out a regulation-size basketball and began twirling it with his finger.

"Yeah, I saw it. You was killin' that Frankie dude out there, and I heard he was one of the top kids in the borough. Didn't look like it tonight though," Chris replied, dapping Dennis again.

"I know, right. Had my jumper going, and he couldn't take that, so he starts trash-talking me, and I almost lost it for a second."

"Yeah, I saw you was getting' heated over there by the bench, but I knew you was gonna come back and eat him up in that second half."

"You know what I'm sayin'? I almost had a double-double tonight. Could've had it if Coach didn't bench me."

"I feel you. Anyway, I got something I need to talk to you about."

"Yeah, what's up?"

Dennis sat up on his bed, shuffling through his Apple playlist. Chris had contemplated whether to tell Dennis about his friend, but after a trip back to when he first met the guy, and remembering his attitude, he cast all doubt aside and decided not to beat around the bush.

"Listen, Dennis, I know you don't know me all that well, but I gotta keep it real wit' you, B. You know yo' boy Gerard? You gotta stay away from him, bro."

Dennis chuckled slightly and raised his eyebrows in suspicion, thinking that Chris was joking. When Chris didn't laugh, Dennis stopped laughing. "What, you serious?"

"As a heart attack, bro. Yo' boy livin' foul out here, man. He ain't who he says he is."

"Man, you buggin'. I've known G for three years, bro. That's the homie, and now you tellin' me to stay away from him like you know him or something."

While saying all of this, Dennis was lying on his bed, throwing the ball up almost hitting the ceiling before catching it again.

But to make a point, Chris caught the ball in mid-air to emphasize how serious he was. "Look, dawg, Gerard—if that's his real name—rolls wit' M.O.B., my old set...the gang that smoked our pops, remember?"

Snatching the ball back, Dennis gave Chris a sarcastic look. "Gerard rolls wit' M.O.B.? Get outta hea' with that shit."

"Betta' not let yo' moms hear you cussin' in the house, bruh. But I'm serious about Gerard. I know the kid. His a.k.a. is G-Block, and he runs drugs for Tadarius. Look, I know how they roll."

"That's right cuz you used to be a dope man too, right? You ever thought that you might be talking about another dude, and Gerard maybe looks like G-Block?"

"Nah, dawg, trust me. It's him. He came to you to after the game, right? He wanted to talk to you about ways to make more money, right? That's how they get you. They don't see you as a person. They see you as a commodity, someone they can use."

Dennis turned away from Chris and stared out the window of his room into the starry night. He did not want to admit that Chris was right about Gerard approaching him about an opportunity to make money, but he did not bother to ask.

"Listen, they used the same playbook on our dad too. They knew he was All-City as a football player, but because he rolled wit' M.O.B., he was still runnin' wit' Tadarius because all he saw was the money. Then when he broke away from them after T got locked up, he was a target to Tadarius and others. I'm just lookin' out for you, Dennis."

"Look, I ain't a punk, man. I don't need anyone lookin' after me."

Dennis stood up and confronted Chris face to face. Although Chris was two years older than Dennis, his half-brother was just about the same height, with Dennis just a few inches above Chris.

"You wrong about Gerard, man. He wouldn't play me like that. You've been rolling with the same crew over half your life, so you're seeing them everywhere. Maybe you need help."

Chris shook his head. If he was so determined to find out the hard way about his so-called friend, maybe it was best for him to fall back and allow Dennis to walk into the mouse trap on his own. "Aight, bro, believe what you wanna believe. But just ask him when you see him again. Ask him what he wants you to do. If he's tryin' to make you run a package somewhere, then you know I was right."

With that, Chris left the room, and Dennis promptly closed the door behind him. Chris walked into the visitor's bedroom, which served as his room. *Stupid kid. I'm trying to save him from falling into the same trap that our father and I fell into, and yet he's walking right into it.*

Chris knew if Dennis was discovered as David's son, Tadarius would spare no expense in eliminating anyone who remotely resembled those who opposed him. Taking his phone out, Chris called Edward Reed, silently hoping that he was home.

"Hey, Chris, what's up? Staying out of trouble this time, I hope?" he greeted.

"Hanging in there, Eddie. Yo, I got a situation."

"What's up? Hopefully, not another fight at school?"

"Nah, man, nothin' like that. So, I went to Dennis's basketball game tonight, and after the game, I saw a kid talkin' to Dennis, and the kid's wit' M.O.B."

There was a pause on the other line as Edward processed what Chris had just revealed to him. "You sure about that? Do you have proof?"

"I actually met him when I was still working for them. He was an asshole then, and he's still one now. Ain't nothin' changed."

"Okay, Chris, you gotta do your best to convince Dennis to stay away from him. The last thing I need on my conscious is another dead Anderson."

"I tried talkin' to him, but he won't believe me. Even Mrs. A. is saying that Gerard was always welcome into their home and how she used to make lunches for Dennis and Gerard. I had to sit the whole car ride to hear how perfect Gerard was, blah, blah, blah."

"I see Tadarius ain't changed up his recruiting style. So, what I'm gonna need you to do is to keep a close eye on Dennis. Make sure he doesn't get in over his head. You know the game as much as I do, and as long as M.O.B. is keeping tabs on him, I need you to keep him away from that stuff, and if I were Mrs. Anderson, I would check the locks on my door and see about replacing the locks if any of them are old."

"I wish I can tell her that, but she thinks Gerard can do no wrong either."

Chris did not hear Edward respond immediately, so he guessed that he was thinking about his next move.

"Okay, don't worry about that. I'll talk to her. Just keep an eye on your brother. By the way, I spoke with Renee last week. She said the first progress reports dropped, and you're getting A's and B's in your classes. Good work, man! Keep it up!"

"Thanks, man, appreciate it. Yeah, this whole juggling school and work thing can get hard sometimes, but gotta keep chuggin' straight ahead though."

"Who you tellin', my young brotha? Try workin' over twelve hours a day on a hundred plus cases. Just enjoy being young right now. By the way, how's the situation with the girl going?"

Chris laughed. He did not expect Edward to ask about his relationship status because it seemed irrelevant with everything else that was going on. "It's going good, I guess. I've been working four days a week and trying to get all these assignments done in time, so I don't have time to hang wit' her."

"Probably for the best anyway. Hang in there, kid." Suddenly, Edward heard knocking on his door. "Look, I gotta go. Keep me posted on Dennis's friend."

Hanging up the call, Edward heard rapid knocking on his door again. Aside from his father, who left after his abrupt visit, Edward did not expect anyone else at his home. Reaching into the drawer in his computer desk, he pulled out a box. Inside was a small handgun, complete with a round of bullets. Opening the barrel, he loaded the bullets inside his gun, closed the barrel, and locked it in place. Warily, he approached the door.

"Who is it?" he asked.

"It's me. Can I come in, please?"

A familiar voice replied to him from the other end. Placing the gun back in the drawer, Edward sighed deeply and opened the door. Andrea stood there looking concerned but more subdued than she was the previous time that she had visited him.

"Hey, Edward, can we talk?"

"Depends. Am I gonna need a faceguard or a helmet if I let you in?" Edward asked, chuckling, as he reminisced on the previous time Andrea appeared at his door when she slapped him angrily for defending LaToya at the trial.

"No, you won't need those. I actually wanted to apologize for that. I understand now that you were put in a very tough spot, and you wanted to protect your family."

Edward stepped aside and invited Andrea into his home. He graciously offered to hang her coat on a nearby coat rack on the wall, which surprised Andrea because she did not expect the kind gesture, especially from someone whom she violently reacted to during their previous interaction.

"Would you like something to eat or drink? I got water, ginger ale, wine, and as far as food goes, I think I got some leftover Chinese."

"Water would be nice. Thank you."

After retreating to the fridge to get Andrea a bottle of water, Edward invited her to sit on the couch in his living room. Andrea looked around. She could not help but to notice how meticulously clean Edward kept his house. His couch was clean, his tables were dusted clean, the floors were vacuumed, and his home office was neat and organized.

For all the great character traits that Quentin had, cleanliness was not one of them, and it drove Andrea crazy. *Why can't he be clean like Mr. Reed over here?*

"So, how's everything in the music industry?"

Andrea looked down at her water bottle. She appeared to be embarrassed about expressing her true feelings to Edward. "Honestly, things have not been going too great. I mean, I'm releasing good music. I'm writing my own songs, and I've even got into producing for myself and for other artists. But the sales have been dwindling lately. My PR reps and my agent are telling me that the songs I write no longer have that appeal or the pull for today's audience, and with dwindling sales comes lower pay, and when you're not raking in as much as you were before, it's tough to book shows. Normally, I can survive a sales drought if I go on tour because the fans will come out. Then I get paid by the venue, and it's all good. But without the tours, I don't know if I'll be able to stay afloat."

Edward listened to Andrea and felt a pang of remorse. Here was a woman who suffered a tragic loss early in her life and worked to build her career in the face of sorrow, and where most people would have folded, she had managed to rise above her obstacles. But he sensed the vulnerability in her voice and her struggle to keep the music alive in her.

Artists always had a burst of inspiration or a beacon of motivation that kept them going, and for Andrea, it was Loree McAfee and the consolation that her murderer saw justice and that her soul was resting in peace. But since the verdict, Loree was not resting in peace, at least not to Andrea, and it was affecting her creatively as well as financially.

"Andrea, I'm so sorry that things are rough for you now. I feel that, somehow, I'm responsible for it. I should have never defended LaToya in court. If I could take it all back, I would."

"Even if it meant never seeing your brother again?"

Edward shrugged. If his brother was hurt or killed, it would rip him apart. He would grieve and maybe take a sabbatical from work, but eventually he would find the strength to recover and move on. He was not sure that he could say the same for Andrea because, if she did not get the justice that she needed for her sister, it would not only jeopardize her career, but it could also lead Andrea down an emotional spiral down to a point where she might not recover.

"I see what they said about you in podcasts and the news. I'm sorry about your approval rating going down," she said.

Taking a swig of his water, Edward shrugged again. "Well, I never got into law to appease or make people happy. The approval rating was a bonus. I got into law to give others a fair shot at justice, the shot that I never got when I was younger. I wanted to use the law to defend people, especially people that looked like me. I just got caught playing a very dangerous game with a very dangerous individual. I underestimated him, and now I'm paying the price for it. But this is a game that I ain't gonna stop playing, not until I see to it that Loree gets justice."

Andrea smiled. Although she was not sure what plan Edward had up his sleeve, she knew that he meant everything that he said. "Thanks. And as if my professional career wasn't already hanging on by a thread, I think Quentin might be cheating on me."

"You mean your fiancé? What makes you say that? That man loves you. He's a square, but he loves you."

Andrea laughed. It was the first time someone had made her laugh in days. "Boy, stop! He ain't no square."

"You're right. He's a rectangle. His fingers probably gotta make an appointment to scratch his face. But why you think he's cheating on you?"

Andrea stood up from the couch and started pacing the floor, reminiscent of her sister whenever she was confronted with serious issues. "Well, for one, he returns home from work late at night. I mean, really late at night. I understand that he has a stressful job, and he works overtime, but how much overtime can one person have in a month? We've been arguing about this situation with LaToya's case. He feels like I'm investing in the case more than our relationship. He's already mad that I've called off the wedding, and we don't go out as frequently as we used to anymore."

Although he was listening, Edward's thoughts were all over the place, and they were thoughts that he should not be having. *Quentin is a goddamn fool. You got a woman as fine as Andrea, and you fuckin' around on her? I mean, on a scale of 1-20 in terms of the women I used to bring around here, Andrea is at the top of the charts. The things I would do to her...okay, Ed, keep your mind right. Don't start letting your thoughts wander. I have to remember the fact that she's in my home, obviously because she needs someone to talk to, and she's got those brown leg warm-up pants that hug her curves perfectly, and her skin is shiny and smooth. She drinks a lot of water. I can tell. She probably rubs aloe lotion on her skin too.*

While all these thoughts were running through Edward's mind, Andrea was still discussing the reason for the rift in her relationship. "He's also been very secretive lately, like there's something that he doesn't want me to know. I've always wanted to see where he worked at because the tech that we use for Omega Studios was manufactured at his job, but he's never once taken me to visit his job. Then his phone keeps vibrating when we sleep. I know his phone is underneath the sheets, where he knows I can't get to it, obviously. He would just dismiss it as a notification from his job, but how many employers out there message their employees at 3 a.m. to 5 a.m. in the morning?"

Edward listened, and when he finally allowed his racing thoughts to cease for a moment, he was all but convinced that Quentin was cheating on Andrea. "Look, Andrea, I don't know what to tell you about that. I'm an attorney that doesn't practice in domestic couple disputes. If you never married him yet, then that means you did not sign any type of prenuptial agreement, so he still gets to keep all his assets. I know it don't look good now, but I'm sure ya' will work it out."

Feeling defeated, Andrea stood up and started to head for the front door when Edward grabbed her arm to stop her from storming off, and Andrea looked back at him.

What the hell am I doing? Ed, let this woman go, acting all desperate.

Andrea could have hit him again for grabbing her roughly, but in a strange, unexplained twist, she was aroused by the sudden way Edward handled her, like he was in control and would not relinquish it to anyone. But as quickly as Edward grabbed her, he let her go.

"I'm sorry," he apologized, looking down as if embarrassed about grabbing her hastily.

She smiled and looked down to the ground as well. He smiled sheepishly, and Andrea could not help but notice that his teeth were dazzling white. There was a genuine warmness about his smile, and she was taken by it.

Lord, what am I doing? I'm engaged, and yet all I can think about is how fine Edward looks right now. His smile, his body, his confidence, he's clean-cut...makes me completely forget that he was once a gangbanger. I might as well be eleven years old again when I saw him for the first time when he came by while my friends and I were jumping rope.

"I-I gotta go," she stammered, while opening the door and walking outside.

"Yo, Andrea, you forgot this," Edward said, holding Andrea's jacket that he helped remove for her when she entered the home.

"Silly me. Thanks," she replied shyly, taking the jacket.

"Wouldn't want you to freeze out here."

Oh my God, let me go because I can't control the way I'm thinking about you right now.

Deon Taylor was in his one-room flat in Hillside, Queens, celebrating his birthday the only way a drug runner knew how: excessive drugs, strippers, and music blasting. Cup after cup of Patron, wine coolers, and juice were tossed down as Deon, his partner Maceo, and his close cousin Finley enjoyed their libations and their access to women.

Deon worked for various gangs and sets, so his loyalty was to his pockets. Any way that he could get quick money, he was on the job. M.O.B. happened to be one of his drug suppliers, and they made their rules clear to him: sell the product, and bring all the profits back to the safehouse. The percentage sold would determine the amount of money that was paid.

Deon scoffed at M.O.B.'s money policy, and he hated that he had to give a percentage of the money that he felt he earned back to M.O.B. *If they were going to do that, then why do they need us to sell this shit for them? Nah, what I'm finna do is keep a larger cut and give a reduced portion back to them.*

So, for a long period of time, Deon split the money and started giving the smaller percentage of the revenue to M.O.B. But unfortunately for Deon, they had Edward's brother Tony handling the books at the safehouse, and Tony, who had excelled in mathematics, knew that Deon was cheating the gang out of thousands of dollars, but due to the violent nature of M.O.B.'s leadership, he kept it private until the leaders who normally received the final income from Tony discovered that their monthly revenue was declining each month.

When Tadarius, Pooh, and Jermaine had discovered the profits missing, Tony was confronted, and after coercing Tony, they discovered that Deon had been holding back a larger percentage. Affectively, Deon became a wanted man, and members started packing their weapons to head over to his apartment to deal with the treacherous drug runner. Oblivious that he was a target, Deon continued partying and throwing extra money around his bed as the strippers continued gyrating and shaking their bodies at the men.

Deon decided to get frisky. Under the influence of the leftover weed and cocaine that was available, he reached out to one of the strippers and pulled off her bra, revealing her pierced nipples. "Damn, baby! You know I like 'em pierced. Shit, they taste better that way." He then proceeded to suck on her right pierced nipple as the stripper giggled.

Suddenly, he heard a loud knock on the door. "Who that?" Finley asked, his head tucked between two strippers.

When the knocking stopped momentarily, the partying continued, and the men resumed their debauchery. But then the knocking resumed, and this time, the music was cut off as Deon, now fed up, rose to answer the door. Unfortunately, he did not pack his firearm with him, and as soon as he unlocked the door, it flew open, knocking him back. The strippers screamed in horror as four hooded masked figures barged into the apartment, brandishing loaded guns.

"Shut the fuck up! If you ain't Deon, get yo' shit, and get out now!" one of them shouted.

The strippers did not wait for a second warning, and they all grabbed their clothes and ran out the apartment. Some of them did not have time to dress fully, but out of fear, ran out in the nude. After the last stripper left, Maceo made a dash for the door, but one of the masked men, opened fire and shot him square in the back. He sprawled to the ground, motionless with blood pouring from the exit wound.

"Damn, I really liked that cat too," one of the figures chuckled, pulling down his mask.

Deon saw who it was right away, and he trembled in fear as Tadarius stood before him, gun pointed at his temple.

"Deon, Deon, Deon, now it was brought to my attention that I was missing about $500,000. Now after further investigation, it took me a minute to figure out that I had a snake in the fold. You stole from your family."

Deon sat there frozen in place, his eyes darting around, hoping to find his gun, which was mysteriously missing.

"If there's one thing I hate more than strangers stealing from me, it's family stealing from me. What was yo' angle? Tryin' to level up to be me? Wanna be a shot-caller so that everybody knows you?"

Before Deon could reply, Tadarius fired into Deon's head, causing blood and brain matter to paint the walls.

"Congratulations, you got yo' wish. Now you on the six o'clock news."

Finley stood there, petrified as the gunmen moved in on him.

"Yo, Block, this one's on you," Tadarius said as one of the gunmen pulled off his mask, revealing G-Block's face.

"For the Fam..."

A shot fired, and Finley slumped against the wall.

CHAPTER 16

DIVINE VENGEANCE

THE ENTIRE APARTMENT resembled a war zone as the bodies of Finley, Maceo, and Deon were lying in puddles of their own blood. The entire apartment was a grim color of red as the gunmen made for the door. They knew they did not have much time to make their escape. Although the apartment was dilapidated, which would have affected the market value of the neighborhood, the gang members were positive that there were other tenants that heard the entire commotion leading up to the executions. Their theories were confirmed as police sirens were heard blaring not too far away.

As they made a dash for the door, Tadarius looked at G-Block with admiration and pride. "Good work, young blood. What you did was pass swift judgement on a mu'fucka who thought he could cheat us. This is street justice right here."

G-Block, who had never killed anyone before, had a look of regret on his face, but it was quickly replaced with pride. Tadarius told him that he would be tested one day, and if he passed the test, he would be a permanent member of M.O.B. For the longest time, G-Block was anxious, wondering what the test was, but once he found out that his test included making a quick decision, he felt included in the street family.

"Aight, let's get the fuck outta hea'. Pooh already got the ride out back."

As the gang members headed out the door, the fourth gunman looked back at the grisly scene once again. Pulling his mask halfway down, Cochise looked at the faces of the men slain, lying on the ground. Maceo's eyes were still open with death's stare. Cochise felt his stomach turn. *It wasn't supposed to be like this. This was not the way this was supposed to go down.*

Cochise originally thought that Tadarius and Pooh would go to Deon's home with the intentions of leaving a message but not killing anyone. Even though Deon was a shady character himself, Cochise did not believe that Deon deserved to die in the matter.

"Yo, Chise, you deaf or something? I said let's roll," Tadarius repeated, while suppressing a cough.

During the last few days hanging in the M.O.B. safe house, Cochise started to notice that something was wrong with Tadarius. He would suddenly get into these cough fits that would prevent him from speaking, so Pooh would normally address the other members in the room. Tadarius would often rush into the bathroom, where the cough fits continued, sometimes for as long as ten minutes. By the time he would emerge from the bathroom, his eyes would be bloodshot red, his appearance would be more haggard, and his face drenched with perspiration.

But despite these brief health scares, Tadarius maintained his leadership, refusing to show weakness in front of the other members, but as the days went by, it was getting tougher for him to conceal his health concern.

After the triple homicide that was committed, Cochise followed the other members in their car as they sped away from the scene. The police would arrive on scene, but it would be far too late for them to catch the suspects.

After M.O.B. left the scene, the members took off their masks. Pooh drove the car while Tadarius rode on the passenger side with him. G-Block and Cochise were in the back seat. As the three other men discussed and described the scene as if it was an enjoyable day at the park instead of murder, Cochise remained quiet as ever.

It wasn't supposed to be like this. I didn't think the game would get this messy. What have I gotten myself into? Is this what they do to initiate young boys into this mess? G-Block can't be no more than fourteen years old. He could be my son. I can't see my son taking somebody else out like that.

Arriving at the trap house, the first order of business was to ditch the car used to dispatch the drug dealers. They wanted to discard everything that tied them to the murders. After volunteering to discard of the car, Cochise got into it with the intention of meeting up with a contact that was awaiting him at an undisclosed location.

Cochise may be part of M.O.B., but Caris Grant is not a part of this group.

Receiving a pin on his phone to follow the directions to meet his contact, Cochise, a.k.a. Caris Grant, made his way to the location. Parking his car under a subway overpass, he stepped out of his car. Lighting up a cigarette, he waited for thirty minutes. Finally, his contact pulled up and stepped outside.

Edward Reed stepped out of the shadows and made his way toward Caris. "Yo, C, what's up?" he greeted.

But Caris was not in the mood for pleasantries. "Yo, man, you did not tell me how this group rolls. I just witnessed some crazy shit back there. Tadarius literally smoked three guys without hesitation. I know you said they were dangerous, but these men are volatile, and what's even more crazy is that they had some schoolboy out there shooting grown ass men."

"I know it's hard out there, but I need you to stay inside a little longer," Edward said to his cousin.

"How much longer, Antonio? How much longer to want me to stay inside?"

"I need you to stay in there for at least four more days. Then, you book it. How's Tony doing? They didn't hurt him yet, right?"

"Yeah, Tony's good. He's working their books there, and from what I heard, they're planning on keeping him there longer."

"Look, that ain't gonna happen. First chance you get, get Tony up out of there. He's in there because of me. He shouldn't have to suffer while dealing with my shit."

Caris thought it over. As a young promising upstart law enforcement officer, he was initially excited to take an undercover role for the first time in his life, but if he had known how messy it would be, he would have rejected the job. *Antonio warned me that it would get messy. I just didn't know how messy it would get. All I was looking for was an undercover role and my first drug bust.*

DECEMBER 2019

Caris Grant stared half asleep from his desk at the 83rd Precinct in Flushings, Queens. Only two months removed from his police academy graduation, he had been lauded on his ability to investigate tough cases and being able to crack those cases, many being small drug rings and lower-rated kingpins. He knew how dangerous his profession was, and he knew it could cost him his life, but he was no stranger to taking risks.

As a kid, Caris helped bring a serial rapist to justice. Jasper "Bag Em" Manfield, a former New York City construction worker, was responsible for several assault cases on young women during the early 2000s. Known as one of the most slippery criminals in history, he had managed to evade law enforcement after committing one of his heinous crimes. But unbeknownst to him, there was someone that was watching his move. Young Caris Grant, then twelve years of age, had begun tracking Jasper's movements.

Jasper just so happened to live in the same apartment complex where Caris and his family lived. Jasper was usually kind to Caris and his mother whenever they encountered each other on the way to work. There was nothing odd about Jasper at first, but then Caris noticed the carousel of women who entered Jasper's apartment with him, and it seemed as though Jasper had a different woman every week. At first Caris thought nothing of it because in his mind, what man would not date multiple women if he wanted?

But one late night on the way back to his apartment from the movies, Caris heard blood-curdling screams from Jasper's apartment. They were not the screams of a woman in pleasure. However, they were the screams of a woman in pain.

Caris then decided to scope his mysterious neighbor out the next day. But he was in for a surprise when he returned from school to find that Jasper's apartment had been cleaned out, and there was a "ROOM FOR RENT" sign on his door. *Damn, I missed my chance to call the police on that dude. I might have saved the lady.*

The next day, there were news vans, police cars, and the local network news anchors interviewing different people in the apartment. Caris found out later that the woman whom Jasper was with the night before had called the police and reported being raped by Jasper. Although the police took statements, Jasper was "in the wind" and nowhere to be found.

Caris, who was focused on becoming a detective one day, decided to take the case into his own hands because he felt the police were not doing enough to bring the man to justice. Through an anonymous tip, Caris walked into a local pizzeria and noticed a familiar face throwing up the dough of the pizza. It was Jasper, who managed to pull a part-time job at the pizzeria. *The nerve of this guy. His name is all over the news, and come to find out, he's working here?*

The pizza parlor was in Long Island, and Jasper, who only worked parttime, had another job as a part-time photographer. Adding onto his social media that he has worked with various celebrities, Jasper was able to lure young women under the impression that they were getting new headshots for modeling/acting careers.

One Saturday, Jasper took a Korean girl with a modeling potential into his studio. The day went as planned with Jasper taking pictures of her, but while he was showing her the proofs, the girl realized that Jasper had become extremely physical, grabbing her in areas that she did not ask to be grabbed. Jasper forced her on a cot in the studio and pinned her down before proceeding to sexually assault her.

The next day at school Caris attended one of his classes when he realized one of the students in his class, Lina Chan, was absent. Lina never missed a day of school, so it was odd, but Caris remembered overhearing Lina at lunch one day, boasting proudly about how she was going to be taking photographs for her acting portfolio. When one of the students asked Lina who the photographer was, the photographer's description matched that of Jasper. Caris was suddenly suspicious, but at the time, he thought that maybe it was just an odd coincidence, and it was not Jasper.

However, Lina being absent raised red flags, and Caris knew that if she was alone with Jasper, there was a good chance that he molested her. Determined to get the man locked up, Caris decided to investigate on his own. First, he visited Lina's home.

"Hey, Mrs. Chan, my name's Caris, and I just wanted to know if Lina is okay. I didn't see her at school."

Her mother then proceeded to tell Caris that Lina was home sick and was not in the mood for visitors, but before she closed the door in Caris's face, Lina stopped her mother.

"It's okay, Mom. Caris is cool. Let him in."

After Lina invited Caris in, he asked her about her encounter with the photographer.

"I don't know what I did wrong. All I wanted was a headshot, and that was it. He started touching me in weird places, and before I knew it, he…"

Lina's voice trailed off, and Caris shook his head angrily, knowing that Lina had been another one of Jasper's victims.

"I'mma get that sick bastard locked up, Lina."

"No, don't put yourself in danger, Caris. My mom already called the police, and they went back to the studio, but he was already gone. They don't know where he is, but they said they would keep looking."

But Caris knew where Jasper would be the next day, and he planned to take the serial rapist down. Caris went to the police station and informed them that the photographer who molested Lina was the same man who was responsible for a string of assaults back at his apartment building and that he was all but convinced that Jasper was the man they were looking for.

Jasper, who had been working at the pizza parlor under an assumed name, walked into work the next morning as if nothing was wrong, put on his apron, and proceeded about his day, when four police officers entered the pizzeria. After confronting the manager about Jasper's whereabouts, a few moments later, Jasper was walked out of the pizzeria in handcuffs.

He was charged with multiple counts of rape and sodomy and sentenced to fifty years in prison. The man who managed to avoid authorities for years was quietly foiled by a courageous pre-teen who had grown tired of seeing criminals getting away with crimes. The ordeal with Jasper awakened a desire within Caris to pursue a career in private investigation, and after his academy graduation, he officially became a P.I.

It was a turning point in his life. He also happened to be the second cousin of Edward Reed on his mother's side. During their younger years, Isabelle would take Edward, who was known as Antonio back then, to family reunion gatherings, where he would meet his extended family.

Caris happened to be on hand for many of those events, and Antonio got to know his cousin firsthand. Antonio had heard of the boy who helped bring down a serial rapist in the news, which turned Caris into somewhat of a celebrity, but Caris never allowed that case to change his personality.

Now, sitting at his desk, after working a couple of small-time drug-bust sting operations, Caris was becoming restless. He had grown weary of the small cases that he took, and most of the time, he was reviewing past cases or working with forensics to tie up unsolved murders dating back about twenty years ago.

Caris was familiar with his cousin Antonio's brush with the law and his key testimony that helped exonerate some gang members back in 2003. So, one could imagine Caris's surprise when he received a call late December 2019 from Antonio.

"Ayo, cuzzo, what's good?" Caris greeted.

"Not too good, cuzzo. Listen, I need to holla at you for minute. Tony's been kidnapped by M.O.B., and I just got a message from Tadarius saying they gon' kill him if I don't do what he says."

"What? Tony's been kidnapped? You gotta call 911, cuzzo."

"Nah, they already said not to get the police involved, or he's a dead man. Look, come by my place. I'll text you the address, and we can break this stuff down."

A few hours later, Caris was at Edward's house. After preparing a meal and a bottle of beer for his cousin, Edward explained the entire scenario, from Tadarius being released from prison, to LaToya nearly killing him as well as her own son and Andrea McAfee. It took nearly an hour for Edward to break down the series of events that took place the entire year leading up to his Tony being held hostage by Tadarius and his crew.

"Damn, man, you are in way too deep. So, this crew, M.O.B., that you rolled with, they want you to defend this LaToya lady even though she killed David and killed Loree back in '03?"

"Yeah, this shit's gettin' crazy, Caris. It's outta control. It's clear that I can't come to this guy directly. I'm gonna have to play just as dirty as him to bring him down."

"What do you suggest?" Caris asked.

Pacing the living room, Edward decided not to beat around the bush about his intentions for his cousin. "Caris, for years all I've heard was how you wanted a big case. You want to help bring drug lords, pedophiles, and serial rapists down. How'd you like to help me take down a gang?"

Caris raised his eyebrow at Edward, silently wondering if his cousin was joking. "You want me to help you bring down one of the biggest gangs in the city? How are we gonna do that?"

"We need someone on the inside, someone who can gain his trust—a person who can infiltrate his operations and tip me on his progress so we can get the drop on him and bring him down permanently so we can get Tony out of there."

"Look, Edward, if that's what you callin' yourself now. I still don't get that name change, but it is what it is. You want me to infiltrate M.O.B. as one of his gangbangers to bring him down?"

Edward stared at his cousin intently. He could scarcely believe that he was putting yet another family member's life at risk, but in his eyes, there was nobody better suited for the job than Caris Grant. "Yeah, that's exactly what I'm asking. These people don't give a damn about law enforcement. They see the boys in blue, they'll start blasting, and we've already lost people in the ranks dealing wit' these monsters. Remember the shootout on Merrick in 2003?"

Caris acknowledged the infamous tragic shootout, and he was not too crazy about taking on the assignment. "Look, Antonio, I hear you, man. But you think I'm ready for something like this?"

"I know you're ready for something like this. Caris, you were known for bringing down drug rings and sex offenders. This is some next-level shit you're getting into now. Tadarius is a ruthless dangerous leader of M.O.B., and he will shoot first, ask questions later if he doesn't get his way. He's got two co-leaders in charge. One is named Pooh. That's his cousin. He took over as second in charge after Malik and David died. Then he's got another cat by the name of Jermaine. He's the enforcer of the crew. Then you got Tina a.k.a. Bunny. She's lethal, cuzzo, and she was the one who lured my brother back there. Caris, I'm warning you, right now, this game can possibly get us killed if we don't play it carefully. It's a chess game out there. Tadarius is back, and he's spared no expense on expanding his influence and his reach. So, if we're gonna do this, it has to end with M.O.B. destroyed, Tadarius back behind bars, or we need to take it up another notch."

Edward filled Caris in on M.O.B.'s usual haunts and arranged for his first meeting to be with Pooh at the club where he would announce his arrival and inclusion in the gang.

"The goal is to get Tadarius to trust you. Once he trusts you, you're in. How many tatts you got?"

Rolling up his sweater sleeve, Caris revealed his unusual array of body art on his arms, upper back, and chest. "C'mon, bro, I'm a tattoo enthusiast, unlike you, who only got like what, three tatts?"

"Yeah, but I got the one that matters the most for you," Edward replied, holding up his forearm to reveal the M.O.B. gang emblem tattoo. "You want them to trust you to the point where they get this tatted on you. When you're inside, it's real important that you do whatever you have to do to gain their trust, even if you have to go against the code."

Turning away from Edward, Caris rubbed his chin in deep thought. Here was a deep infiltration assignment that was going to demand more out of him than any other venture that he had taken in the police force. "So, what you're sayin' is that when it comes down to it, if they want me kill somebody, I gotta do it?"

"Yeah. You gotta do it. This is why I can't have anybody in the police force running this operation. We gotta color outside the lines here, okay? Knowing Tadarius and his crew, they're gonna test your mettle to try to see if you a man, and they want to know if you down for the Fam. If you are, then the transition will be easy, and we might be able to get away unscathed."

"How long you need me to stay inside?"

"Let's start with two months. I need you to get in, take as many pictures of their operation, act like you working wit' them, and when the time is right, they're gonna let their guard down. When they do, that'll be the time we move in on them."

"Cuzzo, you're making this sound so simple when you know it's gonna get complicated. What's in it for me?"

Edward checked his account and wrote a check with a sum over two thousand dollars. "That's two months' pay in advance. It's all worth it if we can bring M.O.B. down. If we succeed, there's more where that came from. So, you down?"

Smiling, Caris took the money and prepared himself for the biggest mission of his career and life. "By the way, I already thought of a new name for my character."

"Lay it on me, fam."

Nearly two months later, Cochise was on his way back to the trap house, hands slightly trembling in fear. Tadarius and his crew just eliminated a nest of drug dealers, and he was a part of it.

Is it worth the $2000 at this point? Was it worth me exposing myself to gunfire, picking up women who murdered their buyers, and witnessing children killing adults? What have I signed up for?

CHAPTER 17

DIVINE VENGEANCE

WAITING FOR SOMEONE at the Diamond Bar late that evening, Edward ordered a gin and tonic from the bartender. Although he had arrived at the bar moments earlier, the television that was mounted just above the bar was turned on the news. There, he saw the coverage of the grisly scene on Hillside Avenue, and although the suspects were still at large, Edward suspected that M.O.B. was behind the shooting.

They gettin' sloppy day by day. All I need is for one of 'em to slip up, and when they do, I'll be there to catch 'em. Someone's gotta put an end to this bloodshed.

Edward took the liberty to snack on some gourmet peanuts being served at the bar when his contact finally arrived. Caris sat at the bar beside Edward and ordered a beer.

When Caris had returned to the trap house with M.O.B. earlier that evening, Tadarius, fighting another coughing fit, had given a sort of impassioned speech that involved crediting the three other hitman that accompanied him in Deon's execution. He credited G-Block for his quick trigger and decisive judgement on the perpetrators that had been stealing his stock. Pretending to celebrate the night's conquest with M.O.B., Caris was internally disgusted and appalled by the company he currently kept.

As he continued to play the part of Cochise, he texted Edward and asked to meet at an undisclosed spot. The Diamond Bar was unmarked and outside of M.O.B.'s normal haunts. Caris needed to make sure he was not seen by anyone because he knew Tadarius had eyes everywhere, and if word ever got out that he was a spy in their midst, he would share the same unhappy fate as Deon and his cronies.

Waiting for members of the crew to leave the house or fall asleep, Caris snuck out of the house, and after two subway train rides a bus stop away, he arrived at the bar.

"So, were you with them when this went down?" Edward asked, gesturing to the news coverage, which was still covering details of the shooting.

The bar was empty, except for the bartender and an old man that sat in the far corner of the bar, passed out drunk. Checking if the bartender was out of earshot, Caris thought about how to answer the question. He initially hesitated because he knew Edward had friends in the police department, and he did not want to implicate himself.

"I had no choice, Tone. I had to ride wit' them fools there. I ain't shoot nobody though. There were three cats ova' there, and I knew they were dead from the moment we arrived at the spot. Pooh smoked one of 'em. Tadarius smoked the other one, and get this, Deon was killed by a newbie called G-Block."

Edward raised an eyebrow. "G-Block? Never heard of him."

"He joined up wit' 'em about a year ago. Damn shame too. Young buck should be in school. He way too young to be mixed up in all of this."

"How old is this G-Block?"

"Shit, he can't be no more than fourteen. Just walked up and popped Deon in the head like it was nothin'.'"

G-Block. That's the kid Chris was tellin' me about. Anyone that's cold-blooded like that is extremely dangerous. I need to call Chris and remind him to watch Dennis closely, or he might end up like his father.

"Look, how long do you want me to stay inside? The longer I hang around these fools, the more suspect I look to them."

Taking another small sip of his alcoholic beverage, Edward decided that he no longer was going to risk Caris's life by having him stay in the fold with M.O.B. "Aight, check it. You can bail out anytime you want. Just please take Tony wit' you. He's been helpin' them long enough."

"Bet. So, what else did you need to know?"

"What's the weapon situation looking like at the trap house?"

"It's more than just guns there," Caris replied. "They got a whole artillery of high-grade military style weapons in a designated room in the back of the house. Tadarius is very particular about how his weapons are stored. He wants to use them himself, and he wants to sell the rest for a profit. We talkin' Uzis, AKs, and pistols, just to name of few. He's also changing the game by buying bombs too."

"Hold up. He's buying bombs too?"

"Yeah, he got C4, grenades, flares, and other types of weapons over there. He's planning to plant explosives in random locations around Queens, just to cause havoc."

Edward shook his head, grateful for the intel that he was receiving from Caris. *I could nail Tadarius's ass on an illegal weapons charge if I play this out right. All I need is evidence, and I know he don't suspect anyone in the Fam telling anyone about his stock.*

"To me, it sounds like he stockin' up for war. He was shot back in 2003 in Merrick because he was outmanned and outgunned. He's trying to prevent that from happening again."

"Yeah, I heard people talkin' about that. Tadarius lost two of his guys that night."

Terrance and Malik. Those were the guys that were killed in that standoff. All the more reason who I should pull Tony out of there sooner than later.

Suddenly, Edward's phone vibrated, and checking it, he saw that it was Andrea that texted him, thanking him for a contact that he gave her recently. Earlier in the day, Edward was looking through her social media page where she updated daily events in her hectic schedule. He again found his thoughts wandering as he stared at Andrea at one of her celebrity party events.

That woman's got it going on. Okay, Eddie, get yo' mind right and out of the gutter. Obviously, you are attracted to her, but why would she give you the time of day? She's an artist with millions of songs on livestream. Meanwhile, you're a second-rate lawyer with a diminishing approval rating in the city, all because you took a chumped-up case defending a killer.

Caris finished his drink and prepared to leave the bar as Edward informed him to keep him posted. While talking to Caris, another piece of breaking news blared on the screen that grabbed Edward's attention and caused his heart to skip a beat. Terrell Washington, the incarcerated member of M.O.B. who first introduced Edward to the gang, was found dead in his cell earlier in the evening.

Quentin Stevens arrived home shortly after 3 a.m. This marked the latest that he had ever spent outside of work. *Kim was not going to take no for an answer. Every time I try to leave, she begs me to stay, and when lays them begging brown eyes on me, I gotta go for mine. If not for her, I'd be going crazy right now. But I can't leave Drea out in the cold like this. I'm gonna have to come clean with her.*

Closing the door behind him, he strode to the kitchen to grab a snack when he flipped on the lights, and to his surprise, Andrea was sitting at the kitchen table in her bathrobe, her hair tied back in a ponytail and her legs crossed.

Usually, a man would enjoy coming home to see his lady waiting for him in a similar fashion, but Andrea's stern expression already told Quentin that he was not going to see any action from her this evening. "Andrea, you scared the hell out of me. What you doing up so late?"

"I could ask you the same question, Q. Where were you today?"

Quentin's eyes started shifting sideways, and even though he tried not to make it obvious, Andrea had been with Quentin for years, and she memorized all of his mannerisms, so she knew Quentin was looking for a story to tell her. *Let's hear it. This should be good.*

"Baby, you know I get off work late sometimes, okay? Rick has been on my ass lately about these new software developments, and I've been determined to knock that out. We've been working on it for a few months, and it's taking up most of my time—" he started to explain before Andrea abruptly cut him off.

"That's good." She was chuckling slowly, but it was a laugh that Quentin picked up as sarcasm. "You know, Quentin, I'm always all ears to hear what kind of story that you would come up with, and you never cease to disappoint. If I had a dollar for every excuse you've given me, I'd be making a helluva lot more than I'm making right now!"

Noticing the sharp rise in her tone, Quentin tried his best to deescalate the situation. "Okay, baby, calm down, all right? Don't get worked up for nothing."

"I'm gonna ask you again, Quentin, and this time I want you to tell me everything. Where were you tonight?"

Fidgeting in his shoes, Quentin tried his best not to break in front of the woman that he had intended to marry. "I already told you, I was at work," he replied.

"Don't lie to me, Quentin!" Andrea yelled angrily. "I just got off the phone with Rick, and he told me that the software that was being worked on was fully developed, and you left the office before eleven last night. So, I will ask you one more time, and while you rack your brain looking for another story to tell, make sure you stumble on the right one!"

When Quentin realized that the game was up, he lowered his head.

Andrea angrily brushed a tear away from her eye. "How long have you been seeing her Quentin?"

"Look, Andrea, it's not what you think."

Andrea then rose from where she was sitting and walked over to a cabinet drawer. Opening the drawer, she revealed a yellow manila envelope that was already ripped open from the top. She had already seen its contents, but now she wanted to hear the details of the contents from the source.

Opening the envelope, she pulled out surveillance photos of what appeared to be Quentin exiting work shortly after eleven two nights earlier. She pulled out another set of photos that showed him pulling up to a brownstone home, and the sequence of photos showed Kim opening the door and pulling him inside by his tie as he anticipated another night of intense lovemaking. Then the last group of photos showed Quentin exiting the brownstone and entering his car to leave the premises.

"What's wrong, Casanova? Cat's got yo' tongue now? Or are you still shoving it down that trick's throat? What story are you gonna make out of these tonight, hmmm?"

Quentin looked at the photos in shock. Unbeknownst to him, upon Edward's referral, Andrea had hired a private investigator to follow up on Quentin's activities after work after being suspicious about his late home arrivals. He was positive that he was being discreet in his nightly activities. He had no idea that he was being followed by anyone once he got out of work.

"Where did you get these?"

"Does it matter?"

Quentin looked at Andrea in shock. He always thought she was in his corner, but he realized that she was playing him for a fool, pretending to be in the dark about what was going on but having him followed.

"So, you had someone follow me and take unauthorized photos of me without my consent. Is that it?"

Andrea could not believe what she was hearing. Was Quentin serious right now? "You gotta be kidding me. You're out here screwing some office freak behind my back, and all you're worried about is someone taking unauthorized photos? How could you do this to me?"

Quentin walked over to the doorway, ashamed to face his fiancée, who was on the verge of tears and on the verge of breaking off the engagement entirely. "I didn't mean for it to go down this way. You were so invested in this LaToya Richardson case and getting justice for your sister, we stopped talking like regular people. Emotionally, I was fragile, and Kim came to me at a time when I really needed the support."

"Oh, don't give me that BS! I'm not taking the blame for your insecurities, Quentin! Not anymore. I deserve better than this."

"Yeah, I deserve better than you leaving me out in the cold whenever I want to spend time with you. You'd rather go with your girlfriends than invest in this relationship, and it's too much for me to handle. I'll take a backseat to you when it comes to your music but not when it comes to our relationship."

It was the last straw for Andrea. She stood up and walked over to Quentin. Pulling off her engagement ring that she still was wearing, she handed it over to Quentin. "Then I think it's best if we handle it like this. I think we should go our own way."

Now it was Quentin's turn to beg for another chance. "Drea, come on. I've made a mistake, and I'm sorry for it, but there's no reason to break down what we've built all these years."

Andrea walked over to the window. Staring out into the starry night, she was reflective of her past. "You know, I've been thinking about the people I've been with and people I've encountered over the years and people that I no longer talk to these days. De'Von Franklin, he was an artist on the same label as me, and he was a public figure. When he cheated on me, it hurt, but I understood why. It was because of who he was. Women would go crazy for him, and I did not want to share him with anybody. I guess that's my problem. I love hard, and maybe I love too hard, and people mistake that for weakness, and they take advantage of me."

She walked over to Quentin and for a moment, Quentin was afraid that she would smack him or retaliate by force, but she lovingly caressed his face. "But I thought I found someone different when we got together. My high school prom date...I still remember when you picked up the courage to ask me out. You had those glasses, and you were mad awkward. Vanessa was asking me why I decided to go to the prom with you. There was nothing that stood out about you, but you were honest, kind, and chivalrous. Then when you went to college, and I went into the music industry, we reconnected years later, and even though you grew out of them frames and you filled out, I still saw the shy boy in glasses, and that was who I fell in love with. But I don't see him anymore."

Unable to stop her tears from falling, she walked over to the door. Quentin, whose eyes welled up with tears, was inwardly cursing himself out. How could he have been a fool and not realized who he had? *Andrea was the only girl that was down for me in high school during them awkward years, and I gave it all up for a jump off with Kim.*

"When I needed emotional support from you, where was it? When I needed a shoulder to cry on, where was it?"

"It was always here. I'm sorry I couldn't be there for you all the time. Please don't do this."

But the damage had been done, and there was no point of return. Andrea opened the door and held it open for Quentin.

"I think you should go, Quentin. I'll pack your things, and you can come pick them up in the next couple of days. I don't hate you, but I can't continue this anymore. I hope that girl is everything to you that I'm not."

Taking the cue, Quentin knew it was useless to argue with her. He gathered his work supplies and walked out. Andrea figured that he was going to call a hotel and book a room to stay in for the night, and then after that, it was no longer her concern. As her second ex-boyfriend walked out, Andrea closed the door behind him. Slumping to the floor, she cried uncontrollably. *Lord, what am I doing wrong? Am I cursed to be lonely for the rest of my life?*

The next day at school, Chris focused on an exam about the Mid-Atlantic Slave Trade system. After checking his answers, he handed it to Mr. Thompson. While making his way back to his seat, the bell rang, ending the block period. As students grabbed their belongings, Chris was heading out the room before he was beckoned back into the classroom. He hoped that he was not in trouble. *What's going on?*

It did not escape Chris that Mr. Thompson seemed to look out for him more so than any other student in the class. He treated all the students the same, but Chris seemed to be Mr. Thompson's favorite. Anytime Marlon opened his mouth to give a slick remark about Chris, Mr. Thompson would shut it down right away, and he would always routinely remind Chris not to let his emotions get the best of him.

It had now been three weeks since the infamous fight between Marlon and Chris, and Chris had been working hard in class, handing in all his assignments and steering clear of Marlon as instructed. But Mr. Thompson never missed a chance to give Chris some words of advice.

"You wanted to see me, sir?"

"Yeah, I just wanted to make sure that everything was okay. You're not as engaged in class as you were earlier in the week."

"Yeah, a lot's been going on lately, you know—school, work, the whole nine. I'm cool though."

"You sure that's what's bothering you?"

Chris's eyes darted around nervously. *Why is this dude sweating me?*

"Yeah, but I'll take care of myself. I'm good."

Although Chris did not know about it at first, Mr. Thompson had received word from an unnamed source that a former member of M.O.B. died in prison inexplicably. Mr. Thompson knew that Chris was a former gang member, and if the M.O.B. was doing a bounty, then he was possibly still targeted.

As Chris focused on getting to his next class, he felt a tap on his shoulder.

"What's up, stranger?" Shantay greeted, smiling.

"What's up?"

"Feels like it's been years since we talked. You ain't been around to see me lately."

"Well, I've been working at Associated for four days out of the week, so I ain't had time to chop it up with you."

"It's okay," Shantay replied, hugging his waist. "So, check it out. My older sister is having a kickback at her house, and I was invited to go. She wants me to meet some new man that she's been dating for about two weeks. So, you down?"

"Sounds dope, but when is the kickback gonna happen?" Chris asked.

"It's next Friday at 9:30 p.m. There's gonna be drinks, music, food, and hookah there."

"Damn, for real? I don't think I can come through then cuz I work Fridays."

"Oh, come on, Chris. You mean you can't take a rain check for one day for me?"

"Look, I just started this job, and I'm doing real good now, so the last thing I wanna do is jeopardize my position there."

Shantay laughed as they entered the other side of the building where they shared the same math period. "Chris, they ain't gon' fire you for missing just one damn day. C'mon, please?"

Shantay edged closer to Chris, and he could feel her cool breath on his face. *Mint strawberry. That girl been chewing mint strawberry gum. Her breath is smelling too right. Not to mention, she looking fine as hell right now with them jeans and tight blouse on. How can someone say no to her?*

To increase the tempting offer and the physical allure to attend the party, Shantay leaned forward and kissed Chris on his right cheek. "Please come. I'll definitely make it worth your while," she said.

As they headed inside the math room, Chris thought to himself. *I really don't want to draw attention to myself here. I don't think going to this kickback's a great idea, but I'm just going to accompany her and chill for a few minutes, then take off. I ain't planning on staying. Besides, Officer Renee Anderson's gonna be on my case if I stay too long over there anyway. What's the worst that can happen?*

CHAPTER 18

DIVINE VENGEANCE

TONY HAD BEEN a prisoner of M.O.B. for nearly one month, and he feared for his life every day since being held hostage against his will. But he had lent his accounting services to the gang, and because Tadarius and Pooh still found him useful, he was still alive. He was given a separate one-room flat nearly a block away from the M.O.B. trap house to keep a close watch on him until Edward made an appearance.

Tadarius, although he was a dangerous criminal, held up his end of the bargain after LaToya managed to avoid jail time. But he was not wired to trust anybody, so at night when Tony returned to the flat, which was run-down, insect-infested with paint peeling off the walls, Tadarius normally sent two members of the gang to stand outside his door to keep watch.

Eventually, Tadarius was impressed by Tony's work in keeping the books, and there had been no funny business from him or Edward lately, so in the evenings, Tadarius sent only one member to stand guard outside of his flat instead of two.

On this particular evening, Pablo "Piccolo" Javier was the man on watch. While stifling a yawn, he noticed Cochise approaching the door. Piccolo knew Cochise, and when he approached the door, they dapped, using the usual gang sign.

"T told me to relieve you. I got the rest of the watch," Cochise said.

"Aight, cool. Catch you on the rebound, B," Piccolo said before handing Cochise the keys. Then he turned around to go home.

After standing outside the door for thirty minutes, Cochise made sure that he was not being watched before he turned the key into the lock and walked inside. *Damn, it smells like old cabbage and unwashed gym socks in this piece. Least they could've done was spray some Lysol.*

Walking into one of the rooms, he saw Tony sleeping on a single mattress on the floor. He shook Tony so vigorously, the man woke up with his fists up as if he was ready for a fight.

"Who the hell is this? What you want?" Tony asked sharply.

"It's just Cochise, dawg. Hurry, and wake yo' ass up."

Confused, Tony sat up in the bed, rubbing the fatigue out of his eyes. "What does Tadarius want? And what the hell are you doing here? You keeping watch on me too?"

"Nah, it ain't nothin' like that," Cochise replied, handing Tony a change of clothes and two thousand dollars in cash.

Tony was stunned, staring at the cash in his hands, confused. "What's this for?" he asked.

"Let's just say, you're being bought out of your contract with M.O.B.," Cochise replied.

Tony's facial expression went from surprise to confusion immediately. "So, you mean—" he started to ask before Cochise finished the sentence for him.

"Yeah, we're outta hea'. We ain't got much time, so pack whatever you got, and take this."

Giving Tony an Amtrak train ticket, Cochise finally decided to fill him in on his true intentions. "Look, I'm not really Cochise, all right? I'm an undercover officer for the NYPD, and I've been working with your brother Edward to infiltrate M.O.B., and when the time was right, I was gonna break you outta here."

Tony looked at the man sitting right in front of him until he began wondering if he could trust this individual. When Cochise's story checked out, Tony wasted no time in gathering his clothes and throwing them all in a blue burly knapsack that he had stored with him.

"What's yo' real name then?"

"Caris Grant. Okay, now that we got the specifics out the way, hurry up. I don't know when the other guys will be comin' back, and when they realize you ain't here, they're gonna hunt you down. This ticket will get you a train right to Palmer, New Jersey. There's an Airbnb house on one of the streets there waiting for you. Everything's been taken care of already, and trust me when I say that it's an upgrade from this shithole."

Even though Tony knew that he was breaking out, he still shook his head. Tadarius was a smart guy, and if he could hold Tony hostage for weeks on end, there was no telling what he would do to the other members of his family, not to mention Edward, who was still in his crosshairs.

"You comin' to Jersey too?" he asked.

"Nah, I gotta stay here. Somebody gotta bring this whole thing down."

"Look, man, you've been here long enough to know that ole' boy is crazy. When he figures out I've dipped, he's gonna go into overtime to try to hunt my ass down."

"Don't sweat that, all right. Let me take care of all that. Right now, get your brothers, and get up outta here. I've already made accommodations for you there. You'll have everything you need. When we finally take 'em down, then ya' could come back. But the next week is gonna get hot, and I need you to get out today."

"How's my brother doing?"

"Edward's good. But he ain't comin' with you cuz he has to deal with M.O.B. his way."

"What you mean 'deal with them his way'?"

Cochise closed his eyes, inwardly cursing himself out for opening his mouth. "Look, never mind all that. We got this. Just round up the rest of yo' brothers and go."

Taking heed, Tony finished packing his clothes, and while tying up the bag, he took one more look at Caris. "Look, man, just look out for Edward, man. He was the one that got caught up wit' these cats first, and if he's fightin' them, his head's gonna be on a swivel."

After Tony packed up his things and left the apartment, Cochise took out his phone and texted Edward. When he received confirmation that the message was successfully sent, he then left the flat and went back to his home. He vowed he would not return to M.O.B. because Tony's disappearance would anger Tadarius, and he knew that Piccolo saw him, and he would no doubt put two and two together and figure out that Cochise was involved in Tony's escape. Cochise knew he would be a marked man after this night, so he prepared to change his identity once again as he looked forward to the future.

Back at his home that next day, Edward stood up from bed. He received a text from Caris that read, "Tony's out the trap and he's safe.

I gave him the ticket and told him to go to Jersey with the rest of your brothers."

With the reassurance that his brothers were now safe from Tadarius and M.O.B., Edward had another emotional rollercoaster to contend with: the dynamics of his relationship with Andrea. He wanted to keep his interactions with Andrea as cordial as possible, but he soon realized that he had feelings for her that could not be repressed, despite constantly reminding himself that she was a young woman who was dealing with severe emotional trauma and bouts of depression that all stemmed from when her sister was murdered.

Even though Edward had convinced himself that he was not the person who pulled the trigger, he was in concert with those who pulled the trigger, and Tadarius had given him the deadly mission to carry out. His guilt over not stopping the murder still ate at him as he was now remembered by the gang as the one who cowardly retreated during a mission and left the mob family high and dry.

Although she had been upset that he defended the woman who killed her sister, Andrea regretted striking Edward in the face that day, and their bond grew closer. Andrea recently sent Edward a message inviting him to attend a show at a club where she headlined a performance from amateur and guest singers in the R&B industry.

The Fusion Lounge in South Richmond, New York, had seen better days. The club, which had once been a hot spot for different artists, producers, movie actors, and record execs, was going through a period of economic struggle as Internet livestreaming and large corporations had taken a chunk out of Fusion's regular clientele, and as the attendance dipped, the owner of Fusion was forced to make difficult decisions in order to keep the doors open at one of Queens' most prestigious clubs.

They eliminated Amateur Night, the event that had propelled Andrea to sign a deal with Metro Records at the age of eighteen. Fusion also laid off more than twenty-five percent of its staff and started downsizing the club with the extra space being renovated into a daytime fitness/spa center. It was the only way Fusion could afford to continue paying the lease on the building.

With Fusion hemorrhaging money, they started booking established acts and artists to bring much-needed revenue back into the club. Constance Yardley, the owner of Fusion Lounge was beside herself when Andrea McAfee signed to perform at Fusion Lounge, the place where her singing career launched. It would be a full circle moment for Andrea and for those who were present at the club on the night Andrea brought the house down with her epic performance years earlier. It was also an opportunity for Andrea, whose career needed a boost after the record label's recent money troubles and dwindling tour dates.

When Andrea texted Edward about the event at Fusion, he agreed to attend. Placing a long-sleeved sweater on him and wearing a cap on his head, Edward went to the club, not wanting to be seen or recognized by anyone there because he remembered that the area was heavily occupied by M.O.B. members, so he wanted to remain discreet.

Ordering a glass of Merlot, he sat back and enjoyed the opening artists that performed. After the opening performances concluded, the host introduced Adia to the loud applause from the audience. When she emerged from behind the curtains on stage, Edward had to do a double take because it was a crime how breathtakingly beautiful Andrea was. Her light blue eyeshadow had a hint of glitter, and her natural hair was wrapped in a tight bun behind her. She wore a long, flowing silver dress with slits at the side, showing her long, shapely legs.

Edward took out a handkerchief from his pocket and wiped the perspiration from his head. He was not sweating because of the heat. Rather he was sweating out of nervousness. Andrea's dress, as elegant as it was, did not leave much to the imagination. The sequined gown was slightly see-through, and Edward, inwardly regretting his carnal nature, was wondering how her fiancé could be such a fool to let this exquisite woman out of his grasp.

"Thank you, Fusion! Many years ago, I came to this club as a shy, underaged teenager, not knowing what to expect at the Open Mic night performance. But you've welcomed me, and that night changed my life forever. Now I want to show my gratitude through the songs that I will be performing this evening for you."

Closing her eyes, Adia allowed her emotions to carry her through her first track, which was playing off her first EP that she recorded through Metro Records.

Your touch has got me thinking I'm in love/A sensation pure as the angels sent from above/When you kiss me, my body reacts to the emotion/A love so deep it fills up more than the ocean.

Edward was hypnotized by her words and the lyrics she sang on the first song. It was easy to fall for Andrea if one closed his eyes and allowed her to serenade him.

She ain't like none of these manufactured artists that are out this year. Many of them can't hold a tune to save their lives, but Adia got it all: looks, talent, and stage presence. It's a shame that these artists are not appreciated more in the mainstream.

After Adia finished performing, the crowd roared itself hoarse and screamed for an encore. Adia, who was on the verge of tears because she had never been asked for an encore in a live performance in years, decided to sing one more song for the audience.

When the next song played for the audience, they cheered as they heard her voice harmonizing in the background with De'Von Franklin's voice rapping to the beat, and out he came with his signature styled NY cap. And although now he was a few pounds heavier than he was when he recorded with Adia more than ten years ago, he still showed that he could move his audience.

The crowd went into complete bedlam upon seeing De'Von on stage with Adia again. De'Von, who had spent the last couple of years in obscurity in the industry, was overjoyed to hear his ex-girlfriend when she called him to invite him to the Fusion Lounge to perform once again with her as they had done back in the day.

After apologizing for his part in their break-up, Andrea forgave him and decided to surprise the Fusion audience with a throwback performance of their song.

Boy, you know I got you in a trance/On the dance floor I can feel your glance/The excitement in yo' eyes tells me what I know/ Come wine wit' me as we let da music flow.

Edward smiled and nodded his head as the crowd rocked to the rhythm of the song. It was a great moment because Andrea had mentioned on more than one occasion in each interview that the moment she left Metro Records, she was never going to sing R&B music again, and she had made the transition into gospel music. It was a change that helped Andrea spread her wings and attempt her hand at a different musical genre as well as to display her spiritual journey after the passing of her friend Emiline, who she had once vowed to make a gospel track with before her untimely death.

But as the fans clamored for her to sing the songs that catapulted her into stardom, Andrea decided only for one night to bring the old Adia back, not only to prove to her old fans that she still had some performances left in the tank, but to also boost her own self confidence as well, which had been waning after her break-up with Quentin.

After the duo's performance, the crowd cheered, and Edward joined in. As people began filing out of the club to make their way out into the starry evening, Edward made his way to the door that led backstage.

Holding a bouquet of flowers to give Andrea after her performance, Edward waited outside for about twenty minutes. When she still did not come out, he heard one of the club's employees call out to him.

"Hey sir! Club's closed. You're gonna have to go outside."

Acknowledging the employee, Edward started to make his way out of the club with thoughts of possibly delivering the flowers to her home, when he heard another voice.

"Edward! Leaving so soon? Wait up!" Andrea finally emerged from backstage, wearing a jacket over the dress that she wore for the performance.

"I thought you might've left already. I was headed out."

Andrea walked hastily in her heels to catch up to Edward. "No, I was just tied up backstage for a while." Her eyebrows raised when she saw the flowers in his hands. "Are those for me?"

Edward's eyes shifted nervously. "Oh yeah, here you go. I just wanted to show my appreciation for the show. You were amazing up there today."

Andrea smiled genuinely. "You think so?"

"Yeah, you definitely ain't lost your mojo from that time. You can still sing up a storm. So how was it singing with De'Von again?"

Andrea lowered her eyes. "It was just like old times being up on stage with him again. I think about all the good times when we were on tour, and we're laughing together, joking together and even going out on different dates together. But then, I think about the fallout from our relationship and everything that went down ever since that time, so I'm happy to keep it as just a one-time thing."

"Oh okay, that's cool."

As Edward and Andrea walked outside, she noticed the shift in his body language when she started describing the nostalgic moments with De'Von. He seemed a little aloof and indifferent whenever De'Von was mentioned in her recollections. *If I didn't know any better, I'd say he was jealous of De'Von or the fact that I was with him.*

"By the way, did you drive here? I could walk you to your car," Edward offered.

That is so sweet and gallant of him. "Actually, I didn't drive here today. De'Von sort of gave me a ride here. It was one of his conditions for performing with me tonight."

Edward nodded as if he understood, but in the back of his mind, he wished that De'Von would go back under the rock he had so recently emerged from.

"So that probably means that he'll be giving you a ride back to your house, right?"

Andrea stared at Edward, smiling, and for the first time, batting her eyelashes at him. "Not tonight. I was actually wondering if you could give me a ride back home."

"Word? Oh, well you ain't gotta ask me twice."

Walking Andrea over to his car, he opened his passenger seat for Andrea to enter. Once on the road, Edward asked, "So, forgive me for this stupid question, but why did De'Von insist on giving you a ride to Fusion?"

"He just wanted to catch up with me and see how I was doing. We didn't leave on great terms last time we saw one other, and he wanted to make amends, I guess. I told him I would see him at the club, but he said, 'Nah, baby, I'm driving you there.' He always had a way with words."

Edward could not explain why, but he felt a pang of jealousy towards De'Von, and he did not even know the guy well. *Even as a washed-up rapper, dude still has a net worth of three million, and he's a smooth talker...two things I don't have.*

"As a matter of fact, that was the reason I was still backstage. He wanted to drive me back home, but then he started talking about getting back together because he was the happiest when he was with me, and at that point, I had to shut him down."

Edward tried to hide his look of glee because he felt now maybe there was a chance for him and Andrea. But there was one more person whom he had to be sure was out of the picture as well. "So, how are things going with Quentin?"

It was as if a switch flipped within Andrea when she heard the question. She went from happy to disappointment and consternation. Edward immediately regretted asking the question.

"It's over between us. There's no engagement, and there's no relationship." Andrea bared her left hand, which still had the imprint of the engagement ring she had once wore proudly every day.

"Damn. I'm sorry to hear that. He wasn't so bad, you know, for a L-7 weenie," Edward replied, smiling and wondering if Andrea would get the *Sandlot* reference.

"Boy, stop!" Andrea exclaimed, laughing. "Quentin was not a square, okay?"

"I'm just playing. But I don't know. I see ya'll together in public, and it just never seemed like ya had anything in common."

"Oh really? Please, do explain," Andrea challenged.

"I mean, he was always keeping tabs on you. He never wanted you to do anything fun or go out anywhere. He was the insecure type to me."

Andrea stared at Edward with a mock look of shock. "Wow. Okay, Edward. Tell me how you really feel."

"Look, it ain't like that, Andrea. It's just…you deserve better. Whoever you hook up with in the future, I hope they treat you better than those two clowns did." While Edward kept his eyes on the road, he glanced at Andrea through the dashboard mirror and sensed that she was staring at him.

"I'm right up this street here."

Edward pulled up to her house and parked in a perfect parallel position. Opening the door, he walked around and opened the passenger door so Andrea could get out.

"Well, home sweet home, right? Guess I better get going," he said.

As he turned to head toward the driver's seat, he felt Andrea's hand grab his arm. "Do you wanna come in for something to drink? I think I have some water, ginger ale, or some Moscato or White Zinfadel wine."

Edward stopped in his tracks and walked back towards Andrea, approaching her until they were nose to nose. "Are you trying to get me drunk, Ms. Adia?"

Andrea raised her eyebrow and laughed derisively. "No. I just wanna offer one of my friends a drink. I do that all the time. Is that okay, Mr. Reed?" She answered him teasingly, and she started walking toward the door.

Suddenly, Edward started having dirty thoughts once again. *Damn, the jacket she wearing ain't covering that thang enough. She got a booty on her. I think hers is probably bigger than Loree's was, and Loree wasn't flat by no means.*

Andrea knew Edward was staring at her from behind, and if she swayed her hips right, she would be able to entice him even further. He followed her into the house, and she welcomed him into her living room, where he sat down. After five minutes, she came out holding two glasses of Moscato. It was peach-flavored, which happened to be Edward's favorite.

For a minute, they sipped in silence while Edward looked around. His eyes fell on a framed photo of Andrea at age twelve with Loree, who looked just as beautiful as Edward remembered before her tragic death.

"I have a question to ask you, Edward. What did you think of Loree when she was still alive?"

Edward found himself at a loss for words. The question came out of left field and was not what Edward wanted to talk about. "You mean what did Antonio think of Loree?"

Andrea laughed, which had Edward sighing in relief. He wanted to lighten the mood for the evening.

"Boy, you know what I mean. Obviously, you're Antonio, fool."

"Um…well, from what I remembered, she was headstrong. Confident. She was bad, and she knew it too."

The answer satisfied Andrea. "Yeah, that was her. She always wanted things her way. She used to talk about you sometimes too."

"Really?" Edward asked, surprised.

"Yeah, she would say that her crew started adopting little boys, and they got one of the most nappy headed, tallest little boys she'd ever seen and that his nickname was Tone."

Edward rolled his eyes. He tried everything in his power to block out that deplorable name as it was a reminder of the low-class thug that he used to be. "Listen, Andrea, I'mma keep it a hundred wit' you. I didn't know Loree all too well, but I never had beef wit' her at all. I saw how down she was with everyone that she knew, and some people just couldn't stand her. But I wasn't one of them people."

"I know. You've been so helpful to me, and you've been there since that day in the courtroom when you testified, knowing that they could've killed you for it. You're not just a town hero. You're my hero too."

Edward hung his head. "How? I could've done so much more."

Andrea stared him in the eyes. "You did everything you could, and you're still doing everything you can. I'll never forget that."

With Andrea caressing the back of his head, Edward became intoxicated by her touch rather than the wine going through his system. "You are so beautiful."

Their lips met, and Andrea and Edward were in their own world, unbothered by her relationship drama, and he was unfazed by the gang problem. Slowly unbuttoning his shirt, Andrea ran her hands down Edward's well-toned chest as he slowly unzipped the back of her dress.

"Is this really happening right now?"

The dress slipped off Andrea's shoulder's, revealing her bare chest, and Edward, unable to hold back, buried his head in her chest and kissed her everywhere.

"It's really happening, Mr. Reed."

CHAPTER 19

DIVINE VENGEANCE

IT WAS A FEELING of physical bliss and exuberance for Andrea and Edward as they held each other as if they would be permanently separated if they let each other go. Working his way down her lips, chin, and breasts, which gleamed in the moonlight, Edward was initially reluctant to proceed with his seductive actions. *What am I doing? This girl sings the Lord's music, and here I am, gettin' down with her. But I can't stop. Nor do I want to stop.*

Edward found out very quickly that Andrea was no innocent woman by any stretch of the imagination. She intended to live out all her sensual feelings that she had lacked with Quentin for so many months. Her lack of intimacy with Quentin created sexual frustration that even she could not describe.

Sensing Edward's uncertainty, Andrea whispered seductively in his ear. "It's okay, Mr. Reed. Do what you want with me."

That was all it took for Edward to unleash what Andrea was waiting for, for weeks. Edward buried his head between her legs and used his tongue to pleasure her. He went to work, licking her vaginal spaces and using his finger to rub the moisture out of her. The sensation was so intoxicating that Andrea, who had her hands cupped on her mouth to prevent herself from screaming in pleasure, could no longer hold back, and she moaned in response to Edward's oral skills, releasing all her pent-up frustrations in one dramatic orgasm.

Although it was a cold February night, temperatures were high in Andrea's bedroom as they both made sensuous love. Andrea playfully pushed Edward on his back onto the bed with her feet, laughing in complete satisfaction.

"Oh my God, Mr. Reed! That was intense! What am I gonna do with you?"

Then, Edward took her perfectly manufactured feet and proceeded to suck on her toes, one by one, causing her legs to quiver. "Do whatever you want with me. And call me Eddie. This ain't *Fifty Shades of Gray*."

Andrea replied by getting on top of him, kissing his perfectly chiseled chest, barely able to contain herself by how good he looked shirtless. Pulling her to him, Edward kissed her intensely, and Andrea licked her way down his chest, until her mouth found his throbbing member under his briefs. After two minutes, Edward found himself moaning as Andrea's mouth turned what he thought belonged to him into her very own plaything.

Edward found himself clutching the sides of the bed to prevent himself from ejaculating prematurely. Out of all the women that he had been with, Andrea's oral skills rivaled all of them. *Damn, this girl sucks dick better than I thought. No wonder she had Quentin feening for her for years. Her game ain't no joke.*

Then Andrea truly showed her carnal side, wrapping her breasts around his penis, rhythmically ascending and descending it between them.

Edward laughed in complete euphoria. "Damn, girl, I never took you for a freak like this. I ain't mad at you though. You feel so good, Andrea."

Placing her finger on his lips, she said, "Don't call me Andrea when we gettin' it in. Call me Adia."

Okay, she wanna take control now. I can dig it. I'mma give it to her. "Yes, ma'am."

As Andrea climbed onto Edward, he caressed her breasts, which were soft and supple in his hands, and traced his hands up to her lips, where she started sucking his fingers. They both moved to the tune of each other's bodies, and finally he could not contain himself anymore. He exploded while she was on top of him, and Andrea climaxed as well. After they both were satisfied, Andrea slept on Edward, their bodies covered in perspiration.

As they slept, the room suddenly lit to a bright white color for a moment. Alerted of another presence in the room, Andrea opened her eyes, and there she stood, staring at her with an expression of both serenity and concern as she looked at the man and woman in bed.

Loree McAfee was just a few feet from the foot of the bed. She was wearing a flowing white gown and glowed dazzlingly white, which contrasted to the cold, lifeless, individual that was in the casket on her funeral day.

Edward did not stir from his sleep. Perhaps he had not seen the light that exuberated from the ethereal being in her room, but Andrea was convinced she was dreaming, which was why she was not alarmed. Loree routinely visited her, especially during the difficult few years following her murder.

"Loree, what you doing here?"

Loree walked over to her sister and caressed her chin. Even though Andrea was now in her late twenties, and Loree still resembled her eighteen-year-old form, she laid her head against Loree's waist.

"I could ask you the same question, Drea. Why are you making love to one of my killers?"

Andrea drew her head back from her late sister. "No, ReRe, not Edward. He had nothing to do with your death. He's a good guy who's been there for me."

"It doesn't matter, Drea. He was with the people that took me away from you. Why did you hurt me like this?"

Tears fell from Andrea's eyes. She could not believe what Loree was saying. "You're wrong, ReRe. Edward don't want anything to do with M.O.B. Your true killer has already been caught. I have feelings for Edward, and he's determined to see justice for you."

"Is he? Or is he dragging his feet to protect his crew? How do you know he ain't leading you to the same trap he led me?"

Before Andrea could reply, Edward suddenly stirred next to her. After realizing that he was not waking up, Andrea turned back to where her sister stood, but she had already disappeared.

Andrea was not sure whether she closed her eyes again, or if she stayed awake, but when the few cracks of dawn appeared through the window, she looked up at Edward, who was still sleeping soundly. *What have I done? I mean I enjoyed last night. It was the best lovemaking experience I've had in years. Before Edward, I've only slept with two other men, and both never took their time to love me and care for me like him. But is Edward the one? Or am I playing a dangerous game?*

While these thoughts ran through Andrea's mind, she felt him stirring next to her. Edward did not wake up immediately, rather he repositioned himself in bed, turning at an angle that allowed Andrea to wiggle herself free from under him. Taking slow steps so she would not wake him, Andrea went to her bathroom. Splashing water on her face, she stared at the mirror. She had a few drinks last night with

Edward, and it exceeded her normal alcohol consumption for years. The headache that she felt was evident of her unusual drinking.

But she remembered last night, and it was the most beautiful romantic night that she'd had in years. What was it that drove her to her actions? Was it a mixture of grief, anger, jealousy, and spite that she felt toward Quentin, or was it the growing infatuation she now felt with Edward? Both possibilities were true, and Andrea was not sure where she was with anyone, and she did not know how far her relationship with Edward would carry her.

Hearing her wash her face in the bathroom, Edward woke up. Upon realizing that she was not lying down in bed with him, he rubbed his eyes. "Baby, you okay?" Checking his phone, which was nearly dead because he had left his charger at home, he realized he had to return home to prepare for work.

"Yeah. I'm fine, Eddie."

But Edward knew Andrea was reflecting on last night, and he wanted to find out where her mind was the morning after. "Lemme ask you something. Do you regret what happened last night?"

The question threw Andrea off because she was still questioning herself and her role in the entire ordeal. "Last night was amazing. It's been a long time since I've felt this way, and I just don't know what comes next."

Getting up out of bed, Edward walked into the bathroom and massaged Andrea's shoulders. She looked at Edward's toned abs and strong hands as they gently caressed her shoulders. *Oh my God, he looks even better in the morning. Get a grip, Andrea. Control yourself. You've already failed the first temptation test last night. Don't fail it again this morning. I've got to withstand this.*

Edward sensed Andrea's apprehension while massaging her, and he was not sure where he was on Andrea's mind.

"I'm willing to find out if you are."

Chuckling, Andrea took Edward's hands and kissed them. "Are you sure, Mr. Reed? Cuz my life is pretty much a mess right now. I wouldn't blame you if you didn't want to stick around."

"Hey, I'm not gonna leave you now," Edward reassured Andrea. "I'm still determined to see that your family gets justice and make sure Tadarius doesn't hurt you or anyone again. I mean that." Wrapping his hands around Andrea, Edward kissed her on the cheek.

"Speaking of, I have to get back home and get ready for work. Is it cool to call you when I get off so we can talk about us?"

Andrea raised an eyebrow and smiled sarcastically at Edward. "Boy, you better call me when you get off, or you might come up missing."

Edward laughed at the joke threat. It felt good to be with someone who shared his sense of humor. "I got you. I always got you, no matter where or when."

"All right. I'm gonna hold you to that."

Edward washed his face and brushed his teeth with a spare, unused toothbrush that Andrea kept in her bathroom vanity. He did not mind using it, given that it did not share the same DNA as the cheating chump that Andrea once shared her home with.

Chris stumbled outside, donning his favorite Nike hoodie and fitted cap. Waking up late, past his alarm, he managed to brush, shower, and grab a Pop-Tart from the pantry before heading out. He missed the first bus, so he walked over to the stop to catch the next one to school. Dennis, Cree, and Katrina had already left for school.

Renee decided to allow her kids independence after weeks of dropping them off to school by allowing them to take the bus on their own to go to school. Dennis would accompany his sisters by taking one bus line to go to middle school while dropping Katrina at elementary school along the way, and Chris took another bus line to go to Townsend Harris.

He was stuck at work late the night before, cleaning up an aisle mess just minutes before he was due to clock out. A kid had accidentally spilled a bottle of Juice-Up fruit punch on Aisle 8, and because Chris was the only stock employee still working at that time, he was left to clean the mess. It took nearly half an hour to clean the aisle, mopping it up and placing a caution sign over the spillage area. By the time Chris got off and took the next bus home, it was thirty minutes after midnight. He barely remembered getting into bed.

To make matters worse, in his haste, he forgot to complete a workbook assignment for Mr. Thompson's History class, something that he had stayed consistent with over the semester. Mr. Thompson assigned students weekly workbook exercises to complete in preparation for his quizzes and although Chris found them pointless and cumbersome, he always managed to complete them on time, until this morning.

Inwardly cursing himself and the kid who spilled the juice at the store, Chris headed to school, expecting to receive his first zero on the assignment, and it was certainly going to drop his overall grade. He had managed to maintain a B average in school thus far, and Renee began to trust him more at the house.

After getting off at his stop, Chris made his way to school when he saw Shantay talking to another boy, whom Chris recognized as a senior. Although Chris and Shantay never made it official that they were exclusive, he could not help but to feel a pang of jealousy. The girl was not shy about putting out for other boys, and Chris was weary about her.

Charity's words were on repeat in Chris's head: *She likes guys like you as long as she could get something from you—either money, rep, or she might just wanna fuck. But once she gets what she wants, she's on to the next one.*

Maybe this senior was the next one. Making his way to Mr. Thompson's class, Chris opened the door to a surprise. An older white male sat at Mr. Thompson's desk, which was confusing to Chris.

As the other kids filed in, including Shantay and Marlon, the last bell rang, and the man stood up to address the class. "Good morning, class. My name's Mr. Daniels, and I'll be subbing for Mr. Thompson for three days. He's away on a business trip and will return next Monday morning. He's given me the lesson plan and advised me where everyone is on this block, so with that said, please open your textbooks to page sixty-eight."

Chris found it difficult to contain his smile because not only had Mr. Daniels failed to bring up the workbook assignment to collect, which bought Chris time to make it up, but Chris would also not have to worry about Mr. Thompson's close watch of him. But the day that he saw his teacher in the car with a confirmed member of M.O.B. raised questions in Chris's mind, and he could not help but to wonder. *Where is Mr. Thompson, and what kind of business is he involved in?*

LAKE GEORGE, NEW YORK

The luxury stretch limo pulled up in front of the dock at Lake George, New York, and after the vehicle parked, the driver opened his door and made his way to the passenger side towards the rear end of the limo. Opening the door, he gestured to a young lady to step out.

Bunny stepped out of the limo and looked around. She was not in familiar haunts. This area was as far removed from the city as anything she knew. Having been upstate for two days, Bunny had been showered with gifts and luxury since she stepped foot in the area.

A few days before he liberated Tony, Cochise received an offer from a perspective, affluent real estate tycoon by the name of Percy Blackwood. Cochise knew that Tadarius had always had ambitions of tapping into the real estate industry while still selling weapons and drugs at a premium, and he was always looking for partners in this venture.

So when he was approached by Cochise with the opportunity to increase his cashflow and the area in which to expand his empire, Tadarius leaped at the opportunity and was enthusiastic to take on another client and add him to the M.O.B. family. But inexplicably, Tadarius began to feel sick, but while he dismissed his condition as a common cold, he recruited Bunny to represent the family on the trip to close the deal with Mr. Blackwood on a partnership with M.O.B.

When Cochise showed Bunny the picture of Mr. Blackwood, her jaw nearly dropped, astounded by how gorgeous he looked. So, she did not delay in participating in the deal, which she hoped to close on in more ways than one. Graciously, Mr. Blackwood had arranged for Bunny to be picked up by his private limo and whisked to a nearby hotel near Lake George, where she would enjoy fine living and every decadence the hotel had to offer. The penthouse room was set with bottles of Moet, hookah pipes, and a pound of weed.

Bunny, who smoked routinely, did not waste time in sparking up on the first night at the hotel. But she did not see Mr. Blackwood the first night, and it struck her odd that he did not introduce himself to her the first night that she arrived. *Where is this man at? I want to show him my appreciation for all this. No better way to do it than in person.*

I might not kill this one. He's so fine, I may have to keep him all to myself. He got them washboard abs, unlike that fat clown Mr. Khaimov, whose got a paunch so fat, kids mistake him for Santa Clause at Christmas time.

Later in the evening, she received a text from an unknown contact, informing her that Mr. Blackwood would be arranging the same limo to pick her up from the hotel and drop her off near the dock, where she would be joining Mr. Blackwood on a luxury yacht. There, he would treat her to dinner, and they would be discussing the partnership with Tadarius and M.O.B. Bunny dressed in her finest sky-blue dress, which was low cut at the top, revealing her cleavage, and she was wearing her finest Jimmy Choo stilettos. She made sure she showered, washed, and bath for over two hours before dressing up because she wanted her mere presence to intoxicate Mr. Blackwood.

The limo had gourmet chocolates in the fridge, and Bunny, who was a huge chocolate lover, ate about three of them. Two of the chocolates were caramel-filled and had a strange aftertaste when she swallowed them, but she eliminated the bitter taste by drinking some red wine that was also in the car.

When Bunny walked onto the dock, she saw the yacht. It was a basic two-deck luxury mariner with lights and a clear holding bar for the edge of the deck, and in the middle of the wide first deck, there was a small, decorated table, complete with two towel doves' beaks meeting as if they were kissing. A card reading, "Welcome Bunny!" lay on the table.

Wow, this is sweet. No man has gone through lengths to do this for me. Well, Tony has tried, but he just don't have the money that Mr. Blackwood has. He is finna get all the goods tonight.

Finally, after boarding the yacht and taking it all in, Bunny made her way to the table with the doves, and two candles were lit. There were two covered plates awaiting them. Bunny uncovered one, which revealed fettuccini and veal. Hearing a door open behind her, Bunny turned around on full alert. Mr. Blackwood emerged from below deck with a bottle of Settle House white wine.

"Mr. Blackwood, to whom do I owe this wonderful reception?" she asked.

Mr. Blackwood was the very definition of tall, dark, and handsome. He smiled serenely at Bunny and pulled out her chair for her so that she could sit. Bunny, who suddenly felt slightly light-headed, but shook the sensation away, sat down.

"You don't owe anyone, Ms. Tina, and may I add that you look absolutely beautiful in that dress."

Even though she had received her share of compliments from other men, most of whom were no longer alive, there was a way Mr. Blackwood complimented her that caused her to blush. "Thank you, Mr. Blackwood."

"You're welcome. Now why don't we have some dinner?"

With his fork, Mr. Blackwood tapped the side of his glass, and a server came out from under the deck, where Bunny assumed the kitchen area was located. The server placed a calamari dish next to Bunny's main plate and then placed an identical dish next to Mr. Blackwood's. Bunny, who was no stranger to fine dining because of her call girl days, folded her napkin on her waist and began to dine on the calamari.

It was exquisite as the whole presentation, from the dinner to its flawless host, was unmatched. But Bunny felt uneasy, not only because the light-headedness sensation had re-emerged, but she also could not understand the reason for Mr. Blackwood's expensive treatment on her behalf.

"Mr. Blackwood, I want to tell you that I'm thoroughly impressed with your presentation, but it seems as if you think you can wine and dine me into accepting your partnership, and I'm afraid it takes a little bit more than this to impress my employer."

Mr. Blackwood chuckled and waved his hand dismissively as if to state that it was not his intention to bribe her with hotels and dinners. "I completely understand your position, Ms. Tina. My intention is to explain why I believe M.O.B. LLC and Blackwood Enterprises can create a firm partnership. I have spoken with Tadarius Hill and his representatives, and he is aware of the number that I'm willing to invest to my shareholders to forge this union."

Mr. Blackwood then pulled out a folder from a briefcase that he carried with him.

Bunny, who was always observant, noticed specific initials on his briefcase. "Mr. Blackwood, what does the THHS on yo' briefcase stand for?"

Mr. Blackwood looked at her curiously, as if he did not understand what she had asked before looking on his briefcase. "Oh, this old thing? I've had this briefcase for a while now. I never really paid attention to what it meant. I just needed a place to carry all my documents."

While they continued eating, Mr. Blackwood went over the value of the amount that he was willing to pay M.O.B. to embark on a joint business venture. Bunny did her best to listen to him, but she found her eyes drooping at times. She became even more light-headed than she was earlier, and now her vision was beginning to blur. *What is wrong with me? I feel like shit right now. Was it something I drank or ate that got me feeling like this?*

But she dismissed her own personal suffering and focused as best as she could on Mr. Blackwood. She could not quite put her finger on it, but his face resembled that of a man she knew in the past. She was not sure if it was an ex-boyfriend or a victim as there were so many of them, so they all seemed to blur, just like her vision.

"Mr. Blackwood, I'm sorry, but can I be excused? I need to freshen up for a minute. Where is your bathroom?"

"Sure, just down these steps on the first deck and to the right."

Making her way over to the bathroom, Bunny nearly lost her footing while walking down the stairs to the lower deck, saving herself by holding onto the railing. Stumbling to the bathroom, she splashed water on her face and examined her eyes. They were nearly bloodshot, and suddenly, without warning, the contents of her dinner forced their way back up, and Bunny leaned over the toilet and heaved heavily, vomiting into the toilet.

Expecting the excursion of food from her system to heal her, Bunny still felt lightheaded. Placing her hand to her chest, she could feel her heart beating rapidly like a drum, and sweat rolled down her face. As a former medical assistant before her days with M.O.B., Bunny knew the side effects of a person who had harmful chemicals coursing through his or her system, so it did not take long for her to realize that she had been poisoned.

She needed to get off of the yacht and find help immediately. Kicking the bathroom door open, she rushed out, but with her vision blurred and odd shapes appearing in her line of vision, she collapsed at the foot of the staircase, unable to summon the force to walk up the stairs. Time seemed to slow down before she felt her head being cradled by Mr. Blackwood.

"What happened? What the hell did you do to me?" *Did this fine specimen of a man just poison me?*

She was not sure if she imagined it or if it really happened, but she saw a cold smile curl the lips of Mr. Blackwood before it was met with a solemn grim look.

"A long time ago, you went out with my brother. He was also affiliated with M.O.B. He put in work for Tadarius, David, LaToya, Malik, and all you other weak-minded muthafuckas, and what did he get? He got nothin' but death."

Bunny began to slip in and out of consciousness, unaware that she was part of a plot to eliminate M.O.B. in retribution for the death of one of its own members. Before she blacked out, she saw Mr.

Blackwood's eyes as tears welled up in them, and before he mentioned the name, she finally remembered who he was.

"Imagine my mama gettin' a call from the New York Coast Guard, saying they found Theo at the bottom of the Hudson River. They said random hit, but I know ya killed him. Now it's yo' turn to swim wit' the fishes."

A few minutes later, Tina "Bunny" Richardson suffered cardiac arrest, and after he tossed her motionless body overboard, Sean Brunsen-Thompson watched Bunny disappear into the depth of the sea.

CHAPTER 20

DIVINE VENGEANCE

Two Weeks Earlier

MR. THOMPSON LEFT Associated Food Source with his bags of groceries, grateful that he was finally able to find time to do some shopping. Aside from being a high school History teacher, Sean Brunsen-Thompson was also a real estate investor and part-time Wall-Street broker who dabbled in cryptocurrency, so he had multiple streams of income that allowed him to amass a certain amount of wealth. But no amount of money could fill the emptiness of his heart.

Having been married, then divorced, Mr. Thompson was in his late forties and lived as a single bachelor in Queens, where he also completed his formal education. Graduating from Springfield High School and St. John's University, Mr. Thompson held a bachelor's degree in World History, a master's degree in Education, and was working on his PhD program while also teaching at Townsend Harris High School.

He loved his job, and he loved teaching children, but he always felt that there were certain types of children that did not warrant his teachings, and those were the kids who thought learning was a waste of time, kids who would rather hang out in the streets at all hours of the night, getting into trouble with themselves and with the law. Mr. Thompson was no stranger to the streets. He easily could have been drawn into the life of trapping and gangbanging, but if it were not for his older brother encouraging him and steering him away from the life, he might have been coerced into it.

Theo was a few years older than Sean, and he was the darling of the family. Normally, the baby of the family typically received more attention from the family, but that was not the case for the Brunsen family as Theo would often receive more of the attention, which often made Sean envious. But as they grew older, Theo learned to appreciate his brother.

Then he found out that Theo got mixed up with a local street gang that called themselves M.O.B. Theo had just started college, and he ran his tuition fees dry. One day while looking for a job, he was confronted by someone who offered him an opportunity to make fast money selling drugs, and unbeknownst to Sean at the time, the man who offered Theo the job was a member of M.O.B. Although Theo felt strange about this line of work, he could not deny the payday that he would receive, which would help pay for his fees.

Theo met his employer, Tadarius, and his associate David Anderson, who was still in high school. While working the streets, Theo fell for a young lady who was street smart, wily, and gorgeous. Tina Richardson was a laid-back girl, someone who used to visit the Brunsen family on several occasions, and Theo was happy to introduce his new girlfriend to the family. Tina took a liking to Sean and always stated that he would be a perfect addition to the M.O.B. family one day.

But Theo one day made the mistake of shaving too much money from Tadarius's cut. When he found out, Tadarius was enraged, and from that time, it was decided that Theo had to pay. Tina, whose true loyalty was with the gang and its notorious leader, went by to accompany Theo on what seemed like a date.

Sean remembered the day as if it were yesterday. He had asked Theo to give him a ride to the park to play basketball that day. Theo had a green Mazda that he earned from months of working with the gang. But Theo told Sean he was busy and that Tina wanted to see him. Sure enough, Tina came along. However, there was a different tone to her on that day. Normally very reserved, Tina appeared impatient as if pressed for time and asked Theo to hurry up and get ready.

At the time, Sean was not appreciative of the sudden switch in moods when it came to Tina. Theo waved goodbye to Sean and promised he would give him a ride to the park another time. That time never arrived because it would be the last time Sean saw Theo alive.

When his family had not heard from him, they reported Theo missing and posted flyers everywhere. The police brought in various people to question for more information, but nobody knew of Theo's whereabouts, and Tina, his supposed girlfriend, suddenly vanished.

Then a local fisherman at the Hudson River noticed a strange object floating in the water. Theo's body, which had been submerged underwater for weeks, floated up in plain sight, and the authorities were called. They could not even identify the body until they saw a billfold with his school ID in it, which finally identified him.

The Brunsen family's world crashed that evening as the autopsy revealed that Theo had been slashed several times with a bowie knife at close range. Then the blow that finally killed him was the cut across his neck, which severed his carotid artery. His body was then dumped in the Hudson River to dispose of the evidence. Although Theo's murder was never solved, there was no doubt in Sean's mind that Tina and whoever Theo sold drugs for, were responsible for his demise.

Sean tried for weeks to report M.O.B. to the police, but without substantial evidence tying him to the crime, Tadarius was still a free man. From that moment forward, Sean decided to take matters into his own hands. If the police would not seek justice for Theo, then he would. He then put his plan into motion.

Adding the last name of Thompson over the years, Sean closely watched and made secret alliances with various professed members of M.O.B. to get close to Tadarius while focusing on his own career. Working at Townsend Harris, he recognized one of the gang members, David Anderson, who had now reformed himself at this time and had a family of his own.

Sean initially had animosity for David for no other reason than the fact that he was part of the crew that killed his brother. But David renounced M.O.B. and separated himself from the gang. As a witness, David even shared the details of Theo's last night alive with Sean and told Sean that Tina led Theo into a trap, and Tadarius confronted Theo about missing money. He proceeded to slice up Theo as if he were Freddie Krueger and had his body disposed of at the river.

David did not come forward to the police with the story, perhaps out of fear of retaliation by the gang. But he encouraged Sean to go after them, and for weeks he scouted his first target—Tina, or as everyone liked to call her, Bunny—and he started plotting her demise.

Now emerging from the store, Mr. Thompson made his way to his car when he saw a figure leaning against it. Recognizing him, he opened the door while the man sat in the passenger seat. Caris, a police detective who was infiltrating M.O.B. as ruthless gang member Cochise shook Mr. Thompson's hand.

Both men had been contacted by Edward Reed, and together they plotted to take the gang down from within. Two minutes later,

Chris ran out with the celery that Mr. Thompson had forgotten. After Chris re-entered the store, Mr. Thompson turned to Caris.

"Has Edward briefed you yet?"

Caris nodded. "Yeah, he said everything is in place for that weekend. I've managed to get their trust. But I gotta tell you, Tadarius is one crazy bastard, so you can't confront him with kid gloves."

"Nah, you ain't gotta worry about that. We stick with the plan. We cut down his guard, one by one, starting with her," Mr. Thompson replied, referring to Bunny.

Caris rubbed his forehead. It was not his nature to look the other way whenever somebody clearly mentioned killing another person. But Caris wanted to see M.O.B. off the streets as much as anybody, but he wanted to do it the right way, without casualties. "You sure there ain't no other way?"

Mr. Thompson's eyes glowered in deep concentration. "You weren't there, man. Imagine getting the call from the Coast Guard and NYPD saying they found yo' brother who'd been missing for years. They call you to morgue at the hospital to identify him. I never got to say goodbye to him."

Looking at the vanity mirror, Caris realized that Mr. Thompson had a wallet-sized photo of Theo attached to the mirror. Caris shook his head. He understood the need for vengeance, and after living with the gang for weeks, Bunny was one of Tadarius's right-hand ladies, the one he used most in the parlays and deals with underworld figures and business investors.

"What else do you know about her?"

Caris looked at Mr. Thompson, and a sly smile crossed his face. "Did I tell you that she loves gourmet chocolate?"

That was all it took for Mr. Thompson to devise his plan. As a student of history and science, he was familiar with different poisonous plants around the world. He learned how to extract juices and poisons from certain plants during his college days. He would inject the gourmet chocolates that he would gift Bunny within the limousine, and if she did not resist or ate the chocolates right away in the car, she would eventually eat them, and the poison that he injected would course through her body, causing cardiac arrest and death.

"Thanks for the heads-up."

Looking back towards the entrance where they saw Chris bagging groceries, Caris asked, "Is that him? David Anderson's kid? He's a spitting image of his pops."

"Yeah, that's him. One of the last things his old man told me before he passed was to make sure his kids were safe. I've been watching him like he was my own child."

Mr. Thompson looked at Caris again. "Let's do this for David, Theo, and everyone else who fell victim to the fake family."

PRESENT DAY

On Friday morning at the M.O.B. trap house, the scene was chaotic as Tadarius stormed the rooms in fury. It was not just the fact that Tony was missing without a trace, and Cochise was also in the wind, but Bunny had not been heard from in days. Tadarius tried calling her cell and left her a dozen messages, but not one call was returned. It was not like Bunny to ignore calls from the Fam. *Where the hell is she?*

Tadarius wanted to know if the deal with Mr. Blackwood was successful, but without Bunny's confirmation, he became more uneasy and unhinged. Two random members of M.O.B. were laughing, playing video games on the TV as if they were drama free. With his fury reaching uncontrollable levels, Tadarius went to the TV and unplugged the box to the dismay of the players.

"Yo, what the fuck, T?"

"What'd you say to me?" Tadarius threatened, with a tone indicating he was not in the mood.

The member who blared the question remained silent.

"Playing video games and being a waste of space, that's all ya know how to do. Open yo' eyes and realize we in some shit right now. If any of ya were real ridas, ya would help right now."

In his fury, Tadarius seemed physically weak. His voice dropped from his normal high-pitched command voice to a voice of someone struggling to breathe. While pacing in place, Tadarius continued coughing rapidly, which concerned his followers.

Turning to Pooh, Tadarius said, "Listen, I know that he had something to do with this. Leave a message. He thinks he can do this to me and get away with it?"

There was no doubt that he was talking about Antonio. Jermaine, Solieks, Andrew, and Kendra got up and started getting their inventory and supplies for the day, when Tadarius unexpectedly put his hands on his chest, heart pounding rapidly, and he started sweating profusely. Loosening his tank top, Tadarius made his way to the kitchen area, and it was there that the other members heard a loud thud coming from the kitchen. Rushing into the kitchen, they saw Tadarius lying unconscious on the floor.

"Oh shit! Yo, J, call 911. Now!" Pooh exclaimed as they called 911 to their spot.

While the health of the notorious gang leader hung in the balance at Queens General Hospital on Friday evening, Pastor Michael Hillman unlocked the doors to the Rock of Jacob Baptist Church in Richmond

Hill. As he turned on the lights to the sanctuary, he waited for the sound technician and musicians to arrive.

Friday nights were usually the nights that he conducted Bible study for college students and young adults. He had Bible study for married couples and older members of his church on Wednesday nights in addition to the normal Sunday morning services. Pastor Mike, as his members referred to him, was grateful to finally have a sanctuary for the young adults, which was a ministry that he had prayed for, for years.

Having been pastor of the church for over twenty-five years, Pastor Mike and his wife, Robyn Hillman, had begun a spiritual journey for their family as well as the community. He wanted to rehabilitate Richmond Hill and Queens, which had seen their fair share of gang activity, drug dealing, police brutality, and prostitution.

After a series of meetings with the New York Clergy Evangelical Commission and days of prayer, Pastor Mike was able to convince them to give him permission to hold Friday night Bible study at the church for young people. He sympathized with the upcoming generation, and he saw the spiritual guidance that he could provide them with through the Word of God.

One of his inspirations for beginning this ministry was his daughter, Shania Hillman-McClain. His daughter had been heavily involved in ministry since she was a young girl, and she aided on Sundays, singing with the choir and teaching Sunday school for the younger students. Shania went through a dark period in her life when her best friend, Loree McAfee, was brutally murdered, and she spent days blaming herself for Loree's death.

It was not until later that Shania realized that Loree had been living a double life for most of her teenage years, with her secret life working on street corners and associating with the gangs of the area. Shania also dealt with family secrets and betrayal when her boyfriend at the time, Trevor McClain, who is now her husband, discovered that he was adopted and that his biological mother had been killed in a botched drug deal and that his father abandoned him as a baby. It left Trevor wondering if anyone loved him and trusted him. If Shania had not been by his side during the most difficult part of his life, he could have fallen victim to depression and uncertainty for his future.

Pastor Mike himself was going through a rough period in his life because he had experienced infidelity for the first time in his life and ministry. He made the terrible mistake of being intimate with a member of his church, which caused waves of gossip among the community, and it almost threatened to destroy his family and his union with Robyn.

But both Robyn and the Lord had given him a second chance, and he decided to take full advantage of that second chance. Not too long after their marriage hit that unexpected roadblock, Robyn and Mike renewed their vows and continued their ministry. Michael's church family increased in member population, and he was pleased that people from his past were starting to join the ministry.

Pastor Mike's old friend Nate Plummer, the former drug dealer who, like Mike, was a former high school athlete, reunited with his best friend and finally started to attend church services regularly every Sunday. He even found love after years of seeking revenge for an old friend's death and constant bitterness in his heart. Felicia Givens, a middle-aged boutique store owner had taken interest in Nate, who was currently the basketball coach at his old alma mater, Richmond Hill High School. They began dating, and not too long after, they tied the knot. It was Nate's old friend Michael Hillman who had married the couple at his church, and it was the most joyous occasion that he remembered, along with the birth of Michael's granddaughter, Loree Emiline McClain.

As young college students who were members of the church began to arrive, Pastor Mike greeted each of them at the door as he usually did every Sunday. Pastor Mike was not a stereotypical pastor that only greeted certain people and shouted at the pulpit for shock value. One of the reasons that Pastor Mike was beloved in the community was the fact that he was genuine. He generally cared for anyone in all walks of life and welcomed everyone into his church doors. He did not care about a person's sexual orientation or their background because Jesus welcomed everybody around him.

"He doesn't love your sins, but He is still open to everybody who is willing to walk in and accept Him," Pastor Mike would always say.

Shania McClain led the small group in praise and worship to start the Bible study before her father took over to talk about the subject of the day.

"I would like to welcome everybody to Friday night Bible study," he addressed in his deep voice as he opened his Bible. Although Pastor Mike was still strong from his days as a football player, signs of age began showing, from the specks of gray hair on his beard, to the slight hunch in his back.

Before the Bible study began, Shania had told her father that a special guest would be attending that evening, but as Pastor Mike looked around, he only saw the members who normally attended Bible Study.

"Today, our Word will be found in the letter of Paul to the Romans, Chapter 12 verse 19. It reads, 'Beloved, never avenge yourselves, but leave it to the wrath of God, for it is written, Vengeance is mine, I will repay, says the Lord.' Brothers and sisters, we all have that one person or group of people who have wronged us throughout our lives, and it is natural for us to want revenge on those who did us wrong, whether it's our own family members, our friends, our co-workers, or a person that just cut you in line at the local bodega."

The last example drew some chuckles and laughs from those in attendance.

"But I'm here to tell you today, do not become a victim of your own anger. Don't let your emotion cloud your judgment, and most importantly, don't allow it to compromise your faith."

One of the attendees raised her hands, and Pastor Mike paused his lesson to allow the person to speak, which made Friday night Bible study more interactive. The pastor wanted an open forum for debate and conversation. He did not want the same environment as Sunday morning, where everybody would just sit and listen to him speak for a lengthy amount of time. He wanted participation from those who attended.

"So, Pastor, you mean to tell me that if someone hurts me, I'm supposed to turn around and not do nothin'?" she asked.

Pastor Mike chuckled. He knew this subject would bring a lot of questions to the forefront, and he expected the reaction. "I know it sounds extremely difficult to do because as human beings, we're wired to react or run. But the Lord is fighting your battles, and those are battles that you don't often see. Let me put another verse on you. Deuteronomy chapter 32 verse 35 says, 'Vengeance is mine, and recompense, for there is a time when their foot shall slip; for the day of their calamity is at hand, and their doom comes swiftly.' That means that God already has a plan for your detractors because those who have wronged you are bound to slip up one day, and their day of reckoning is at hand. So, you will not need to lift a finger because the Lord wants you to keep your heart. Don't lose it on account of someone who's not worth losing it over."

As he continued teaching, the doors opened, and the surprise guest Shania was referring to walked into the sanctuary. The church was silent in shock and amazement as Andrea McAfee walked down the pews and looked for a place to sit by herself. The other members could scarcely believe it. Most of the attendees to the Friday night Bible study did not attend church on Sundays, so they were not aware that Andrea used to lead the choir on Sunday mornings. They only saw Adia, the R&B and gospel artist, and she was in their midst.

Shania smiled at Andrea as she glanced around nervously and opened her Bible to the highlighted verse of the evening. Andrea did not ask any questions. She just sat quietly and listened as the study continued.

Finally, when it ended, and most of the members walked out for the evening, many of them, as usual, asked Andrea for a picture, and she was happy to pose for them.

Shania was the last to leave the sanctuary. "Girl, you have to stop being a stranger every time you walk up in here." Hugging Andrea tightly, she sensed that Andrea was troubled. "Are you okay?"

Andrea tried to convince her spiritual sister that she was fine, but Shania knew Andrea from when she was a little girl, and she knew when she had a heavy heart.

"I'm good, 'Nia. Just trying to get a grip on life, you know."

"Oh, I know. Trust me."

"So, how's my little Loree doing?" Andrea asked, referring to Shania's daughter.

"She ain't so little anymore, and boy does she keep me and Trevor running around. Girl, she got a lot of energy for five years old. And she keeps on asking me, 'Where's Auntie Drea?'"

Andrea laughed. She regretted not taking more time out to visit her goddaughter and the family more, but due to her schedule, recording, touring, and making appearances, family visits were few and far between.

"Tell her that Auntie Drea will be coming by soon, and she'll be coming with a gift too."

"I definitely will. Thanks again for coming."

"No problem. I miss coming here. It always brings me back to the old days with you teaching Sunday school, and we were in class with Jamal, Omar, and Loree…"

Andrea's voice trailed off when she realized two of the names she mentioned were no longer among the living. Omar Keaton had been tragically murdered in a drive-by years earlier, but his widow and his son would often attend Rock of Jacob Baptist Church upon Jamal Samuel's invitation. Jamal still attended from time to time, but with his busy professional basketball career, he was unable to attend frequently. However, his wife, Tracy, and his newborn daughter, Onyx, still attended church services each Sunday.

"Hey, we have to continue living for them. It's what they would have wanted," Shania replied.

"You're right. It was great seeing you though. Say hi to Loree and the bighead for me."

Shania laughed, knowing that Andrea was referring to Trevor. "I will, sweetie. Take it easy, okay?"

After Shania left, Andrea walked to the pastor's office, where Pastor Mike was filling out the church attendance and offering sheets. Looking up, he beamed proudly when he saw Andrea. Standing up from his desk, he gave her a fatherly embrace.

"When Shania told me that a special guest was coming, I didn't know she meant a superstar. How have you been?"

Andrea smiled. Out of all the spiritual leaders and pastors that she had encountered in her life, especially during her most traumatic moments, Pastor Mike was always present, praying for her family and encouraging her. Pastor Mike had every right to avoid the McAfee's after one meeting following Loree's death where they asked Mike to stand witness against David Anderson, the suspect accused of killing Loree.

When Mike refused to accuse David, Amos McAfee stood up almost face to face with Pastor Mike, and it almost came to blows. Andrea was present during that tense meeting, but she never blamed Pastor Mike for Loree's death being unsolved, and as it turned out, David was innocent, so Pastor Mike was right in not joining the angry mob.

"I could be better, Pastor," Andrea admitted with a sigh.

Right there in the office, she spilled the events of the past few weeks that had been troubling her heart, from partying with her sister's actual killer and the anger and guilt she felt afterwards, to cancelling the engagement with Quentin, which eventually led to his infidelity and their separation. With a heavy heart, she also talked to Pastor Mike about her latest flame, Edward Reed.

"Pastor, I didn't know what to do or where to go. I wanted things to work out with Quentin. I really did. But I was feeling emotional, upset, hurt, and the way Edward swooped in and just became the comforting presence I needed, I didn't expect things to unfold like this."

Pastor Mike sat at his desk in deep thought. He sympathized with Andrea because Robyn had been in her shoes and knew exactly how it felt when he cheated on her with Isis Samuels. Their marriage survived that drama, but Andrea's union fell apart.

"For starters, I don't blame you in walking away from Quentin if you had proof of his unfaithfulness. An institute of marriage cannot be built on secrecy and lies. But I believe you made a mistake in prematurely sleeping with this Edward Reed."

Andrea rolled her eyes. Pastor Mike was dismissing Edward as a stranger.

"Pastor Mike, you know who Edward is. He changed his name. Do you remember Antonio Franks?"

It took Pastor Mike a few minutes for the name to register in his memory bank. "The star witness at the trial. The former gang member."

Andrea nodded.

Pastor Mike sighed. The last thing he wanted to do was be mixed up in a domestic situation that involved a gang member. But if what Andrea stated was true, and he had reformed himself, then as long as they wanted to do so, he did not see why Andrea should not pursue a relationship with the lawyer.

"Andrea, whenever I look at you, I still see the little girl that my daughter taught all those years ago, who is still scarred by her sister's death. I feel that you are not at peace with it, and as a result, you're looking for ways to find that peace, whether it's in your music or in your relationships. Loree's death left a void that has never been filled."

Tears filled Andrea's eyes because she knew that Pastor Mike was right.

"You've carried the burden of your sister's death for too long, and you've been trying to compensate for it. You'll never be truly happy unless you let that burden go. Loree's death was an unspeakable tragedy, and our family misses her, but we don't want you to suffer because of it. Psalm 55:22 says, 'Cast your burden on the Lord, And He shall sustain you; He shall never permit the righteous to be moved.' When you lay all your burdens at the door of the Lord, he will sustain you. That means He will take care of you. He will see that all your needs are met, both spiritually and emotionally."

Andrea nodded, indicating that she understood clearly what Pastor Mike was saying.

"Now I have another question for you. Do you love Edward?"

"Yes, I do."

"And does he feel the same way about you?"

"I think he does. He's been there for me, and he's not perfect, but he's loyal."

"Then you let Jesus take control of your relationship and let the chips fall where they may. He seems like a good guy. I heard his reputation took quite a hit when he defended your sister's murderer, but something tells me he didn't have a choice in the matter."

"Tadarius didn't leave him much of one."

Pastor Mike rolled his eyes. "Lord, I pray that man goes back to prison. I couldn't believe when I heard that he was paroled and released after all the things he's done. Well, God still reigns on the throne, so I'm sure the Lord will see to it that justice is served or that he sees the light and repents."

"Me too, Pastor. Thank you for everything." Hugging Pastor Mike, Andrea felt reassured and knew that if she wanted to move on, she had to let her guilt about Loree go and move on with her life.

"You're welcome. And you're also welcome back here anytime for Bible study. Please invite Edward as well. We would love to have him."

Promising that she would invite Edward, Andrea left the church reaffirmed in her faith and ready to get her career back on track.

That same Friday night, Chris had a fitted Yankees jersey on with black sweatpants and a new pair of Jordan sneakers that he bought. Earlier that evening, he called out of work, stating that he had a family event to attend.

It would be his only occurrence since he had never called out of work before. Renee was out of the house for the weekend, having gone to a work retreat that her job was hosting. Cree and Katrina were sleeping over at a friend's house in Rosedale, New York, which left

Chris and Dennis at the house alone. Renee trusted Chris to watch Dennis and left money for them to order out when they were hungry. Unfortunately, Chris was going to have to betray Renee's trust for this one night.

Chris had ordered Chinese food for himself and Dennis earlier, and while Dennis retreated to his room to play video games, Chris intended to go to the party that Shantay invited him to. He had hoped to sneak out the house before he heard a voice.

"Yo, Chris, where you goin'?" Dennis was at the top of the staircase, eyebrows raised in suspicion.

"Don't worry about it, dawg. I'm headed out. I'll be right back."

"You goin' to a kickback, ain't you?"

"What you talkin' about, B?"

"I ain't stupid, man. Hold up. I'm coming wit' you."

Sighing, Chris saw no way out of this situation. If he left Dennis, he would tell Renee that he snuck out, and she would not trust him again.

"Aight, c'mon then. Hurry yo' ass up."

CHAPTER 21

DIVINE VENGEANCE

AFTER A 20-MINUTE subway ride and a couple blocks away from the closed warehouse on Forest Hills Parkway, Chris and Dennis finally arrived at the address that Shantay texted him. It was a small single-story house with a small fence in the front yard that opened at the center. The house was already filled with high school and college kids playing music, drinking alcohol, smoking weed and hookah, and dancing in the living room.

Chris recalled Shantay telling him that the house belonged to her sister, who recently started going out with a new guy that she met while at work. Chris had second thoughts about bringing Dennis with him because of his age, but Dennis was already a couple of inches taller than Chris, so people would already figure him to be a high school student, unless they recognized him from the eighth-grade team.

As they approached the door, Dennis said, "Maybe we should knock."

But Chris had been going to these types of parties for years. Dennis was the novice in this situation, so Chris thought it was the best time to school the rookie.

"Knock? Man, ain't nobody gonna hear us with that music blasting. Door should be open."

True to form, the door was indeed unlocked, and they walked in and took in the scene. There were college frat boys, sorority girls, and some students Chris recognized from Townsend Harris. It was a chill vibe type of scene, but there was a feeling Chris could not shake off, as if someone in his soul was telling him that he should not be at the party. It was bad enough he called off work just to get to the party, and as much as he tried to enjoy himself, he felt uneasy. But a beautiful vision blocked those doubts away at once.

Chris saw Shantay standing near the kitchen, holding a red cup and talking with a few girls. Deciding to stroll to her space nonchalantly, Chris and Dennis made their way over to the kitchen area. It did not take Shantay long to notice her two latest visitors, and she went over to Chris and hugged him, while welcoming him to her sister's house.

"And who's this?" she asked when she saw Dennis.

"Right, that's my brother, Dennis." Chris refrained himself from telling her what grade he was in because it was not relevant to the introduction, but he was tall enough to pass for a high school student, so why not let them assume he was sixteen or seventeen?

"Aight well, make ya selves at home, you know what I'm sayin'? We got drinks in the fridge, and I know we still got some pizza left over. That's if Avery's fat ass ain't eaten it all."

Upon hearing his name, one of the boys who was watching a boxing match on TV turned around to glare at Shantay. He was a chubby guy with a little belly fat or "gut" as Chris referred to it.

"Damn, Shantay, you dissin' me like that? That's cold, mama."

Chuckling, Chris went over to the table where all the drinks and food were located. Chris did not tell Shantay right away, but he had no intentions on staying at the party long. He just wanted to make Shantay aware of his arrival, eat a little bit of food, then make his way out. The table was filled with pizza boxes, chicken wings, soda, juice, Hennessey, 1800, and other wine coolers/beverages.

While loading up his plate, Chris's suspicions grew again. Looking around, he did not see anyone he recognized right away, and he could not wait to get Shantay next to him again, even for a few seconds.

"Man, she wearing them jeans. Yo' I'm about to holla at Shantay again real quick. Then we outta here."

When Dennis failed to reply, Chris looked behind him and realized that Dennis had wandered off. Looking around frantically, Chris finally located Dennis, who had wasted no time talking with a couple of high school cheerleaders, who were blown away by his height. *Okay, Dennis, go get yours, son. But make it fast cuz after I tear this food up, we outta here.*

Chris did not realize that Shantay had snuck up behind him. "You got a cute brother."

Turning around, Chris took in the sight of Shantay. *God damn she fine. I might have to stay a lil' longer.*

"Yeah, he cool. So, where your sister at? I don't think I've seen her yet since I got here."

"Why? Are you tryin' to get at her too?" Shantay asked, fake pouting her lips.

"No, never that. I just wanna know cuz I ain't neva' met her yet."

"Well, you'll meet them later. Come on, I want you to meet my girls, and you owe me a dance."

Chris followed Shantay into the living room, where college and high school students talked, danced to the music playing, smoked, and drank their fair share of beverages. Some girls and guys were making out, and Chris had to look twice when he saw two girls kissing each other, and they were going at it harder than the other couple kissing. *Damn.*

For about thirty minutes, Chris and Shantay talked, and Chris sipped on some juice mixed with a little bit of white liquor. Chris was no stranger to drinking alcohol although he was underage because he drank habitually when he was still a member of that gang he would like to forget.

A slow R&B song played, and Shantay swayed her head and closed her eyes. "Oooh, this my jam right here. Come dance wit' me." Pulling Chris by his shirt, she guided him to the dance floor, and Chris, slightly buzzed, followed.

Shantay gyrated her body to the beat, grinding her hips against Chris. Between the drink and Shantay grinding up on him, Chris could feel himself getting aroused. He tried to move a centimeter away so Shantay would not know that he was getting hard, but it was too late. She brushed against him, and she felt him.

Smiling when she realized she had his member hard, she whispered in his ear. "So that's how you feel? Don't be scared of me. I'll give you whatever you want."

A few minutes later, Chris and Shantay were kissing uncontrollably as she pulled his arm and led him to one of the bedrooms. Pulling off his shirt, Shantay was kissing his chest. She wanted every part of Chris, and Chris wanted her. Pushing him onto the bed, she mounted on top of him, and Chris could not control his erection at that point. Shantay was ready to go to town, when suddenly the door opened, and an older girl in her twenties with two mini afro puffs looked inside. Shantay and Chris looked back at the door.

"Tay, I know you ain't out here givin' it up to some random nigga."

Shantay rolled her eyes. Rolling off Chris, she was upset that she was interrupted, and honestly, Chris could not blame her. The moment was ruined.

"Klea, can't you knock?"

"Girl, it's my house. I could walk in anytime I want. Ain't you gonna introduce me to yo' latest boy toy?"

Boy toy? Chris looked at Shantay in confusion.

Frantically, Shantay tried to ease the tension. "Baby, she just playin'."

"Look, man. Don't feel bad. You ain't the only one. So, what's yo' name?"

"Chris Anderson."

"Well, you are a cute one, cuter than the last boy she had in here."

"Klea, shut up!"

Taking it as his cue to leave, Chris took his shirt and put it back on. He had to find Dennis and leave the house right away.

"Where you goin'?" Shantay asked, visibly upset.

"I just remembered I had something to do back at the house. I promised Mrs. Anderson I'd be back before ten."

Shantay hung her head in disappointment. Throwing an angry glare at Klea for ruining the moment, she hugged Chris and thanked him for coming to the party. While he was taking off, he heard a male voice behind Klea.

"What's up, baby?"

"Nothin' my baby sister was in hea' bout her get her freak on with one of her classmates. Puppy love...you know how it be."

"Oh word? Where he at, Shantay?"

By the time Shantay tried to point him out, Chris had disappeared among the party guests, frantically quickening his pace, when he realized the male voice. Klea was dating Jermaine, one of the members of M.O.B. and his former mentor. Chris looked around the house before seeing a glimpse of Dennis walking out of the house with G-Block.

Looking around, he noticed some guests were members of M.O.B., and he had walked into a trap. Internally praying that he would get out, Chris followed Dennis and G-Block from a distance, taking out his phone to check the time.

"Yo, Dennis, what up?"

Upon hearing his name, Dennis turned around and saw G-Block calling to him. "What's up, G.?" Dapping each other, they walked toward the front of the house.

"Yo, I ain't expect to see you hea', dawg."

"I came wit' Chris. I was just looking for him. There's a lot of people here."

"Chris is here too?" G-Block smiled, but secretly hiding his true intentions.

If Chris was discovered by a member of the Fam, he was as good as dead, and G-Block had been waiting to smoke that scrub since last year. He already killed one man which all but solidified his place within the family.

"Well, don't worry about Chris. He'll find us. Lemme holla at you for a minute, B" G-Block walked outside with Dennis, and they made their way toward the warehouse.

"Yo, I think we should go back. I gotta get Chris. I can't leave him there by himself."

"Yo, you sweatin' that man too much, bro. What is he, yo' boyfriend or something?"

Dennis laughed, still under the impression that G-Block was joking. "Nah, he's my half bro, dawg. We rolled up in here together, and we gotta take the same train back to the house."

"Man, he'll be aight. Anyway, remember what we chopped it up about after the game? The money opportunity?"

"Yeah, I remember. What you want me to do?"

"All right, so what I'm thinking is that you run wit' our crew and run some of our shit. Let us represent you, and you represent us in high school. We'll pay for all your tournaments, game kicks, jerseys, and all that. You'll go to college, and then you'll go to the pros, and NBA money is where it's at, right? When that contract hit, we all rich, you know what I'm sayin'?"

Dennis thought about the investment offer that G-Block made to him, and as enticing as it was to accept it, he declined. His father made sure that he was taught never to accept handouts from anyone. It was about working for what he had and staying in class. "Nah, I'm good, bro."

"What you mean you good? Boy, I'm giving you a good-ass offer right now. You one of the top players in the state right now. We can invest in you, and you invest in us."

"You're talking all this 'we' and 'us' stuff. Who you rollin' with, G?"

G-Block stopped in his tracks and looked Dennis square in the eyes, and at that moment, he knew his tone had changed, and he was not looking at his one-time friend anymore.

"Let's just say I got special crew that I consider my fam, and we look out for each other. Now you got a chance to be a part of that too. It's yo' birthright, so let's put our big-boy pants on and do the smart thing. Don't make the same stupid decision yo' pops made."

Dennis glared at G-Block. "What'd you say about my pops?"

G-Block laughed, clearly unfazed by Dennis facing him. "I said, don't be the law-lovin' simp that yo' daddy was cuz in the end, it got him six-feet under. That's what happens when you disrespect the Fam."

"Fuck you, nigga!" Dennis yelled, pushing G-Block in the chest.

But his adversary only laughed and stepped up to Dennis again, and while approaching him, Dennis saw the gang tattoo on G-Block's arm. It was the same tattoo that Chris had, and it matched the tattoo that his father had.

"Chris was right. Wasn't he? You roll with M.O.B.? Ya killed my pops, and you expect me to join ya? That ain't gon' happen."

Unbeknownst to Dennis, G-Block walked him away from the house and lured him near the warehouse, where about three other members of M.O.B. were waiting. Dequan, Armitage, and Freddie emerged from the shadows and surrounded the two boys. Dennis looked out of the corner of his eyes and saw the crew making their way towards him.

"Now, are you gonna accept our offer, or are you gonna join your pops?" G-Block threatened.

Dennis looked down at his side pocket and saw the outline of a gun, and sure enough, G-Block reached for it. But before anyone moved, G-Block was suddenly knocked down by a blow to his left chin. Chris, who had been trailing the boys, saw what was happening and knew that M.O.B. was at the cusp on initiating Dennis or eliminating him, and without warning, he walked up and landed a punch on G-Block that knocked him down.

"Dennis, get outta here now! Get back to the house, and call 911!"

Dennis wanted to stay and help Chris, but he listened and got out of there. Chris was backed away from G-Block, who was bleeding from his mouth. Seething in rage, he reached for his weapon, but Chris knocked it out of his hand and kicked him across the forehead. Armitage rushed at Chris, but he was leveled as well by a left blow.

When the other two boys reached for their firearms, Chris made a dash to the warehouse before the boys finally had their firearms in their hands.

Pow! Pow! Pow! pow! Shots rang out through the warehouse, but because there was no lighting, all the shots missed Chris.

Scrambling to find a back way out of the building, Chris thought he eluded all the members of the fake family, and he was making his way out when he was struck in the side of his head with a large metal object that knocked him unconscious.

Standing over him, Pooh dropped the metal pipe that he used to strike Chris and pulled his gun out. "You know, T made me promise LaToya not to smoke you, but talk is cheap."

Before he pulled the trigger, he heard a click at his ear. "Better drop that heater fast, son." Edward Reed had his own gun pointed at the side of Pooh's head.

An hour earlier, upon receiving a surprising location pin and message stating that Chris and Dennis were at the party, he groaned. At the moment, he was spending time with Andrea as they discussed the next step in their relationship. Excusing himself, Edward mapped the location and sped over to the scene.

When he arrived, he saw the confrontation with Dennis and G-Block from the next street. Following the boys into the warehouse, Edward managed to disarm G-Block, Dequan, and Freddie as they pursued Chris. A minute later, Dennis emerged and ran to the subway station, while on his cell phone calling 911. Edward snuck into the vast warehouse and only managed to arrive after watching Pooh knock Chris out.

When Pooh heard Edward's voice, he laughed. "If it ain't the star witness himself. Or should I say the star snitch?"

A third figure emerged from the opposite end of the warehouse. Believing it to be G-Block and his other companions, Pooh shouted, "Yo, ice this dead muthafucka!"

But it was Cochise who emerged from the door.

"Yo, Cochise take yo' shot, son. You claim to be part of the Fam. Prove it!"

Cochise took out his weapon, but Pooh had no clue that he was working with Edward. One could imagine the look that Pooh had when Caris "Cochise" lifted his T-shirt, revealing his police badge and a bulletproof vest.

"You're under arrest for first-degree murder, assault with a deadly weapon, and criminal conspiracy. You have the right to remain silent…" he continued, reading Pooh his Miranda Rights.

All Pooh could do was shake his head. "You son of a bitch. You wear the symbol of our family on yo' arm, and all this time you was a pig, workin' for this bastard."

But before Pooh continued, Edward saw an infrared beam pointed directly at Caris. "DUCK!" Edward shouted.

Without hesitation, Caris dove to the ground as the bullet narrowly missed him. Jermaine, who had fired the first shot, fired again as Caris ran behind a wall to load his gun's barrel.

"Where you at, 5-0? M.O.B. ain't goin' nowhere!"

During the gun battle waging between Caris and Jermaine, Pooh turned around and tried to disarm Edward by punching the gun out of his hand, but Edward still held on and ran to take cover as Pooh himself unloaded about five or six shots.

"These dudes shooting at law enforcement officers? Oh, they gon' get buried under the jail!" Caris said.

Edward needed an exit strategy quickly. He decided to buy Caris some time. "Listen, I'll cover you. Get Chris outta here now. First responders are on their way."

Caris stared at his cousin. Was he out of his mind? "Man, you got a death wish? I'm the one that got the bulletproof vest. I'll cover you, and you get Chris out of here."

When Edward agreed to this plan, Caris jumped out and returned fire. Jermaine and Pooh shot wildly at Caris, but neither were trained officers, and they were just wasting bullets. Caris took his shots with precision, hitting Jermaine just above the chest. He went down yelling in pain, and Pooh started to panic. He saw Edward pick up Chris and head toward the exit.

With Caris turning on the heat with one man down, Pooh had one more play in his nefarious book. As the de-facto leader with Tadarius in the hospital, Pooh was forced to take the initiative for his fallen brothers. As he retreated to the back exit of the warehouse, Pooh fired another shot, and this time, the bullet pierced Edward's leg.

Stunned by the immense sharp pain, Edward dropped Chris as Caris quickly came to his aid. "Here, get him out of here. Save him," Edward urged.

"What about you?"

"Don't worry about me. Get Chris out of hea' now. I'm right behind you."

Caris grudgingly took Chris and carried him out of the warehouse, where a squad of police cars and paramedics were rushing over to the scene.

Pooh managed to make it outside on the other side of the warehouse. As soon as he was a safe distance away, he felt it was time to put his final plan in motion. *I'm about to bring the whole fuckin' building down.*

Unbeknownst to Edward or anyone who was not part of the family, Pooh and two other M.O.B. members had wired the entire building with a stock of C4 explosives which could only be activated by one remote control detonator, and it was currently in Pooh's possession. Tadarius had often stated how he desired to test the C4 explosives that he purchased from Khaimov. There was no other time like the present for Pooh.

Laughing gleefully, Pooh pushed the button, which set off a 5-second timer. Caris was barely fifty yards away from the warehouse when it exploded. The blast sent Caris and Chris soaring in the air, and they landed onto the pavement, with Caris shielding Chris. The police watched in shock as the warehouse foundation burst into flames following the explosion. Caris turned around in horror as he stared at the warehouse engulfed in flames. *Edward never made it out.*

The last thing Caris remembered was Edward gingerly limping after him with a gunshot wound to his leg.

Countless residents had emerged from their homes as the noise from the gunshots and the explosion sent everyone into a frenzy. The party at Klea's house quickly ceased as the blast shook the foundations of the street. As firetrucks made their way to the scene, Caris, after safely placing Chris in the back of an ambulance, frantically rushed back towards the warehouse, but police were already taping off the area, and he was quickly stopped by two officers.

"Excuse me, sir, nobody can pass through here at this time. We ask that you please step back."

Caris quickly showed them his badge. "Look, I'm a police officer too, okay? I had a friend who was in there before the explosion. I'm just trying to get back there to see if…"

The officers looked at each other, and Caris knew from the somber stares that were exchanged, they did not think there was hope for anyone.

"Officer, we don't think anybody could have survived this explosion. I'm sorry."

Waiting nervously in a waiting room at the New York Hospital Medical Center of Queens, Renee nervously sat and prayed for Chris, who was lying in ICU. She was forced to cut her weekend retreat with her coworkers short when she received the call from Dennis about the events that took place earlier Friday evening.

Initially, she was disappointed and angered when he explained how they snuck out of the house without her permission to go to a party, but it was fear instead of anger that magnified when Dennis told her that he ran away to call the police upon escaping and received a call from a cop by the name of Caris minutes later. Then, Caris informed him that the warehouse where G-Block nearly killed him had exploded, but he managed to get Chris to safety.

Now Chris was at the hospital where he was still unconscious from Friday to Saturday evening, and Renee did not leave the waiting room area. She only stepped out to use the restroom or go to the vending machines to get a snack until she waited to hear from the doctors about Chris's health status. *It's like déjà vu all over again. I was in a waiting room like this just two months ago after David was shot. He didn't pull through that evening, and now his son might not pull through either.*

Finally, the doors to the waiting room opened, and Dr. Rafael Gonzalez stepped into the room. Renee walked over to Dr. Gonzalez after he called to her.

"Any news, Doctor?" Renee braced herself, fearing the worst. How was she going to explain this to Edward?

"Well, Mrs. Anderson, I have good news. Looks like Chris is going to be okay. He just woke up."

"Thank God! Thank you, Dr. Gonzalez."

"However, he suffered significant blunt force trauma that affected the temporal lobes in the side of his brain, and that did cause some form of amnesia."

Renee put her hands over her mouth. Although grateful that Chris survived the terrible ordeal that took place earlier in the evening, she was also concerned about his current state of health. "How severe is the amnesia, Doctor?"

"Well, right now he remembers his name and his age, but that is pretty much it. Everything else is a fog right now to him. He doesn't remember the events that brought him here or the person responsible for striking him in the head."

Renee turned away from the doctor as she angrily brushed away a tear.

"You can go in to see him now though. Maybe seeing you will trigger a memory shot, and some pieces will start coming back over time."

Renee followed the doctor into the room where Chris was lying in the hospital bed with his head bandaged, and his oxygen mask had been pulled below his mouth once he was able to breathe on his own. *He's still alive though. That's what counts.*

When Chris first saw, Renee, he squinted his eyes curiously, and Renee knew that he was trying to figure out who she was. "Hey, Chris, how are you feeling?" she asked gently while caressing his hand.

"I'm okay. I just don't remember too much right now. Doc says I took a real bad hit to the head. All I remember is that I was running down a dark hallway...nothing else."

Renee smiled, but her eyes were brimming with tears. "We'll help you remember everything in time, sweetie. All you need to know now is that because of you, my son Dennis is still alive. You saved his life last night, and I can't thank you enough for that."

Chris stared down at his hospital garb somberly, and Renee knew it was because he did not have a recollection of Dennis or any other members of her family at that moment.

Staring up at her, he asked, "Are you my mother?"

Unable to control herself, Renee wept openly. Chris put his life on the line to see that Dennis escaped unharmed, and Renee, who always had her doubts when she took Chris in, no longer felt obligated to help him. It would be too complicated at this time to talk to him about LaToya or his early upbringing in the gang family. None of it mattered anymore because she wanted to leave that part of his past dead and buried. She would now be there for him as well as her other kids until she took her last breath.

"Yes, I am."

Chris genuinely smiled. "Thanks for staying here with me, Mom."

Renee leaned forward and hugged Chris, kissing him on forehead.

While Chris's health improved in the coming days, the health of notorious gang leader Tadarius gradually worsened. He remained at Queens General Hospital where he slipped into a coma without receiving a single visit from anyone in the family, who were all in the wind after the co-leaders were taken down.

Tina "Bunny" Leigh was dead under the sea, and the younger members of the gang, G-Block and others, were apprehended and sent to a juvenile hall facility as minors while the members that were eighteen and over were locked up waiting to be tried as adults in the New York court systems.

Jermaine's remains were found in the warehouse, and firefighters had searched the charred debris for other casualties after the fire was extinguished, but there were no others.

Edward Reed's body was never recovered, but when the news of his involvement in the gang battle leading up to the explosion went viral, he was presumed dead, and the Schorr Law Group held a memorial service dedicated to his memory.

After being on the run for several days, Pooh was apprehended by a Long Island police task force, led by Caris. He was charged with domestic terrorism and arson, adding to the other list of charges, guaranteeing that would spend his remaining days behind bars at a maximum-security facility in upstate New York.

The doctors announced that Tadarius's diagnosis was an "aggressive form of leukemia." Because he never went to the doctor to check on his health, combined with his imprisonment and his indulgent habits with alcohol, cigarettes, weed, and women, Tadarius was living in the fast lane that was doomed to reach its end.

One day, Tadarius finally had a visitor—a mysterious man who came to him outside of visiting hours. He hid away from the hospital employees so that he went unnoticed. He knew which room

Tadarius was admitted in, and he walked into the room, where he found Tadarius with various tubes in his body.

"You know, it took me years to see this moment finally happen. You've killed so many people and left so many families crying. Loree. Theo. Terrell. Xavier. Craig. David. Deon. The list goes on. You've destroyed countless lives because of your ruthless family. Now look at you. Your main guys are dead or in jail, and everybody else left the state. M.O.B. is history."

Approaching the bed near the vulnerable gang leader, the man continued speaking. "It was only a matter of time until you received your comeuppance for all the crimes you committed because, when you expire, there is no return. Some people call it justice. I call it divine vengeance."

The man walked away. It was not too long after he left that Tadarius flatlined, and doctors rushed in frantically to save his life. Trying to revive him, they worked feverishly, but in the end, the words of the man rang true. Dontrell "Tadarius" Hill, the infamous leader of M.O.B. expired and passed away at the age of thirty-seven.

A month passed by, and LaToya Richardson walked out of her cell at the Queens Female Penitentiary System, completely dressed in orange garb. After Tadarius's death, LaToya's case was reopened by the state of New York, and they found that LaToya's evidence provided to assist with her insanity plea had been tampered with. Therefore, prosecutors were able to take the case to state court.

With Edward Reed presumed dead, which provided little comfort for LaToya, she was assigned a state attorney. At the end, she was found guilty of murdering David Anderson, and new evidence also linked her to Loree McAfee's death, and her previous prison sentence was upheld. Just like Pooh, LaToya would never see freedom in her lifetime again.

Walking into the visitor block with her hands and feet chained, LaToya had lost significant weight while locked up. After hearing about Tadarius's death, she had tried calling her sister multiple times, but each time she called, she would only receive her voicemail. *Did Tadarius harm my sister? Did the police catch her as well?*

The anxiety that stemmed from not hearing from either Tina or her son, Chris. This caused LaToya to lose patches of her hair and suffer a loss of appetite, and her appearance was gaunt and disheveled. As she sat across from her visitor, the person was not who she expected. She expected to see Andrea or even her new lawyer, but a stranger sat across from her. She was dressed in formal attire, even though her visit was anything but formal.

"So, to whom do I owe this pleasure of a visit. I'm sorry I don't know your name, so I don't know how to address you."

"My name is Renee Anderson. David Anderson was my husband, and he was the man you shot."

LaToya shook her head, chuckling slightly. *Figures, Little Ms. Thang would come up in here. What did he ever see in this uppity bitch, anyway?*

"Is that all you got to say to me? You come all this way to show yo' face and expect me to feel some type of way? Well guess what? I feel nothin' at all. David got what was comin' to him. It's all part of the code."

"What code?" Renee seethed.

She had never seen a woman so heartless in person. LaToya truly had no soul, and it showed. Renee could not believe that such a vile woman had once been a mother.

"M.O.B. has a code that we live by—" LaToya started before Renee cut her off.

"M.O.B. is done, LaToya. Do you hear me? Tadarius is dead. Everybody is scattered. We had an undercover cop infiltrate ya'll, and guess what? He implicated everyone that was involved in all the murders, wire fraud schemes, illegal drug sales and everything else that they were involved in."

"You're lying."

"Am I? You know, for all your sense of loyalty and family, you never once showed that same level of loyalty to your son."

Upon hearing about Chris, LaToya stared at Renee right in the eye and realized that this was the woman who had been acting as the guardian to Chris. "So, where is he? He's obviously safe, isn't he?"

Renee glared at LaToya, unable to fathom the level of hate that she harbored in her heart. "He's fine, but you have some nerve acting as if you care for him now."

LaToya hit the table angrily, prompting the guard who was watching the interaction to step forward, expecting a physical confrontation, but LaToya waved her hand at him, as if to say, "I'm good. Don't worry about me."

"So, where is he? Why can't I see him? He's got a right to visit his mama. You can't deny me that."

"Listen, I can deny you anything and anyone right now. Do you know how much you put that boy through? You used him to kill David and make our family suffer. It's like he's nothing but a piece to you, but let me tell you something. He is worth more than that. Chris is a smart, remarkable, resourceful young man who is going to change the world someday. He got that drive and determination from someone, but it damn sure wasn't you."

"Bitch, who the hell you think you talkin' to? Nobody knows my son more than I do."

"Is that so? Don't you see what your choices have done to him? He almost lost his life a month ago because you got him involved with this gang family business. Well, now it's over. I will do what you should have done and stick by Chris as if he is one of my own children because half of him still reminds me of the man I loved that you snuffed out."

LaToya, still glaring at Renee, wanted to wring the life out of her, but the chains restrained her. As the guard signaled the end of visitation, LaToya stood up and made her way back to her cell. But she turned around and addressed Renee one last time.

"Just promise me one thing. Promise me that you'll do right by him and provide him with everything that I couldn't give him."

"I promise I'll do right by him, and when he's ready, I'll see to it that he comes to visit you."

With that, LaToya walked out the door and back into the darkly lit cell block. Renee stood up and made her way out of the facility into her car.

After a month Chris recovered and returned to school, and fragments of his memory began to return. He remembered parts of that fateful evening.

The brotherly bond between Chris and Dennis grew, and so did Chris's bond to the family. He was fully accepted, and he continued attending class and continued maintaining top grades. Although his teacher Mr. Thompson mysteriously resigned, and a new professor took his place, Chris continued to excel in school and work.

CHAPTER 22

DIVINE VENGEANCE

February 2023

RISING OUT OF BED, Andrea McAfee hummed a song from her new soundtrack that she was planning to record for Soul Sisters Indie LLC, based in Newark, New Jersey. Following the tragic events of that Friday nearly three years ago, Andrea had been searching for a new beginning. There were times when she played back the day when Caris, who she recently discovered was infiltrating M.O.B. to cease its operations, came up to her door and asked her to sit down.

Her heart was rendered to shreds when he told her that in his attempt to save Chris, Edward never made it out of the warehouse before it exploded. If Andrea thought Loree's death rocked her to her core, Edward's death certainly sent her over the edge. She had finally found the man she loved, no matter how long it took her to find him, and within days, he was taken away from her.

Andrea was depressed for days and weeks following the tragic news, and although she resumed her sessions with Dr. Ralwinski and continued attending Bible study on Friday nights at Rock of Jacob Baptist Church, nothing could replace the pain of losing Edward. It was at that point that Andrea finally realized she needed a change of scenery. Living in New York just reminded her of endless tragedy, and she wanted to live without having to worry about anyone in her circle dying.

After talking with her best friend, Vanessa, who had moved to New Jersey in March of 2020 just weeks before the nation shut down due to the COVID-19 pandemic, Andrea started making plans to move out of New York and stay with her. Unbeknownst to anyone else, she started making plans for another reason as well.

After showering and brushing her teeth, Andrea walked into his room and smiled serenely as he slept peacefully in his crib. She remembered when she first discovered that she was pregnant, just weeks after everything that occurred. She was violently sick one morning and went to see her physician expecting him to tell her that the reason she was sick was due to her depression and anxiety following Edward's death. But after the doctor ran different types of tests, he called her one morning to give her the news that her ailments were caused by morning sickness because she was expecting a child.

Vanessa, her parents Amos and Alisha, along with Shania McClain, all helped Andrea through the process, and when time came to give birth, Shania made sure that Andrea was under the care of the same doctors and midwives who helped her deliver Loree Emiline. After more than fourteen hours in labor, little Anthony was born.

Andrea immediately fell in love with her son. The midwives and nurses wrapped him in blankets, and Shania and Vanessa wasted no time showering Anthony with love and care. After giving birth to Anthony, Andrea spent a few more months in New York before heading out to New Jersey. Her contract with Omega records came to an end, and she signed a new record with Soul Sisters Indie LLC.

Andrea and Anthony lived in the same duplex with Vanessa and Patrick Charles, her boyfriend, living next door. Since Vanessa now worked remotely from her home, she would watch and care for Anthony when Andrea would leave to go to the studio.

With streaming services now able to stream her music multiple times a day and with constant radio play, Andrea's career was back on track, and she still had time to be a mother, taking Anthony to the park and watching him play on the swings and little slides. Whenever she looked at Anthony, she saw that he had Loree's skin complexion, fair skinned, but it was the eyes that drew Andrea—those eyes that seemed to look into her, and those brown eyes which drew her to him. *He is definitely Edward's son. There's no denying that. I see Eddie in his eyes.*

Checking her clock that morning, she realized that Vanessa was late coming over to pick up her son. She wanted to go to the studio to put the track down as quickly as possible. Finally, her door knocked, and in walked Vanessa. She hugged her best friend, and Andrea rolled her eyes playfully.

"Girl, it is about time you came. What took you so long?"

"Girl, men. That's all I got to say about that. Patrick woke up asking where his special tie was, that it was his lucky tie and all that, blah, blah, blah. You know how them executive types are—always fussing about the small stuff."

"I feel you, Nessa."

"So, where's my Anty-man at?"

"Your little man still asleep. Let me bring his stroller round to his room. I don't think he'll be up for a while."

But when Andrea emerged from the closet with Anthony's stroller, the two-year-old had already woke up and was taking small steps around his crib.

"Well, that was fast. Guess you could put that away," Vanessa laughed as she came and lifted Anthony up. "How is my widdle Anthony doing?"

Anthony laughed as Andrea lifted him off Vanessa to shower and dress him. While dressing him, her eyes glanced onto a stack of letters on the lampstand. The other day, a letter that was not post marked or dated was found among her usual bill letters. She had promised herself that she would open it, but she never had the chance because of work.

After dressing Anthony up, she handed him to Vanessa. "Okay, papi, be a good boy for Auntie Vanessa, okay? Mommy will see you later. We're gonna go to the park later, and after that, we're gonna get ice cream!"

Anthony laughed, no doubt anticipating the day coming up ahead. As Vanessa held Anthony's hand and walked over to her side of the house, Andrea decided to read the unmarked letter. When she opened it and read its contents, she had to hold the kitchen chair to steady herself.

Trying to stop her tears from falling was futile because she could not believe what she was reading. She did not know whether to cry out of fear, grief, or joy. But the handwritten letter was very distinct and expressive. But it was the author that left Andrea speechless.

The letter read:

To the one I never stopped loving:

Hello Andrea, I hope this letter finds you and I hope that when you read this, you do not think any less of me. Throughout my life I have always been pressured to live life as if I was somebody else. I've always felt the pressure to act like a person that I wasn't, and the truth is I was not ready to truly accept myself. I searched everywhere for acceptance, and it led me to dark places that I thought I would never escape from. I've hurt family members, co-workers, friends, and I've even been an accessory to crimes that I had the opportunity to stop. The city hailed me as a hero because I did what I thought was the right thing but deep inside I never felt like I was a hero because a true hero would have sacrificed himself to save the lives of his friends.

I've tried to cover my guilt through work, women, and deep thoughts of anger and revenge, but all I've managed to do was further depress myself. But then I met you and the most extraordinary thing happened. I fell in love and although I tried to deny it, my heart could not deny what it knew to be true, and it was being one with you. On that night, before I went out to save Chris and rid the borough of Queens of an unnecessary evil, I was going to tell you that I wanted to go to church with you and I wanted to find the peace that you searched for many years for and found that evening when you visited Pastor Mike.

Before I went into the building, Caris who you may have met, already warned me about the bombs in the warehouse and he told me about a secret trapdoor underneath the carpeting that I could use to go underground into the sewer system, to shield myself from the blast. That is why my remains have not been found at the scene. One of my brothers picked me up and took me out of the state and I lived off the grid for three years, cut off all social media, and disconnected my phone lines so that I couldn't be tracked until I was made aware that the criminal organization that I was once affiliated with was finally obliterated.

I wish David were here to witness it, as it was his goal for children in our community to have opportunities without having to worry about surviving to see the next day. I regret not coming back to you sooner to explain all of this but I am hoping that I can return to you now so that I can make amends for the sorrow I've put you through for years. I cannot walk without a cane these days, and it's a constant reminder of what I put my body through to see that the next generation does not have to live in fear.

I do not want to disclose my current location in case this letter falls into the wrong hands, but when I was told that you currently reside in New Jersey, I searched for your new address, and I've been watching you from a distance. I see that our son has grown, and one day when I reveal myself to you, I would like to be a part of your lives as father and a provider. I still love you Andrea as I always have. Enclosed in this envelope is a picture Caris sent me that is near and dear to me and that shows me the potential of our youth when we inspire them to work hard and chase their dreams.

Andrea looked inside the envelope and saw a picture of Chris in a red and orange cap and gown proudly holding his diploma as he celebrated his graduation from Townsend Harris High School. Posing with him were Renee, Dennis, Katrina, and Cree.

Chris was able to do this without a father and I commend him for it, but I want our son to have his father every day to help him get to this plateau and beyond. One day, I will come back to you and we can start to live as a family and unite our hearts before God and ourselves. For although Edward Reed died that night, Antonio Franks has been reborn, and he is ready to be the man you deserve. Love always, Antonio Paul Franks.

ABOUT THE AUTHOR

MARC A. BEAUSEJOUR was born on July 28, 1987, in Queens, New York to Haitian parents Jean and Lineda Beausejour. He discovered his passion for writing at the tender age of twelve, with poetry becoming his initial artistic expression. Beausejour showcased his poetic talents in various school talent shows and poetry reading events during his time at North Cobb High School and later at Kennesaw State University after moving to Kennesaw, Georgia in 2001.

Throughout the years, Beausejour continued to hone his craft, writing poems for diverse occasions such as weddings, funerals, and church events. In 2011, he took a significant step by self-publishing his first book, "Words on High," a compilation of spiritually inspired poems from his formative years. Building on this success, Beausejour released his second poetry book, "Rising Higher Than Ever," in 2015.

In the same year, he ventured into a different literary landscape by writing and publishing his first urban novel, "The Preacher's Web." This gritty morality tale marked a departure from his earlier poetic works, showcasing Beausejour's versatility as an author. Expanding his literary horizons, he created the *BlackCyrano* series, demonstrating a wide-ranging creative skill.

While continuing to share his literary work on blogs and social networks, Beausejour remains committed to his education and promotions, earning his associate degree in marketing management from Chattahoochee Technical College in 2018. As a multifaceted writer, Marc A. Beausejour continues to captivate audiences with his words across various genres and platforms.

ALSO BY, AUTHOR

"Marc A. Beausejour"

Title: The Preacher's Web | Publisher: SHE PUBLISHING LLC | ISBN: 978-1-953163-91-2 (paperback) Publication Date: February 2024 (*Second Edition*)

Set in the heart of the city, "The Preacher's Web" unfolds a gripping narrative of former All-City quarterback turned pastor, Mike Hillman, whose dedication to preaching love and forgiveness in Queens, New York is challenged by the return of an old friend seeking revenge. Amidst a community grappling with the scourge of drugs and gangs. As Mike puts his reputation on the line to testify for a young man accused of murder, the story converges with the adolescent struggles of Jamal Samuels on the basketball courts of New York City.

Now, standing at the crossroads of faith, family, and societal challenges, Mike faces a pivotal choice. Will he risk more than his reputation to uphold justice and fulfill his role as a public servant and father? The pages of "The Preacher's Web" beckon you to explore the complexities of morality and redemption. Can Mike Hillman rise above, or will he be consumed by the web of his past?

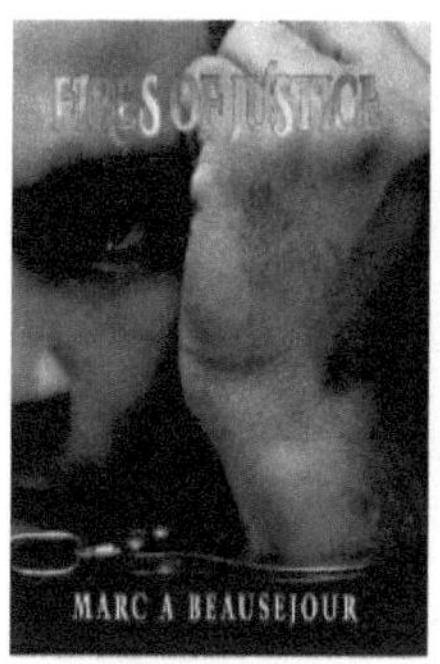

Title: Fires of Justice | Author: Marc A. Beausejour | Publisher: SHE PUBLISHING LLC | ISBN: 978-1-953163-93-6 (paperback) | Publication Date: February 2024 (*second edition*)

English professor Levell Thomas is ecstatic when he receives the opportunity to teach in a metro Atlanta high school. A native of Queens, New York, Levell moves to Georgia with his family and as they settle in their new home, Levell meets his neighbor, a mysterious girl named Raven Roberts. Despite being underaged, she doesn't hide her desires for Levell and pursues him relentlessly. Levell refuses her advances but would soon pay dearly for his decision. The spurned teenager accuses Levell of assault after a physical confrontation and Levell is found guilty in the court of law. Detective Isaac Sands leads the investigation to expose a plot of false accusation and imprisonment in a race against time. Will Sands help prove Levell's innocence by finding the conspirators, or would he put himself in harm's way?

"The controversies confronted, stirred, and then addressed in this story have no choice but to awaken you to new perspectives that might not have ever crossed your mind. Readers, all I can say is be prepared to feel the fire that Beausejour has ignited in this suspenseful masterpiece!"

—D.A. Goodwin, author of The Offender I Once Defended

Title: Adia's Ballad | Author: Marc A. Beausejour | Publisher: SHE PUBLISHING LLC | ISBN: 978-1-953163-92-9 (paperback) | Publication Date: February 2024 (*second edition*)

From the author of "The Preacher's Web", this coming-of-age story explores the life of young Andrea McAfee who struggles to cope with the tragic murder of her older sister. Then a chance opportunity lands Andrea into the music business where she shares a bond with other artists in the hip hop industry and learns she has more in common with them than she realizes. As Andrea immerses herself deeper into the life of recording, touring and partying as Adia, the new R&B princess, she begins drifting away from her family and her loved ones as her star rises too fast for her to absorb. With fame corrupting her relationships with those she loves, will Andrea find the inner peace and closure she seeks, or will she succumb to the draw of money and celebrity?

Title: Split Decision | Author: Marc A. Beausejour | Publisher: SHE PUBLSIHING LLC | ISBN: 978-1-953163-94-3 (paperback) | Publication Date: February 2024 (*second edition*)

Prepare to enter the ring as cultures clash in this adrenaline-filled drama! Under the tutelage of experienced trainer Jim Shaw, young boxer Sylvio Dominique has taken the middleweight class division by storm, winning bout after bout. Nicknamed "Wolf" for his boxing style and aggression in the ring, Sylvio works hard in the ring and plays even harder out of the ring and there is no shortage of women. Reuniting with childhood friend Valentina Cruz, the two become involved in an intense romance. But as Sylvio falls deep in love with Valentina, he realizes that she is more than what she seems. With a fight against the undefeated Dominican champion Felipe Maximo looming, secrets are revealed, and friends turn to foes as Sylvio later discovers that he may not be fighting only for the middleweight crown, but he may also be fighting for his life.

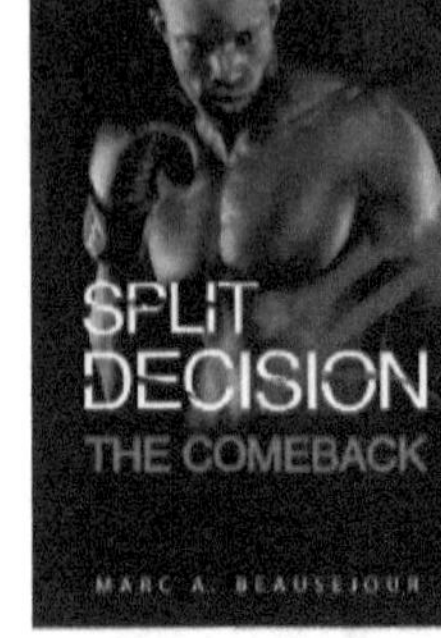

Title: Split Decision II - The Comeback |
Author: Marc A. Beausejour | Publisher: SHE
PUBLISHING LLC | ISBN: 978-1-953163-95-0
(paperback) | Publication Date: February 2024
(*second edition*)

After Sylvio Dominique's sudden retirement from middleweight boxing following a close brush with death, the former champion hangs up his gloves to continue running the Shaw-Dominique Community Center in Queens, New York. When Sylvio's hometown rival and current middleweight champion Barry Taylor; asks him to help train for his title defense against new contender and former MMA fighter Jun Zhang, Sylvio agrees to the proposition. But Taylor is defeated handily, and when Sylvio suffers a tragic death in the family and the center struggles financially, he makes the decision to return to the ring. Meanwhile, his girlfriend, Valentina Cruz find success as an actress and her relationship with Sylvio begins coming apart at the seams. Sylvio's trainer, Jim Shaw is reluctant to help Sylvio, as he finds himself struggling with his own personal demons. Jun Zhang then challenges Sylvio to fight him for the crown. As he prepares for his toughest ring battle yet, can Sylvio and Jim find the fortitude to emerge victorious while putting all their struggles behind them?

Title: Street Retribution | Author: Marc A. Beausejour | Publisher: SHE PUBLISHING LLC | Publication Date: February 2024 (*second edition*)

New York City attorney Edward Reed harbors a secret. He was once known as Antonio Franks, a member of M.O.B., the most dangerous gang in Queens, New York. He was also the key witness in the trial that exonerated another ex-gang member, David Anderson, when he was falsely accused of murdering his girlfriend, Loree McAfee. But years later, both men's lives are in danger, as other former gang members are slain under mysterious circumstances by a femme fatale, prompting rumors that M.O.B.'s ruthless gang leader, Tadarius Hill is seeking revenge on those that turned on him and his organization. Will Edward and David survive the bounty, or will they fall victim to the code of the streets?